The Women's Press Ltd
34 Great Sutton Street, London EC1V 0DX

I emerged in 1945 after twelve years of Nazi persecution, damaged, ill, poor, uneducated, unmarried, independent, with a two-year-old son, longing to leave Germany – which I eventually achieved in 1952, going to New York. I think I have lived one of the most liberated lives of any woman of my generation. I earned my money through office work, not much above the poverty line, got acquainted with English and American literature by incessant reading, went to concerts, educated and entertained my son, kept house, wrote every night, had close and intimate friendships with women and friendly, sexual relationships with men. Since the women's movement became a political force, I have supported the National Organisation for Women and the pro-choice group NARAL. At 55, I began to work part-time in the office and used the spare time for writing. I am now writing full-time. *Dead End Street* is my first published novel.

Helga Hagen

HELGA HAGEN

Dead End Street

The Women's Press

First published in Great Britain by
The Women's Press Ltd 1991
A member of the Namara Group
34 Great Sutton Street, London EC1V 0DX

British Library Cataloguing in Publication Data
Hagen, Helga
  Dead end street.
  I. Title
  813.54 [F]

  ISBN 0-7043-4257-X

Typeset by MC Typeset Ltd, Gillingham, Kent
Reproduced, printed and bound in Great Britain by
Cox & Wyman, Reading, Berks

To my sister Herta

Author's Note

So-called 'half-Jews', offspring of one German (or Arian) and one Jewish spouse, were also affected by the restrictive legislation enacted against Jews in September 1935, even if they had been baptised. Under the Nuremberg Laws they had more rights than Jews and they remained German citizens, though they were not allowed to marry Germans. If they married a Jew, they were considered Jewish. They were only allowed to marry another half-Jew.

The fate of half-Jews depended on whether the breadwinner of the household was Jewish. When the German spouse died, as was the case in Eva's family, the remaining Jewish parent was treated like other Jews, with a few minor advantages. Since commerce for Jews declined drastically after 1933, a Jewish father could no longer provide for his family and the decline into chaos was swift and complete.

After the Nuremberg laws were passed, half-Jews were no longer allowed to finish secondary school or work for a university degree. They were not allowed to become government employees or work in any higher position. They were also not allowed to learn any trade, work in the medical field, work as an artist, own property or rent flats.

During the war, before they were sent to concentration camps, Jews were only allowed to live in a restricted area, which formed a ghetto. Half-Jews looked for rented rooms, and had a hard time finding a German person or family who dared to rent to them. The same was true for jobs. Few companies employed half-Jews, so that many were forced to live underground, hidden and supported by those Germans who sympathised with them. Without the help of these Germans, very few could have survived.

For most of the war, half-Jews had been open to arrest, but this had only been carried out in an erratic way. After the assassination attempt on Hitler in 1944, the systematic arrest and deportation of half-Jews to concentration camps began.

Chapter One

Hamburg 1942

Eva sat at her office window looking out over murky canal waters towards a row of bleak grey warehouses on the opposite side. A seagull perched motionless on a wooden tow pole like an irreverent statue. Eva wondered how often she had stared at the same view with its looming, dark Gothic church tower, enclosed by deep, hanging clouds; she'd been doing it for years, long stretched-out years. She could hardly imagine a different life. Her strength seemed to diminish each time she looked out, then apathy would make her lean back in her uncomfortable office chair.

On the ink-stained, worn wooden desk lay the company's ledger and a pile of unentered invoices. 'I'll never recuperate under these circumstances,' she realised. It became frightening to think of another evening alone in the office, sitting in the managing director's blacked-out room contemplating her dismal life, digesting Else's excellent dinner, drinking wine or coffee, smoking cigarettes and stringing pearls of gloom into an endless chain. Afterwards, when the nightly air raid was over and nothing drastic had happened, she would lie on the couch and try to sleep, praying, full of anxiety, for the advent of unconsciousness. After her last furnished room had gone up in flames she had made the office her home, occupying the president's room at night. The male employees were away in Russia, working for the war machine, collecting skins from slaughtered animals. Only Eva and Miss Ehrlich were left behind to mind the office.

Eva stared at the slowly moving grey clouds above the houses, at the raindrops on the pavement over the bridge, at the barge that passed silently below the window and at the wooden tow pole, which at the moment was unoccupied. She was vaguely depressed. Time had turned her into an invalid. She felt her pulse and diagnosed the symptoms. But it wasn't her sickness that made her wait so desperately for sleep at night, it was her fear of being eradicated completely. There was her fate's balance sheet appearing again behind her closed eyes, debit and credit, with very little chance of escape. She sighed and looked with disgust at the pile of unentered invoices.

Miss Ehrlich would have objected to being labelled an invalid. If she suffered from any affliction (and Eva was certain that her life was one big fraud) she was able to hide it carefully behind a display of cheerfulness. Nothing appeared to bother her or to diminish her energy and goodwill. She was happy as head of the company, she cheered at the great victories of her country, she waited with glee for letters from unknown soldiers with whom she corresponded and who had suddenly put romantic dreams into her sheltered, spinstery life. The war had made all the difference. So near to death, for the first time, Miss Ehrlich experienced some sort of life. Eva would watch her at lunch time opening the envelopes affectionately, smiling, saying: 'They come from the boys.' Afterwards she would hammer out her cheerful and optimistic replies on the typewriter. There were letters which came back marked: 'Died in action'; those Miss Ehrlich put aside without getting discouraged. She was there for the living, helping in her little way to win the war. When she was not involved with the boys she worked out the company's profits, the money that would come their way from the Russian spoils. It never occurred to her that she was involved in a crime. Wars excluded all crimes and victory justified war.

The dark, hanging clouds had been with them for weeks now. One moment it drizzled, the next it began to pour, then it was dry again and the fluff of grey vapour sailed by the Gothic church tower like a floating evening dress of the thinnest voile. The church tower going to a dance. And right away the wind began to blow and the rain to drum, opening the festivity with its usual waltz.

Eva remained paralysed at her desk, contemplating a way out of the monotony of her present situation. There was only Miss Ehrlich sitting at her typewriter. If she refused to be interrupted, Eva could pick up the ladies' room key and walk across the entrance hall, perhaps meeting someone or having a chat with Marion, the caretaker's daughter, who had become a prostitute after her mother's death in 1940. Since her father was away fighting on the eastern front, Marion had inherited his job of keeping the staircases and hallways clean. It was a job for which she lacked the necessary enthusiasm. Most of the time she was sleepy from a busy night and eagerly followed Eva's advice to postpone the scrubbing for another day because it was permanently raining and the floors would look dirty anyway.

Eva got up from her chair, tried not to remember the pile of undone work and walked slowly over to Miss Ehrlich's office. The wooden planks creaked under her feet. The hall was almost dark; they lived in the dark ages. Miss Ehrlich was typing new invoices. 'That's all I need,' thought Eva, 'more work.'

'What time is it?' asked Eva. It was an innocent enough beginning.

'It's a quarter past eleven,' answered Miss Ehrlich cheerfully.

'Seems much later.'

'Have you finished your work?' asked Miss Ehrlich in the voice of a responsible supervisor. 'Here are some new invoices.'

'Thanks,' said Eva, taking her copies and leaving the question of unfinished work unanswered. 'Have you had any letters from the boys today?'

'Not a single one,' said Miss Ehrlich as if this were a good sign. Eva was disappointed. She would have liked to hear a long report on battles at the frontier which might have carried them through to lunch time. It might have distracted her from looking out of the window on to the bleak landscape, remembering her unpromising balance sheet. But Miss

Ehrlich resumed her work, leaving Eva to remain in her gloom, unwanted.

'Is your mother coming later?' Eva was desperate.

'What do you mean?' Miss Ehrlich increased the speed of her typing. 'Of course she is coming, like any other day. What a question!'

'Yes, rather stupid. I only hope she is dressed properly for this kind of weather.' Miss Ehrlich didn't answer and Eva knew that she wouldn't get another syllable out of her. So she picked up the key from a nail on the wall and walked out of the office towards the toilets. She didn't meet anybody in the hall, nobody got out of the perpetually moving lift, the light was dim and grey, the air chilly and damp. Another hour of entries in the ledger lay ahead of her, then the afternoon. It was unbelievable! She felt her despair like a knife sticking between her ribs, something threatening and violent. Of course, she would sit later in Else's little room behind her delicatessen and be comforted by a good meal and Else's and Hubert's carefree lives. But now, at the moment of rising pain, this seemed hardly enough to give her the courage to endure another day of continuous unease when her hand-writing had to be so neat in the company's ledger. She returned to her office and decided to look out for Arlen after the performance that evening. Perhaps he would be acting and she could find him in the theatre restaurant alone. He possessed that special ability to blend with her moods. She would watch him eat his supper and he would look at her with the knowledge of an experienced doctor who had come across such cases as hers many times in his life. He would touch her hand and stroke her hair, he would say, 'Yes, I know. Just come with me, I possess the right medicine.' And she would be grateful and go and take all he could give. It usually had a soothing effect, as if the knife had been removed from her ribs for the moment and only the wound was there to smart and to heal.

She put the copies of the newly typed invoices at the bottom of the unfinished pile and thought of Miss Ehrlich's homely, pale face that was neither pleasant nor repulsive. It even possessed some outstanding features, but they were lost in the overall grey sickliness. Her ash-blond hair was parted in the middle, pulled back straight above the ears and held together in a braided bun by innumerable pins which sparkled occasionally, reflecting the light. She dressed in dark skirts and clean but oversized blouses which hung in baggy folds, hiding her flat chest and slender waist. Nothing in her appearance heralded her cheerfulness. Eva often wondered where it came from, what hidden dreams gave her the courage to endure the steady monotony of her life and the tyranny of a mother who granted her neither a place to breathe nor a future to decide upon, who loomed like a bad fate over her days, ordering and demanding. Still, Miss Ehrlich smiled and laughed in spite of her meagre, paper-thin existence.

The seagull had not returned to the pole. Raindrops splashed evenly on to the muddy waters. Another barge passed by noiselessly and vanished behind the sweeping curve of the canal. The clouds hung deep, touching the church tower. Across the water, people began to turn on lights. Specks of yellow flared up here and there like a flash of hope. 'We haven't had a single spring day yet and it's already the end of May,' Eva thought.

Shortly before lunch time she entered a few invoices in the ledger. Not that it mattered. The pile didn't shrink. It would never shrink at the rate she was going. Another seagull had occupied the pole. Or was it the same one with territorial rights? Why couldn't she – ? But it was wrong to start thinking. It only made her temperature rise.

Else's delicatessen was just a few doors away in one of the narrow old streets that had survived the big fire of the last century. The buildings leaned against each other like old people in need of support. The stairs to the front door slanted in different directions and had worn treads. At lunch time the little store got crowded with pale secretaries and book-keepers who wanted a sandwich, a cup of soup or a quarter-pound of Else's excellent, home-made herring salad. They queued up obediently, started conversations like old friends or stood silent and tired, awaiting their turn. Eva ran down the street, took her place and waited. Else had a package ready for her; it appeared from under the counter like magic. She smiled and said, 'See you.' Eva said, 'Thanks,' and then she returned to the office where Miss Ehrlich's mother was heating her daughter's lunch on a small, electric burner.

'Hello,' said Eva. 'Hope you didn't get drenched. What are you having? Smells delicious.' Eva despised Mrs Ehrlich's hold over her daughter and would have liked to show her disapproval. However, she couldn't afford any disharmony in the office. Miss Ehrlich had the power to dismiss her or to forbid her the use of Mr Lindner's couch at night. 'I can't afford it,' Eva decided. 'I like the district after dark when the streets are deserted, warehouses and offices empty, when I can roam around as if I owned the place. I don't have to travel to and from the office. I'm always there and I don't have to pay rent. Else is nearby. I can run around the corner and get comfort from a friend.' Being a half-Jew was definitely a disease which might or might not prove fatal. It remained a question which the government had not decided upon yet. 'Be nice to the old witch,' Eva told herself. 'Sooner or later she will lose her power.'

It got damper and colder. At three in the afternoon Eva had to switch on the light. She had given up looking at the dreary view. Instead she had turned her attention to the ledger, writing down on to the lined sheets, in her neat, small handwriting, letters and numbers, debit and credit. She touched her pulse again. Was it there? She wanted to make sure something was wrong, justifying her visit to Arlen. At just that moment she heard the Ehrlichs make their communal walk to the toilet. Another ten minutes and she would be alone, Miss Ehrlich's pale cheerfulness and her mother's cruelty gone. Eva had plenty of time. Before dinner she could take the lift up to visit Marion or she could give Werner a call. He'd certainly be expecting her sympathy since his mother had been taken unexpectedly to Theresienstadt. Werner found it easy to cry for his quota of consolation. If she gave in to his request she hated herself afterwards for having wasted all her time without having achieved anything; if she found an excuse for not giving in she felt heartless and cold. She couldn't win with Werner, nobody could.

'Good night,' said Miss Ehrlich cheerfully, carrying a black umbrella hooked over one arm and a shopping bag with her kitchen utensils in it on the other.

'Good night,' said Mrs Ehrlich like a parrot.

'Have a pleasant evening,' shouted Eva after the departing pair.

'Same to you.'

'I am on air-raid duty,' lied Eva.

'Take good care of the building then.' Miss Ehrlich laughed as if air-raids were a joke.

'Don't worry, I will.' The front door closed.

Eva went into the adjacent room, drew the heavy blackout curtains, sat in Mr Lindner's chair, put her feet on the desk and lit a cigarette. She hoped Marion wouldn't drop in suddenly as she sometimes did to report on the lunatic perversions of one of her clients as if it had not happened to herself but to some other battered body. 'Poor Marion,' thought Eva, but she got up and locked the front door. She didn't want to hear of Marion's deprived seventeen years of life on top of her own troubles. She returned to her chair, lifting a curtain to look out. The canal looked like a moat around some ancient castle. The houses opposite formed the high wall. She dropped the curtain and inhaled cigarette smoke. It had become silent except for the remote hum in her ears which came from within. Later at night the sounds of war would burst and roar. Eva never reflected on the chances she had in that game. Somehow she felt immune to the bombs' destructive force. Air raids didn't create much anxiety, at least not in comparison with her fear of the Nazis. That fear never left her, not even under Arlen's purposeful caresses. At times she went through moments of crisis. Nobody who was persecuted could run in fear and pain forever without, at some point, losing all hope. There was no cure. Survival depended on a certain amount of luck. Some days things looked better than others. Today was a bad one. She started to smoke another cigarette.

The cigarettes came from Else's black-market dealings. Hubert, her boyfriend, had the contacts and brought the merchandise to the little delicatessen, where false walls hid the contraband. Most goods arrived at night but occasionally a truck would come during the day as if it were making a legitimate delivery. Nobody suspected the prim, clean, blonde Else of any wrongdoing. She simply wasn't the type. Her conversations centred around herring salad, juicy pickles, the weather or some minor street gossip. People considered Else nice and decent, a hard-working woman, someone to be trusted. If a van pulled up it couldn't be anything but legitimate business.

Eva wasn't sure whether Else hated the Nazis because they punished black-marketeers or whether she had started to sabotage the economy because she hated the regime. Perhaps Hubert had talked her into the profitable business and by engaging in it, she had automatically become an enemy of the government, so the government had to be her enemy in return. She no longer had any choice, since she lived outside the law.

Eva lifted the curtain on the other side of the wall, facing the bridge. The house across the street had been bombed. Its jagged walls stood out against the night sky. Eva walked around and around Mr Lindner's desk, trying not to raise her hopes for the night too high. If only she could find Arlen. It was always a matter of chance. He might have performed that night; then he would come down to the restaurant afterwards. If not, he would be enjoying himself elsewhere. She might meet him but with a 'previous engagement', or he might get too drunk in her company to be of any help. She would have to walk back through the desolate early morning streets after an air raid feeling sicker than before. It wouldn't be the first time. 'Just don't think. Don't look back, don't remember. For heaven's sake don't remember! Look in the mirror and tell yourself that you have never seen that person before, say hello, nice to meet you, how do you feel? Not so well, sort of invalidish. I need a rest cure. A cure!' Apparently she had conjured up the wrong person. Eva needed someone with a bit more health and vigour.

At ten-thirty she left Else's store and walked through the dark streets towards the theatre. It had started to drizzle again but Eva didn't notice. Her mood rose to a state of anxiety.

She saw the cake, that awful yellow cake which her father had devoured in his starved state. She saw his hollowed, pained face greedily eating the artificially coloured junk that couldn't nourish. She saw the murderous intent of the country directed at them. Her pulse was racing at a record speed. 'Stop it! You promised not to think back, not to remember. Hurry up and find Arlen.'

With the show over, the 'Bitendorf' Restaurant was filling. The audience congregated around the bar in a happy, festive mood. There were some men among the women, men in uniforms and men in evening suits. The place still retained its old elegance, its old-fashioned lamps and coat hangers, its old waiters and its reputation for good food and wine. Its greatest attraction lay in the actors appearing after the show in ordinary clothes, and sitting down to eat their supper. People watched from a distance, pointed, whispered, mentioned names, got excited. There sat the great so-and-so and they almost rubbed shoulders with him. It was exhilarating. No wonder the place was always overcrowded at this hour.

Eva studied the programme and noticed that Arlen had been acting that night. She sat down at their usual table, which was reserved, and smiled when the waiter greeted her. Then Renate came asking: 'Wasn't it ravishing – Arlen's acting and Eduard's interpretation of the wise old man? Wasn't it all really like a dream?'

'I wasn't there,' said Eva.

'You'd better not tell Arlen. He might feel offended,' warned Renate.

'He knows. We've stopped pretending to each other.'

'He'll never stop.' Renate laughed.

'Perhaps you're right. Nobody can stop completely. To become utterly honest you have to know the truth and there simply is none, none we can use.'

'Here comes Arlen!' Renate shouted as if she had to herald his entrance. 'You must admit he looks gorgeous.' She offered her lips with a smile and Arlen responded like a well-rehearsed actor, bending down and meeting her lips. Renate put one arm around his neck and held Arlen's head for a prolonged embrace.

'Come on,' said Eva, 'do stop it. Are you free tonight, Arlen? I have to know.'

'Has anything happened?' he asked with some concern.

'Just the usual, only worse. I think it's an accumulation – '

'All right, my pet, don't start crying.'

'She always gets you with her sob stories,' objected Renate.

'You can't imagine what it's like,' said Arlen impatiently.

'Oh, she told me.'

'You don't know anything about it. You've never been on trial.'

'I think you've lost me there,' admitted Renate, 'what trial?'

'Promise to lay off Eva,' Arlen demanded.

'I didn't attack her.'

'All right, just be concerned.'

Eduard joined them. 'I don't have much time.' He sat down and ordered a meal. 'My wife always sits up waiting for me.'

'Why isn't she here?' asked Eva.

'She doesn't like leaving our dogs and birds alone in case of an air raid.'

'Well, pet ownership is a great responsibility, my dear friend.' Arlen smiled.

'I wish I could have seen you tonight on stage,' said Eva, and Eduard blushed as if he had never been praised before.

'What about me?' asked Arlen. 'Why single out Eduard?'

'Because you never stay in character. But I've told you that before. The things we repeat seem endless! They almost fill up our entire life. Have you ever done book-keeping?' She blew her nose, close to tears.

'Calm down,' begged Arlen.

'Everything is getting worse.'

'I know it is. But surely things can only get *so* bad . . .'

'You looked divine in your costume,' interrupted Renate in a seductive tone.

'The food isn't bad tonight,' Eduard remarked as Inge arrived arm-in-arm with Thomas.

'Let me see – ' Inge bent her head over everybody's plate and checked the contents.

'You need glasses,' said Thomas.

'I need something to eat.'

'Have the beef stew,' suggested Eduard. 'I can recommend it.'

'If you keep on "straying" I won't act with you any longer. I'll request a replacement,' Inge said to Arlen.

'What do you mean?' Arlen was perturbed.

'Don't you realise how often you lose your character in mid-part and never find him again? Whom am I speaking to then? How do I react? It becomes a new play that we've never rehearsed, and a bad one.'

'This world is becoming such a nightmare,' Arlen defended himself.

'Pull yourself together!' Inge ordered the beef stew. 'If you don't improve, I'll request a replacement.'

'He drinks too much,' said Eduard, wiping his mouth with a white linen napkin.

'I was the only one who got a standing ovation tonight,' said Arlen. He had finished his first bottle of wine.

'Ovations from shopgirls,' laughed Inge.

'You're too ambitious,' said Thomas to Inge.

'Please don't let me down,' whispered Eva.

'Have I ever, my pet?' asked Arlen tenderly.

'Yes.' Eva was frightened. 'But don't tonight.'

'I swear,' said Arlen with conviction.

An air-raid advance warning gave a muffled wail through the panelled basement. Nobody took any notice.

'I'm surprised they come in this weather.' Eduard felt nervous with his wife all alone with the dogs and the two birds in a cage.

'Haven't you noticed that they come in all weathers now, throwing bombs, finding targets?' remarked Thomas.

'This is our last season in the theatre. We'll be drafted this autumn.'

Eduard lit a cigarette with trembling hands. 'Who says they'll close the theatre?'

'The government, my friend. Your beloved government,' answered Arlen.

'It's not my beloved government and you know it. It is my

beloved country.' Eduard wanted to make the point clear.

'Well, you handed it over to the devil.' Renate was angry.

'And it's costing us,' said Inge.

'You talk as if the war were lost,' Eduard protested.

'Can't you see the writing on the wall?' Thomas looked Eduard in the eyes. 'But anyway, we're not talking about the war.'

'I remain hopeful,' said Eduard.

'So do we,' said Renate. 'We'll see who wins.'

Eva had not spoken a word. She sat silently, watching Arlen. Suddenly, instead of an air raid, the sirens wailed the 'all-clear'. Eduard got ready to leave.

'You swore,' said Eva to Arlen.

'Just one more glass.'

She hated waiting because she never forgot what she was waiting for. One more glass of wine and then?

'Let's go!' shouted Arlen at last.

They stepped into the night, blindly at first. It was still drizzling.

'Please,' Eva asked and Arlen took her into his arms, held her with his wine-induced strength. She felt the warmth of his protection, the end of her long struggle, the relief of a victory.

'Hurry!'

'Hold my hand,' she begged as they ran down the street.

Chapter Two

      Eva was depressed in spite of her night with Arlen. She took her pulse, tried to guess her temperature, felt the threat of her situation. Should she try the drugs Marion offered? No, drugs only added to problems, never solved any.

'We don't have to fight at the Russian frontier,' Arlen had said during the night when she couldn't stop crying.

'We also aren't in a concentration camp.'

'We are alive.'

'I wonder if it's worth it.' She had been too sad.

'You slept and had no nightmares.'

'The worst come when you are awake.'

'I know.'

Miss Ehrlich was hammering with enthusiasm on the typewriter. Eva walked into her office to enquire about mail from the boys.

'Three nice letters,' she said triumphantly.

'Are they fine?'

'At the moment only Ernst is in hospital. But he'll recover. Lost a leg, you know. It was Martin who died last month. Now his friend is writing regularly. There is always so much work.' She returned to her typewriter. Perhaps she was writing to Martin's replacement.

'Glad they're well,' Eva said and returned to her office. She wondered how she could get through the day. She had to cling to detail, use a moment-to-moment survival technique. She decided on coffee, went out and ran down the street to Else's delicatessen. The store was empty. Else appeared, clean and prim, her blonde hair combed up and folded into a crown on top of her head. Her apron looked white and starched, her lips had a touch of red, her eyebrows were pencilled a dark colour.

'What's the matter?' Else asked. 'You look ghastly.'

'It's always the same. Would you have a cup of coffee by any chance?'

'I'll make one fast.' She vanished into her kitchen and reappeared in no time. 'Have to wait until the water boils,' she explained. 'What's happened really?' she asked.

'Nothing. Being frightened, feeling empty – '

'Remember, it can't last for ever.' Else went back to the kitchen.

That evening Eva met Werner.

'You don't look well,' he said.

They were silent, sitting in the elegant living room from which his mother had been taken.

'Have you heard?' asked Eva.

'They won't let them write.' He shook his head.

'She never told me she was Jewish, you know. I suddenly got discharged from the army, requested a reason and heard the truth. When I confronted her she didn't deny it. They had found her papers in Poland. Shortly afterwards they took her away.'

'If only your father were still alive – '

'Yes, it would have saved her,' said Werner.

'Wouldn't it be wiser to forget the entire mess and just pretend to live in the twenty-first century? Put on a record.'

'What do you want to hear?' he asked, infected by her mood.

'Something romantic.' He put on 'In the Steppes of Central Asia'.

'Great,' said Eva and began to waltz around the table. 'All these treasures – ' She stepped from room to room, whirling around. 'Treasures, treasures, treasures,' she sang with the music. 'Between the air raids and the Nazis, something is bound to happen to them.'

'It's all a gamble,' Werner said.

She sank into an armchair. 'My feet refuse to dance, they're too ready to run.' The music stopped. They sat empty among the splendour of Werner's inherited treasures.

'Richard Strauss?' he asked.

'Mozart, please.' They faced each other. A pink flower in a valuable vase separated them. 'Gone tomorrow,' warned Eva. 'Can't you put it in storage under a friend's name?'

'I can't part from it all. I'll sit and wait until they throw me out.' He looked at the clock. 'Dinner is ready, with wine and coffee.'

The table was set as though royalty were expected. He played the butler and host, carrying heavy silver platters and dishes.

'We always dined like this,' he said. 'I used to cook for my mother.'

'It's delicious. How is life otherwise?'

'Incomprehensible.' He lifted his glass and said, 'To her health!' Then they ate in silence, feeling guilty.

'I haven't eaten anything as tasty in years,' exclaimed Eva to break the silence.

'I appreciate a compliment from you.' He smiled.

'But I am very appreciative, really, though I might fail to express it at times. In fact I never forget a kindness.'

'You are selfish.'

'Weak people usually are.'

Later they drank coffee from valuable cups in the library. Several candles were lit, giving a soft, auburn light. Eva smoked a cigarette. A Mozart symphony was playing, filling the silence with its dancing notes. Happiness seemed to lie around the corner, just out of reach.

'If life wasn't so hellish, this could be quite romantic,' mused Eva.

'Don't be such a cynic,' Werner said uneasily.

'I wouldn't come between you and your mother,' Eva reassured him. 'Don't worry.'

'I love her.'

'You forgot to grow up.'

'You forgot to say "poor Werner".'

'All right, poor Werner. Does that make you happy?'

'No. It sounds as if you think I'm a cripple.'

'We all carry our deformities, you know. Don't listen to my nonsense. I've had a very lovely evening, I forgot my pain. What more could you have done?'

Eva returned to the office just before the sirens gave the advance warning. Marion stood in the dark hallway with a customer. Eva could hear his heavy breathing.

'You can use the office,' Eva called out. 'I'm on duty.' Then she sat in Mr Lindner's chair and lit a cigarette, waiting. She had eaten too much, her head spun from the wine and from tiredness. '*Wenn ich ein Vöglein wär* – ' she began to recite, expecting the warning signal at any moment. Nothing seemed to flourish in the underworld. What kind of evening had she spent with Werner? It was hard to define. They had sat in splendour, had appreciated luxuries, while Werner's mother was in Theresienstadt awaiting her murder, and at the same time bombs were being loaded into aeroplanes to destroy them all. What kind of evening could one expect? At that moment the sirens started to warn. 'Blast!' said Eva aloud, putting out her cigarette. She switched off the light and groped her way towards the door.

'Get into my office!' she called to Marion through the outside darkness. 'They'll be coming down any minute.' A lot of people lived in the building these days. She found the staircase and descended into the basement. One by one tired office employees appeared, still drowsy from interrupted sleep. Eva knew most of the women in the building, she knew how many children they had and where their husbands were fighting – if they still had a husband. She didn't feel sorry for them. They had asked for it, these mute, uncomplaining people.

The raid seemed to be concentrated around the harbour. The noise became tremendous. Their building vibrated at every impact. Anti-aircraft guns competed with the exploding bombs.

'That might have been a fire bomb,' said the only man, whose heart and lungs were weak.

'I'll go upstairs to check,' Eva said. Nobody else volunteered.

'Take my torch,' offered one lady.

Eva walked up eight flights of winding stairs, searched Marion's apartment, then the attic. Nothing. From one of the windows she could see the illuminated night sky. Flames burned like torch lights on the landscape of the harbour. 'They can't last for ever,' thought Eva. 'They can't last – ' Then she walked down again.

'The harbour is burning,' Eva reported. 'We are in immediate range.'

'In the vicinity,' corrected the man with the weak heart. 'It makes a difference.'

'All right, but if you get hit, you get hit, no matter where you are.'

'Very unlikely,' protested a middle-aged woman.

'Don't tell me you are exempt,' Eva laughed.

'I refuse to consider it.' The woman was adamant.

'That's the best way of preserving one's spirit,' another woman said.

They sat huddled together, listening to the explosions which sounded more and more threatening. A bomb fell nearby. The building seemed to be lifted off the ground then set down again. The basement lights went out.

'Well, you said we were in the vicinity.'

'Somebody should check the house,' the man said.

'Go right ahead,' said Eva. 'We have a torch.' He didn't reply and nobody volunteered. 'Cowards!' thought Eva. 'If it were my country, I would show more courage.'

Nobody went. They sat in the darkness until the raid was over.

'Sorry,' said Eva when she returned to her office, 'but you'll have to leave now. The hallway is clear.'

'Thanks,' answered Marion. 'Come and see me tomorrow after work.'

The next day there was the same dismal, grey sky and

prevailing drizzle. The wooden pole occasionally had dirty-looking seagulls on it. A barge passed by noiselessly. The buildings still appeared bleak, the black Gothic church tower loomed and the company's ledger was an ever-present reminder to Eva of her duties. She was working at a steady pace. Her boss needed the latest balance-sheet figures sent to a desolate post in a far-off Russian province where he himself kept an accurate count of the number of cattle stolen. Now he wanted to know the company's exact share of the spoils. 'I'll have to work day and night. My own fault, I knew it was coming,' she thought.

She ran regularly over to Else's to be cheered by a smile or an embrace. 'Have a cup of coffee.' 'You need a break.' 'Have dinner with us.' Else offered her riches while Miss Ehrlich's cheerful, commonplace remarks sounded off-key and false.

After the Ehrlichs had gone for the day, Eva went to see Marion. She found her sitting in an easy chair reading a cheap novel. The apartment was tidy, polished and clean.

'Always expecting Father?' Eva laughed.

'He's really dangerous, no kidding.'

'I know he brags about murdering Jews and Polacks.'

'Not forgetting my mother. I should have gone to the police but I was too scared.'

'Perhaps when the war is over – '

'I'll do my best to get him put away,' Marion said without any emotion.

'Back to work. My boss wants his figures.'

Eva moved her work over to Mr Lindner's desk. It was the only room with air-raid curtains. The rays of the electric light on the office's dismal surroundings seemed to add to the weight of her burdens. Why couldn't she overlook those things and have a flair for life like Else, who turned every event to her advantage? A toothache was to be expected – you can't have perfect teeth all your life; a spill was wiped up in a second. Nothing got her down, not even a day with a hangover. That was the way it was, a day of some discomfort and gloom. Who can be happy all the time?

'Who is ever happy?' Eva asked herself and wondered whether her father had realised he was going to be murdered, or whether he had been unaware of what was happening when it came to the end. 'Stop thinking!' she ordered. 'Return to your ledger: debit – credit.' She wrote figure after figure which meant starvation for the Russian people. The room with its black air-raid curtains seemed to grow smaller. Eva put down her pen and left. The hallway was empty. Marion was probably out looking for customers. She tapped at the door of Else's delicatessen.

'Right on time,' said Else. 'I was just wondering where you were hiding.'

'Working,' replied Eva. 'Mr Lindner wants his figures and I'm way behind.'

'Nothing's free in this life,' Hubert said.

'That's for sure!' laughed Else. 'Come on, dinner is getting cold.' They ate with pleasure. Else's food, though simple, was always tasty. Hubert wiped his mouth with a light blue napkin after every bite.

'Hubert is such a neat eater,' remarked Else. 'If I'd let him, he would lick his plate clean.'

'I sometimes do it anyway.' He laughed like a naughty boy. 'Your food is delicious but your lips taste better by far.'

'Now, that's all we want to hear on that subject,' Else said, rather annoyed.

'I expect a shipment in at ten,' Hubert said.

'Do you know what it is?' Eva asked.

'Coffee, tea and cigarettes.'

'How much?' asked Else.

'It's all paid for,' said Hubert. 'They don't deal any other way.'

'It used to be half on ordering, half on delivery.'

'It's hard to get at the stuff nowadays. They can dictate conditions.'

'All right,' said Else. 'As long as they come through.'

'They'll come through. The last thing they need is an enemy,' said Hubert. He liked crooked ways and dangerous games. The military had exempted him from service and Eva wondered how he had managed to get away with it. Now he lay back, stretching his legs, relaxing at the thought that he was scheming against the law. His eyes rested on Else's face and figure while she was handling the dishes in the sink. For a moment he got restless and ran his hands through his blond hair, several times, up and down until he was able to relax again. He looked at Else: 'She is all a man would ever want and she's got a head on her shoulders into the bargain.'

Eva was drying the dishes and putting them away. Then the two women sat down as well, stretching, smoking, enjoying their coffee.

'I don't know what I would do without you,' said Eva.

'I always get high praise after a good meal,' Else remarked. 'Hubert knows at least a dozen compliments.'

'But I mean it. You are saving my life.'

Eva worked through the air raid, which lasted until two, then she fell on to the couch in her clothes and stared into the darkness. Memories attacked her thin resistance. Yes, yes, she agreed without defence, she had stayed in Hamburg while her father slowly starved to death in Berlin. She had tried to slow down the process of malnutrition but it had never been enough. She had hardly begun to alleviate the loneliness he must have felt in that small room in an overcrowded ghetto house. After her mother's death in 1935, he had been thrown into it as though it were a prison, though his half-Jewish daughter had provided him with the privilege of a single room and the freedom to walk the streets without the Star of David attached to his clothes. But they were not allowed to live together – if one could still talk about life. About a dozen people, Jews, squeezed together in the flat, permanently hungry, deprived of anything human. Each time Eva had gone to Berlin her father had looked more haggard, had been less lucid, more confused. He had leaned on her arm like an old man, watching for a place where soup or something else to eat was advertised free of ration cards. So they went up and down the streets into various restaurants though signs at the entrance doors clearly stated: 'No Jews allowed'. They had gone in and he had eaten and eaten. On the way back his legs had shuffled in their weakness over the pavements. 'The days are so long,' he had complained. 'I need a wife.' 'Yes, yes,' she had answered.

The last time she saw him he had talked incessantly about a coffee house where they sold cakes for bread coupons. Could Eva spare them? His eyes had sunk deeper into their sockets, the skin hung over the hollows of his cheeks, his feet dragged, he put more weight on Eva's arm. He spoke of nothing but the cake as if in a fever. They sat at a table. The proprietor viewed them with suspicion but Eva went to the counter and inspected the cakes. They were custard pies filled with yellow jelly and topped with a white foam. She ordered two and coffee. He swallowed the sticky, sweet, soft mass with such greed, as if each bite prevented his starvation. After he had finished hers as well, she realised that his stomach was full but that he had not been nourished. No matter what she did for him, he had no chance of recovery. As long as she was better nourished than he, she felt guilty. He didn't talk of marriage any more. Hunger had taken him over. A few days later he was arrested together with hundreds of other Jews. Eva finally got a notice from the Berlin Jewish Community telling her that he had been dead for six weeks. No other comment. One thousand Jews had been killed. The Nazis blatantly admitted the murders, they didn't hide anything any more by 1942. Eva remembered the last meeting with her father as though she had been transported there by a time machine. She couldn't escape the horror, the pain, the guilt.

Finally, she opened the curtains. The sky was getting lighter, it was purplish-grey with lowering clouds. She found herself in a dark tunnel with no light at the end. No coffee, no kind word, no love-making could touch her in her isolation.

Eva turned on the light and went back to work. She made enough progress to contemplate a visit to the theatre restaurant that night. She needed a bath at Arlen's. Why a bath? It made her feel normal and healthy. People always took baths. If she went to the restaurant table tonight and asked Arlen for the key to his house because she wanted to take a bath, everybody would understand and consider her one of them. It would break through her isolation. She turned on Mr Lindner's radio: 'Partly clearing in the late afternoon. Fewer clouds.' Eva put this into her personal credit column. If only Miss Ehrlich would stay at home for once. But there was no chance. She was never ill. Her cheerfulness prevented it. How did she manage to stomach her mother? Perhaps she had escaped into some form of insanity. The days are so long.

After Eva had moved her work back to her own office, she went to Else's for breakfast.

'One of my nights,' sighed Eva.

'I'll make you an extra strong cup.'

'Did your shipment arrive?'

'Everything is under control.' Else put coffee and bread on the table. 'Help yourself, eat. You look so worn and tired. Remember, it can't last for ever.'

'It could.'

'No, it can't! Don't worry, one day you'll forget what happened.'

'I doubt it.' Eva knew better.

'You are too young to remember the times before the Nazis took over. My dear, those were the days – ' Else smiled as if she were looking at a sky full of fireworks.

'I'm glad to hear there used to be days because now we don't seem to get them anymore.'

'They will come back.' Else had her elbows on the table and held her coffee cup with both hands close to her mouth. From time to time she took a small sip, let it rest on her tongue, then swallowed it with satisfaction. 'You can trust me,' she assured Eva. 'I know what I'm talking about.'

Miss Ehrlich was typing merrily when Eva returned from her breakfast.

'Can I have the figures?' she enquired. 'I had no idea you were this far behind. In future please stay up to date.'

'I'll try.'

'How long will it take you to catch up?'

'Thieves, murderers,' thought Eva. 'Perhaps tomorrow, if it balances.'

'I'm relying on you. You are lucky Mr Lindner is such a kind man.' She resumed her typing.

Eva returned to her office and looked out of the window. The canal was a murky dark grey. The seagull, occupying the rotting pole, looked arrogant and soiled. The ledger was covered with figures. She picked up her pen and wrote 'Invoice No. 3521, dated . . .' 'This will go on for ever, timeless like nothingness. Nothingness balances itself. I definitely need a bath.' She worked in a trance-like state. Mrs Ehrlich arrived and was greeted cheerfully by her daughter. Then the bridge was deserted again. Eva could detect not even a partial clearing in the sky. Her hand became cramped from all the writing but she kept it up, entry after entry, debit – credit.

She hurried along the dark pavement, counting the unlit lamp posts. The theatre restaurant was teeming with people. 'What a goldmine,' thought Eva. 'Except that this is the last season.' Arlen sat at the 'reserved' table with Renate, Eduard, Inge and Thomas.

'I have to think of my own career, Arlen,' insisted Inge. 'You've had your warning. I'm going to talk to the director.'

'Bitch!'

'My performance suffers from your blunders – '

'Stop fighting,' ordered Thomas. 'I can't stand vindictive women.'

'Then look for someone else. Artists should take their work seriously.'

'Inge is right, of course,' agreed Eduard. 'But we should help a friend through a crisis.'

'Granted,' said Inge. 'But not on stage. On stage it's another matter.'

'Being vindictive is not going to improve your situation,' remarked Thomas.

'I want a decent performance.'

'All you can think of is your performance in some stupid play,' complained Renate.

'Hello Eva,' said Arlen. 'Inge is trying to get me into trouble.'

'I just heard. As if we didn't have enough already.'

'Good night,' said Thomas. 'I told you, I can't stand vindictive people.'

'You'll be back.' Inge smiled. 'You always come back.'

'Not this time.' He took his coat and left.

'May I have your key?' asked Eva. 'I need a bath.' Arlen searched in his pocket.

'Here.' He handed her the key. 'The bulb is broken. You'll have to take a candle from the living room.'

'Thanks. I'll leave it in the usual place.'

'Right.'

Eva leaned back in clear, hot water. The candle was flickering. Her own shadow appeared, gigantic, on the wall and ceiling. She liked to be alone in Arlen's apartment. She had lived there once for three months while Arlen was on tour. The only apartment she had ever had to herself. In the beginning, during a period of euphoria, she had run out and bought a huge plant with beautifully shaped, deep green leaves, then danced all night to Arlen's records. Three months later she had vacated her magic island again for some hole or other. 'Murderers, thieves!' Jews were squeezed into ghettos and half-Jews had nowhere to go. They were not allowed to rent or to own anything. 'They're going to take Werner's flat and treasures away from him now they know that his mother's a Jew.'

Eva washed her hair and scrubbed her skin. The water was still warm and soft. She rolled over like a seal. With her wet hair wrapped in a towel she walked barefoot through the living room, touching things as if they belonged to her. Then she listened to a recording of the 'Appassionata' and fell asleep. She was woken by banging at the door.

'Who is it?' She could hardly talk.

'It's me,' shouted Arlen.

'Why did you knock?' Now she was sobbing.

'I called and called – '

'I'm scared.'

'Nothing is going to happen,' he promised, holding her in his arms.

'Don't leave me,' she begged.

'Go back to sleep, my pet. I'll hold you.'

'My God,' she was still crying, 'they have reduced me to infancy.'

'Don't fight any more.' Arlen covered her with a blanket.

24

'Try to go back to sleep.'

The sky was grey, as usual, when Eva walked back to the office. She was shivering from fatigue, though she had slept on and off during the night. She would balance her ledger today. Whenever her brain was at such a low ebb it functioned well for the ledger.

'Are you sick?' asked Miss Ehrlich, full of cheerfulness.

'I'm working too hard.'

'Your own fault if you get behind.'

'I don't enjoy book-keeping.'

'Somebody has to do it. Would you like to have my job?'

'No thanks. I'm amazed how you manage. I bet you could run the company as efficiently as Mr Lindner.'

'It's all a question of capital and getting bank loans. The business end is easy.'

'Any news from the boys?'

'Someone's always writing. Mr Lindner sends his special regards.'

'He wants his figures. Well, I'd better start.'

It began to rain. Tomorrow was the first of June. She attempted to finish the April figures, determined to have the balance sheet ready by one o'clock before they closed. It was Saturday.

The Ehrlichs walked arm in arm under a black umbrella across the bridge into the drizzling fog, out of sight. It was cold and sombre. The filing cabinet, the ink-stained desk, the shabby chair, all had the casual and insignificant look of decay. At least she had a large window.

Chapter Three

Eva remembered that when she had come to Hamburg in 1938 for an interview with Mr Lindner, she had waited in the same room she was now sleeping in every night. Work had been scarce then. Her inexperience and half-Jewishness made it almost impossible to find employment. She had tried several Jewish firms but they were reducing their staff or were closing altogether. One bank had let her stay for two weeks because the boss was interested in her but when she rejected his advances there was no longer any work. She had interviews with other bosses who made it clear that they wanted an efficient secretary who wouldn't mind giving herself as well. At least they made it clear in advance. Eva got despondent and disgusted.

Yes, she remembered the interview. There were two desks standing in the room then and a large picture of a beautiful woman half embracing her daughter. The picture made her feel less tense, so she got along with Mr Lindner. It all seemed to fall into place. When she mentioned her half-Jewishness he just smiled and said it didn't matter. She could hardly believe her luck.

She had been introduced to the staff and felt welcomed by Miss Ehrlich's cheerfulness. Everybody was friendly, the two apprentices, both half-Jewish, the office boy, the book-keeper and his assistant Mondschein, who was Jewish, Mr Hamann for whom she had been hired, the boisterous Mr Schiller, who had a minor job but pretended to run the show, and the sly and slick chauffeur with his pock-marked face and arrogant manner.

'Don't worry,' Miss Ehrlich had told her, 'I'll be here at lunch time in case you need any help.' Lunch time lasted for two hours while the bosses were at the Commodity Exchange conducting their business. After their return the rush of buying and selling began. The employees started work at eight o'clock in the morning and they hardly ever left before eight at night. Eva got a lot of help from Miss Ehrlich in the beginning. Everybody was kind.

'That's all going to change,' Miss Ehrlich had told her. 'As soon as Mr Bertram comes back from Poland. He sees to it that no one smiles.' Eva heard the company's history, about its founder, old Mr Meyer, who had now emigrated to France with his wife and daughter. Of young Mr Walter Meyer who had gone to England and of Mr Bertram Meyer who was sticking it out, still sharing in the ownership of the company because he had acquired foreign nationality. He had an Argentinian passport. He was arrogant and tyrannical, always had been, while the rest of the family had behaved in the most gentlemanly manner. Eva could imagine the rage and frustration in Mr Bertram's soul; he had to stand by helplessly while Mr Lindner and the rest were pulling away, bit by bit, what was rightfully his.

One day Mr Bertram arrived from Poland. He was a tall, broad, powerful man with a fat, sensitive, child-like face. His hair was dark and plastered back with some lotion, his eyes were light blue with long, curved lashes behind frameless glasses, the nose well shaped, slender and slightly hooked. The mouth was soft and finely outlined, the cheeks cleanly shaved and flabby. He had a pronounced double chin and fat, cushioned hands covered in hair which made them look dirty. His tailor-made jacket hung sloppily over his shoulders as if it would fall off any moment. You could see immediately that he had money and that he was used to having money. 'Poor Mr Bertram,' she thought after her thorough investigation, 'your belief in the power game will give you a hard time.'

One day, during the lunch break, while Mr Lindner was at the Commodity Exchange – Mr Bertram was no longer allowed to attend – he asked her into his office for dictation.

'You'd better go,' said Miss Ehrlich, 'or he'll fire you.' Eva entered, rather frightened of the bulky man, but he simply dictated several letters in English and French, looking down at the canal as if he were standing on the bridge of a big ship, using his power to steer it. Then he suddenly turned round and asked her:

'I want to know what they're saying behind my back.'

'What do you mean?' Eva pretended ignorance.

'They hate my guts, I know.'

'They're robbing you blind,' Eva had answered. 'They push you against the wall, humiliate you. Why do you let it happen, why don't you leave?'

'First I'll get as much money out of them as I can, then I'm leaving.'

'It's a dangerous game,' said Eva. 'They robbed my family of everything – and we had a lot to take.'

'I have my plan,' Mr Bertram replied.

The atmosphere in the office changed to one of tension and arguments behind locked doors. Mr Bertram issued orders with the fury of a power-hungry general, and yelled if they were not followed properly. He trembled at the slightest provocation. One day he attacked her.

'You can't fight them,' Eva had been saying. 'They will squash you first.'

'Don't tell me what to do!' he had yelled. It was the Jewish drama. They had to take it out on each other.

Then the company got a letter from the Commodity Exchange requesting proof of owners' and officers' pure Arian blood. If they couldn't come up with a bill of clean health their membership would be withdrawn. Without the Exchange they couldn't exist. It was simple, but it worked. Mr Lindner and Mr Bertram had to part company. It was called Arianisation. However, Mr Bertram was in no mood to leave the country just yet. He was still working on his plan. He rented the two back rooms, founded a new company in his own name and continued to do business, selling goods from one foreign country to another. Mondschein, the assistant book-keeper, Bayer the apprentice, and Eva made up the staff. They really were a miserable lot and Mr Bertram remained tense, demanding and disagreeable. Mondschein took the situation particularly to heart. He was a slight, short-sighted young man with unattractive features. His suit was worn and mended like Bayer's. Bayer was at least occasionally able to make a sarcastic remark which was funny. He was able to laugh at a sad situation too. Mondschein became agitated and anxious about the slightest irregularity.

'I don't like working in a Jewish outfit,' he complained. 'It can't last and I'll be out of a job.'

'You're not starving yet,' Bayer responded.

In the front office, which was on the ground floor, Mr Lindner had given the order to paper his windows, so that nobody from the street could look in if Mr Bertram came over for a discussion regarding the separation of assets and liabilities. Mr Bertram was infuriated by the opaque paper, stuck to the windowpanes as though something criminal were going on. When he began to make a habit of walking over unannounced as often as he liked, as if he still owned the company, Mr Lindner closed the door on him for good. In future any communication was to be held through lawyers. The letter Mr Bertram received from the inheritor of the Meyer spoils included the sentence: 'You are herewith forbidden to enter the front office.'

On the same day, Mondschein arrived in a frightful state of anxiety. He claimed to have been followed to the office by plainclothes policemen, and looked repeatedly at the door as if he expected someone to rush in at any moment.

'They're going to arrest me!' he burst out at noon. 'This is a Jewish outfit.'

'Nobody'll come,' assured Bayer. 'Just do your work.'

'How can I work?' He was ready to break down.

Mr Bertram was making his daily call to Darling which always lasted for a long time, full of endearments. But today their exchange didn't last very long. Mr Bertram let off steam like a child in a tantrum.

'Forbidden to enter my own office!' he yelled hysterically, out of control. And as if Mondschein had needed only a slight push to set the machine in motion, he began to act out scenes from a madhouse, fending off attackers, howling, screaming, hiding under furniture.

'Damn it, calm down!' yelled Bayer. 'There's no one here but us. Get out from under there and sit at your desk. I'll lock the door if it makes you feel more comfortable.' But Mondschein was beyond help. 'Gone mad,' stated Bayer. 'It's one way to escape.'

'I wonder what could be worse than our situation in this God-damned country?' Eva asked.

'Our future in this God-damned country,' Bayer replied.

'What shall we do with Mondschein?' By now he had crawled into the furthermost corner of the office, still howling like an animal and hiding his face in both hands.

'I know a Jewish hospital not far from where I live,' Bayer said. They telephoned, explained the case and were promised help. Mr Bertram walked through the office without noticing that one of his employees had lost his mind. He slammed the door.

'It's amazing what kind of luxuries they still allow the Jews: hospitals and straitjackets,' Bayer remarked.

When the nurse came to take Mondschein away he followed without resistance. Eva began to cry.

'He's never been stable,' Bayer tried to console her.

'It's so sad.' Eva was still crying when Mr Bertram returned and heard the entire story.

'Well,' Mr Bertram said, 'one of you had better learn book-keeping fast.'

That afternoon Mr Bertram called Eva in and attacked her with his dirty-looking hands. She stared at him in amazement and wondered whether insanity were contagious.

'Sorry,' she said, pulling at his hands, 'I'm not interested.'

'I used to have a secretary who couldn't get enough . . .'

'Enough is enough!' shouted Eva.

'Don't worry. I can't get any fun when it's forced,' he said, grabbing her again at the same time none the less.

'Keep your hands off me!' yelled Eva, kicking his legs just as Bayer opened the door and asked if anything was the matter.

'Just a collision,' she explained.

'I hope you're not hurt,' continued Bayer.

'Not at all.' She walked out.

From that day on Mr Bertram had changed his tone in the office. He brought them expensive cold cuts and salads for lunch, he sat with them while they ate and enjoyed it. He told stories from his childhood and closed the office early if there wasn't enough to do. 'Have a good time,' he told them, and they ran across the bridge like happy animals. When Mr Bertram left again for Poland, they began to miss him.

'I never realised he was such a nice man,' confessed Bayer. 'He used to be a pest.'

'I miss him a lot,' Eva said. 'It's so empty now.'

They visited Mondschein in the hospital and found him less demented. He asked about the office and his job.

'It's waiting for you,' Bayer said reassuringly.

'Better get well quickly,' added Eva.

'Very difficult,' confessed Mondschein. 'They say I imagine things, but what they say I am imagining is as real to me as the things they say are real. How should I know the difference? It's all very difficult.' He sighed.

'Don't think too much. Just get well.'

'Very difficult,' insisted Mondschein.

They had nothing to do in the office. Mr Bertram stayed abroad and wrote occasional letters or telephoned to find out how they were.

'We are fine,' Bayer told him. 'Just a little lonely. Aren't you coming back? Mondschein is improving. Eva does the book-keeping.' But for most of the day they talked or read books and forgot that life was dismal. For a while they experienced the luxury of normality.

Mondschein came to visit them. He had been released from the hospital and transferred to a camp where he was being trained for field work.

'It's either South America or Palestine,' he told them.

'Great!' Bayer exclaimed. 'You're getting out.'

'Yes. I'm getting out.'

Each time Mr Bertram returned from a trip he had to

struggle with his new situation. The old anger would flare up; he would yell at Eva and Bayer but apologise afterwards. Slowly, he would grow calmer, would join in their life and then switch to the role of protector, buying expensive treats from the delicatessen, throwing packages on the desk.

'Eat!' he would say with a smile. 'It's good for you.'

Every morning Mr Bertram had long telephone conversations with the mysterious Darling. He sometimes called her Sweetie or Honey too. They discussed recipes for their evening meal.

'Do you know who she is?' asked Eva.

'Must be some girlfriend,' suggested Bayer.

Then Mr Bertram would be off again on another trip. Autumn passed slowly into winter with grey, over-hanging clouds, a dreary office, no work and endless hours of unhampered boredom. Mondschein had gone to his camp and he sent them an occasional postcard. At intervals they received business calls, had to send out cables and make a few entries in the ledger. Afterwards they settled back again and read or discussed the possibilities of getting out. Mr Bertram returned for Christmas and talked endlessly with Darling about preparations for the holiday meal.

'You'd think they were in the food business,' Bayer remarked.

It must have been round January 1939 that Mr Bertram told Eva that he was leaving the following morning for England and would not be coming back.

'Once I know where I'm going to settle, I want my belongings shipped there. What I need now is an inventory. Would you come along and type it?'

Bayer put the typewriter in Mr Bertram's Bentley convertible and they drove off to his apartment. There Eva met Darling for the first time. She turned out to be his elderly aunt. She was short and round, with an ordinary, friendly face and grey straight hair, combed back in a bun. She wore an apron and held a handkerchief in one hand, wiping away tears that came spilling down like drops of water from a leaky tap.

'Are you still crying?' he asked, putting his arms around

her so that she disappeared for a while from Eva's view. 'It's not the end of the world, my darling.' He kissed her on the head.

'To me it is,' she sniffled and sighed.

'Come on. What are we having for dinner?'

Before they started to work, Mr Bertram took Eva aside. Darling had disappeared into the kitchen.

'She loves coming over to cook for me. Please look after her,' he begged. 'She'll be so lonely.' Eva simply nodded her head. What could she do for Darling?

'My father's company ought to pay her a pension. But there are no legal documents, just one letter from my father, promising to pay her a pension for the rest of her life. It's written on company stationery though legally it wouldn't hold water if Lindner contested it. I can't imagine he'd ever do such a low thing, but you never can tell – he's cashed all the spoils of our labour like a lucky lottery winner. Darling could rent out one of her rooms and I could provide the rest from wherever I end up. But then again, there might be times when that will become an impossibility too. I'm worried about her future.'

'Don't worry, it doesn't pay,' Eva said. It was a phrase everyone in trouble used nowadays.

'There will be war. Nobody is ready for it except the Germans.'

'Why not take her along?'

'She refuses, she doesn't want to burden me, she counts on her pension from the company.'

They started to work. His apartment was large and heavily furnished. He possessed more china and silverware than a household of a dozen people. There was an enormous assortment of nicknacks, rugs, paintings, cushions, linen. He called out the items and Eva typed them, making four copies on airmail paper. The progress was slow. Eva hadn't realised that Mr Bertram lived with such a mass of bourgeois paraphernalia.

Darling called them in to eat but later Eva couldn't remember anything about the dinner except for the hours of work stretching into the morning. Darling had left after dinner and promised to be back for breakfast. At four, when only the kitchen remained to be done, she refused to go on.

'I'll do that with your aunt tomorrow and mail the list to you.'

He drove her home in his Bentley convertible. 'You can sleep late. I won't need you tomorrow morning.' But Eva went in to the office at eight just in case. Bayer arrived a little late and wanted to know if the boss was coming in.

'Don't know,' Eva answered. 'Probably not. He's leaving for London.'

So they sat and waited. He didn't come and he didn't call. Darling called the office asking if they had heard from her nephew. No.

'I can't understand it,' her voice was trembling. 'He was gone when I arrived at eight.'

'Had he been to bed?'

'Yes.'

'Is his luggage in the apartment?'

'Yes.'

'Can you see the Bentley parked outside?'

'Yes.'

'There is only one explanation,' said Eva.

'I know,' Darling sobbed.

'We'll get him out,' Eva promised. 'Will you stay at his apartment or are you going home, just in case I want to reach you?'

'I'll stay here.' She could hardly speak. 'I can't move.'

'I'll be in touch.'

Then the airport called. They were waiting for Mr Bertram Meyer.

'I don't think he can come. You'd better take off without him.' Eva put the receiver down. 'Damn the whole lot of them!'

'Busted?' asked Bayer.

'Yes, but why?' she asked, half to herself. 'Just a few hours before he got out.' She couldn't decide whether it had been a freak accident or whether the Gestapo had listened in on telephone conversations with his brother.

She opened the top desk drawer and found it filled with

negatives and snapshots of dressed and undressed women, address books, letters and carbon copies. He had probably left them there on purpose, imagining himself safe in London. She emptied the drawer into a box and went from the small back room over to the forbidden front office, straight to Mr Lindner.

'Please put this in a safe place or burn it. Mr Bertram has been arrested. Thanks.' She ran out again. Then she talked to Mr Walter Meyer in London.

'Get a lawyer and don't call my father. He is recuperating from a heart attack.'

By now Eva felt worn out. She knew what to do; it was all a re-run of previous experience. But today she felt too tired to keep up the necessary optimism. She called Darling.

'Who is your lawyer?' she asked.

'Mr Lewinson was a friend of old Mr Meyer. But I don't know if he's still in the country.'

She called Mr Lewinson who said he would try but that there were no longer any laws to protect Mr Bertram. The Gestapo was taking advantage of it.

'What next?' asked Bayer.

'Look through the files,' suggested Eva. 'It feels like one of those endless equations we used to have to solve in Algebra. Mr Lewinson is trying to find out where Mr Bertram is being held.'

In the afternoon came the knock at the door. Eva and Bayer turned pale. 'Here they come,' Bayer said. It was the Gestapo. They searched the office, took several papers out and put them back. They told Eva to put on her coat since she was now under arrest. She remembered being scared but not to a paralysing extent. Wholesale murder was not yet the rule in January 1939. There were disappearances and everyone knew what happened to political enemies, but even Jews were not arrested *en masse*, shot or deported; that happened later when the borders were closed and nobody could escape.

At the Gestapo headquarters she was accused of having had intercourse with the Jew Bertram Meyer. If of Arian blood this act would have constituted a crime punishable by many years in prison. Eva had an easy time clearing up the matter.

In the first place she had never had intercourse with Mr Meyer and, in the second place, if she had it wouldn't be against the Nuremberg Laws since she was half-Jewish. They eyed her with suspicion but let her go home.

Weeks of frustration followed. The Argentinian Consulate wouldn't lift a finger. The Jewish lawyer was unable to do anything. The Gestapo couldn't even come up with a reason for Mr Bertram's arrest. Eva was in constant touch with Darling. They went together many times to the lawyer and the consulate. Mr Lewinson called Eva one day to report that Mr Bertram had been transferred to a concentration camp. She called Walter Meyer in London, but what could he do?

'I am going to call old Mr Meyer in Paris,' Eva declared later. 'To hell with his heart attack.'

Old Mr Meyer seemed a very reasonable man. He did not blame any of them, just stated that he wished he had been informed before and that he would do his utmost to have Bertram released.

Four days later Darling called, sobbing: 'Benny is home. I have to get a doctor immediately.'

It took weeks before Mr Bertram was back on his feet. He didn't want to talk to anyone from the office. Only Darling cared for him. Eva got daily reports.

'He can't understand how this could have happened to him in his home town,' Darling explained.

'He knew he was in danger. Besides, Jews don't belong,' Eva replied.

'But he doesn't feel like a Jew.'

'Too bad,' Eva said. 'He'll have to learn the hard way.'

One day in April when it had suddenly got warm and the sun came out between high moving clouds, Bayer arrived late at the office.

'Guess what?'

'Good or bad news?'

'Good!' He couldn't hide his excitement.

'You're leaving,' Eva said.

'How did you guess?'

'What else could be good news?'

Later that week Bayer and his parents left for Palestine.

'I am so glad you made it,' Eva said before they parted.

'Yes, it's great,' Bayer replied. 'But let's face it, even under the best of circumstances, life is a hard affair.'

She missed Bayer, and she knew that Mr Bertram was about to leave. He came to the office one day in his Bentley convertible, rather slim and nonchalant, pretending that nothing had happened. He brought expensive cold cuts, returned the typewriter, opened the top drawer of his desk and found it empty.

'The things are in a box. I took them out before the Gestapo arrived. I gave them to Mr Lindner.'

It was difficult for Mr Bertram to thank Eva for anything because to do so would have meant admitting that something had happened. So he just said:

'I'll never forget what you did for Darling. She's singing your praises.'

They began to discuss the winding up of his business, the difficulties in getting his furniture out, the accountant who would come to assist her with the taxes. He was going to stay in Amsterdam for the time being and if there were any questions – he would give her instructions on all pending matters.

'We can wind this up in two months,' he said. 'I'll pay you for three months to show my appreciation.' Eva was embarrassed. She didn't want the money. 'I'm leaving tomorrow,' he announced. Eva almost started to cry. She would be left alone. 'I owe you so much,' Mr Bertram suddenly admitted. 'Look after Darling – promise?' She promised. 'I'll be homesick,' he said. 'I was born and raised in this town.'

'Thank God you're allowed to leave it.'

'But I curse God for making me lose what I need most.'

'The fate of a Jew,' Eva reminded him.

They parted with unexpected emotion, each embracing the other as a substitute for something else that they had cherished and lost. It wasn't easy to part from a home and country which had cradled and aided a person into adulthood. It wasn't easy to part from a friend whom one had just met and saved. Somehow Eva felt torn from a precious possession.

Chapter Four

1942

Mr Bertram was now in South America, selling raw hides and skins and worrying about his girlfriends, while here, in his beloved country, murder had become an organised and exhausting business. Once the machine was set in motion, it all became a matter of killing or being killed. So they had sweated and laboured very efficiently, showing no mercy to Jews. The few remaining Jews sat in their ghettos, waiting to be deported.

Eva felt her pulse. It had jumped to ninety-nine, which was alarmingly high. She picked up her coat to take a calming walk. The weather had not improved; it drizzled in a grey fog. She walked down a deserted street towards the quay. The narrow houses, pitted and discoloured, stood side by side like old teeth, supporting one another. The pavement glistened. The steady fog horns from the harbour and the cries of seagulls sounded muffled in the thickness of the clouds. Rain splashed on Eva's hat, rushed down, hung like pearls for a second on the outer rim and departed, carried on by a steady wind. Visibility was poor. The colours varied from light fluffy tones to a solid, coal black. Background shapes were discernible for a short moment then altered or disappeared completely. Boats and barges bobbed at the dockside below the stone wall. Eva listened to the noises of the harbour and thought again of Mr Bertram, Darling's beloved Benny, who had really been a bourgeois playboy, a big child.

Her shoes were soaking wet. They made squeaking sounds each time she put them down on the pavement. Werner wanted her to come for dinner. But she had plenty of time before then to visit Else, to sit with her, to be near her, to listen to her talk about deliveries, cooking, Hubert and politics. Else also loved to tell jokes and her laughter afterwards was just right, never too loud, never for the wrong reason.

Eva entered the damp office. She dried her legs, changed her shoes and stockings, then walked down the passageway, looking into every empty room, and realised that she was living in luxury. Else had only a small, partitioned, windowless storage room behind the shop where she cooked and ate and slept. But she never complained.

The lift had been shut down for the weekend, so Eva had to walk up eight flights to have a chat with Marion.

'It's me!' she shouted from below. Marion was reading a cheap novel, lying on the sofa, a lamp burning. The sky hung in shifting clouds, the rain hit against the windowpanes.

'You can hardly see across the bridge,' remarked Eva. 'I got drenched taking a walk along the quay.'

Marion folded the corner of the page she was reading, closed the book and put it on the side table. The book was called *Love Forever*. She stretched her arms in the air and yawned. Her face had the blank expression of a doll that had been handled by several careless children.

'I wonder if I should go out tonight and spoil my shoes? What do you think? Saturday is usually exciting; everybody's about, waiting for a good time.'

'Put on an old pair and have fun. I mean enjoy yourself, don't always turn fun into a business deal for a few marks.'

'I might go if Petra comes along. Alone I simply can't refuse a deal. I don't know why. Once I say no, I immediately regret it, as if I'd passed up the greatest opportunity of my life. Crazy!'

'Then take Petra.'

'I might and I might not. She probably has other plans. Would you like a cigarette?'

'I'll smoke my own, thank you.' Eva pulled out a pack and

they both lit up.

'Have you heard from your father?'

'Still at the Russian front. Seems invincible, like the devil. And the garbage he writes – all sentimental lies. How he loves me, his cute sweetie pie, how he wishes he were back in our cosy home. And when he comes, if I don't immediately fulfil his every wish I'm black and blue for weeks.'

'Life's not fair.'

After the cigarette Eva made her way back down the winding staircase in almost complete darkness, holding on to the rough outer wall. We're in the dungeons, she realised.

Else stood behind the counter doing her Saturday cleaning. Each week she wiped every corner from top to bottom with efficiency and good humour.

'It's important,' she explained. 'With foodstuffs you have to be clean.'

'Can I help?' asked Eva.

'Yes, get out of my way. Heat up some coffee and sit down.' She continued her scrubbing, humming and singing.

'I got stuck with a lot of herring salad,' she told Eva later while they were sitting and smoking. 'You can take some to Werner's dinner party.'

'Don't remind me,' Eva sighed. 'It's a chore. But how could I refuse the guy some distraction?'

'I know. His mother was taken to Theresienstadt.'

'Sorry, I told you before. I keep on repeating things,' Eva apologised. 'He's nice and sweet, even good looking, but he's clinging to me for pity as if I were a lifeline. After a while I begin to crack up and give way; I lose my nerve. And all he wants is his mother back.'

'I can't imagine what I would do without Hubert,' Else contemplated.

'You'd do all right. You were born under a lucky star.'

'It's not as easy as it seems, believe me. But I live my life the way I like. If other people turn the world into a hell, to hell with them. I have a right to my own world. We have only one life to live.'

'I wish I could do the same,' sighed Eva. 'But everything

they do affects me deeply. You're not a Jew.'

'I know how you feel, but give it a try,' said Else.

It was dark when Eva stepped outside. The rain had stopped. She decided to take the long walk through the deserted streets to Werner's house. 'Give it a try,' she repeated after every fourth step. 'Give it a try.' She had to learn to see life in a proper perspective. Theresienstadt was a concentration camp, one of the better ones, but still, few inmates remained there, most were shipped to the death camps. How the hell could one forget the whole mess? No, she wasn't born under a lucky star, that was certain. Every murder stared her in the face, made her a special target. How could people like her feel joy tonight for instance? It couldn't enter her world, not even with music or booze. Someone like Else possessed the grace of God in her golden-haired crown to conquer misery, to sell herring salad with a smile and to sing as she cleaned her store. Tonight she was at the movies with Hubert, her lover, her black-marketeer.

Werner had prepared for Eva's visit with the utmost care. It must have taken him all afternoon. The table was set with exquisite taste: Limoges china, cut crystal, a damask tablecloth and napkins; gold decorations, forks, knives and spoons, a vase made of gold with one orchid next to Eva's plate, an orchid of velvety gold with white and yellow touches, candles in antique golden holders. An electric light shone from behind one screen and Eva suspected that her friend had arranged for just sufficient light to pick out the treasures, the Gobelin, the paintings, the irreplaceable ornaments and carpets. Her eyes rested on the single flower in the golden vase and it occurred to her that this above all represented the insanity of the hour.

'Do you think summer is ever going to come?' Eva asked after an embarrassing silence.

'The sun will shine,' assured Werner. They drank golden wine.

'You shouldn't have made so much fuss,' she said finally as if she had to set something straight.

'I do it for myself,' he replied.

'You should save those things, they are irreplaceable.' Eva couldn't help beginning the futile exchange again.

'I know. I can't live without them.'

'But if they get bombed – ?' Eva didn't understand his logic.

'I can't part from them even for one day. It's hard to understand. You don't have to.'

'You ought to save them. They'll burn to cinders in no time. I happen to like art.'

'I'd rather see them destroyed than give them up,' replied Werner.

Later the siren wailed and Werner suggested they move to the basement.

'No one talks to me anymore since my mother was taken away. Just pretend we are by ourselves.'

The basement started to fill as people found their chairs. Most of them sat in small groups, each isolated from the next. They talked as if they were waiting for the beginning of a play or a concert, pre-curtain gossip. The rumble started, as usual, with the heavy anti-aircraft guns in the far distance on the outskirts of town. Soon the city's smaller machine guns were added and the curtain rose to the strange sounds of the World War Two orchestra. It seemed to be a particularly noisy night.

'Is it always like this around here?' asked Eva.

'No, it's usually worse,' answered Werner.

'Crazy, waiting for a bomb to smash you to bits – '

'Don't think of it.'

'I have to.'

The light went out. The air-raid warden shouted to the invisible crowd: 'No need for alarm, stay in your seats.' The people talked louder than before, perhaps raising their voices to compensate for their blindness. Werner took Eva's hand and held it against his cheek.

'Did you ever read Nietzsche?' she asked, pulling her hand out of his.

'*Zaratustra.*'

'He predicted this. He predicted the anti-intellectual nationalist masses turning into barbarians destroying Western civilisation.'

'I can't hear you,' screamed Werner, as the noise from the outside became deafening.

'I've had it!' said Eva but nobody heard her. Bombs exploded in their vicinity, the guns bellowed without interruption, destruction was in full swing. Nothing would survive, Eva was sure. This was the end, the end of civilisation. How long would it take to recreate something worthwhile? Thousands of years. She had been born into a wasteland.

'Are you still there?' Werner asked during a lull.

'Just about,' she replied. 'You should save your treasures.'

It was late before the raid ended. The electricity had not been restored.

'Can't you stay overnight?' asked Werner when they reached his apartment. 'I have plenty of room.' Eva agreed, and they finished the wine.

'Good night,' said Eva. 'You remind me of a teddy bear.'

'Is that a compliment?' he asked. Eva smiled and they walked to their separate bedrooms.

They woke to a blue sky and sunshine, with a few good weather clouds sailing by. Suddenly it was summer, warm and humid.

'A miracle!' said Eva, looking out of the window. Her clothes were wrinkled, she had not taken them off the night before. 'Do I look a mess?' she asked.

'You generally do.'

'I've been bombed out twice. It's amazing I don't look worse.'

'Lots of people have been bombed out but they don't look like you.'

'All right,' she said, feeling offended. They sat at the breakfast table and Eva, squinting her eyes and surveying Werner's expression, wondered why she was putting up with a guy like him. She disliked his egotism. But after a cup of coffee she felt better disposed towards him and he seemed to her to be a more harmless sort of being. He can't help himself, we are all rather weak, she concluded and drank more coffee. She kissed his cheek before leaving.

'You made it very special,' she said. 'Thanks.' The precious Limoges dishes were still on the dining-room table just the way they had left them the night before. The gold looked less brilliant now. Only the orchid still had a special glow.

Eva walked to the station and bought a ticket on the north-bound train to the last stop. The compartment was empty. The train passed ugly, narrow streets, with green squares here and there, a few trees, flower boxes on dirty balconies, bombed out spaces. Every city has its drabness. It looked better as soon as they reached the suburbs. Eva got off at the last station and walked through the tree-lined streets, out into the country towards the river which ran narrow and calm along grassy banks, shadowed by high shrubs and bushes. It was a perfect summer day.

She walked for several miles without checking her pulse rate once. Her pulse rate reminded her that Monday was Darling-day. Since Eva had promised to look after Mr Bertram's aunt in 1939, just before Mr Lindner had taken her back into his firm, she had faithfully attended Darling's bridge club every Monday afternoon at four. She had got Miss Ehrlich's permission to leave early, making up the time on other days. 'As long as you finish your work on time,' Miss Ehrlich had said. But, of course, Eva could never finish anything on time. She did not play bridge herself, she left that to Darling, old Mrs Levy, old Mrs Lowenstein and old Mr Kuhn. She appeared solely as decoration and for entertainment. She also brought a big package of food provided by Else and Hubert. Eva brewed coffee for the bridge players who sat silently over their cards, calculating endless possibilities.

There had been Mondays when Eva felt too sick to make a move, when she had not enough strength left to face the doomed bridge players. But knowing that Else had prepared the large food package made Eva set her steps in Darling's direction like a sleepwalker, and when she arrived, say the words she had learned like a well-trained parrot, always reacting on cue without any inner participation.

'I don't know how I got through the evening,' she would

say to herself on the way home. 'I can't go through another like it.' But then 'next time' was often better and she carried on with her obligation.

The sun was shining on the sandy path along the river. Some bushes grew white flowers, and the water reflected thousands of dancing stars. For a moment she felt some hope and happiness but she knew it wouldn't last, it never did. Don't start posing questions, she told herself, or your temperature'll rise. There was no hope for Jews and she knew it; only the death cell which would come one day soon, excluding joy from every moment in the unbearable space of waiting. She turned round and walked back to the station, seeing without feeling, watching but not analysing. She walked in a state of semi-consciousness, adjusting to her racing pulse and rising temperature.

It was high time she got to the store. Her strength had diminished and Else was the best medicine to bring it back and restore a measure of courage.

Else and Hubert were playing cards for money. Else won, as usual, and Hubert smiled with admiration. 'Wonder how she does it?' he asked.

'Do you want to join in?' asked Else, counting the coins by her side. No, she didn't want to play, just to sit there.

'Something's wrong,' said Else.

'No, no,' Eva shook her head. It had only been the river and the walk, her realisation of how wonderful life could be. Now she felt depressed.

'A cup of coffee and something to eat.' Else went about her business like a doctor preparing for a difficult operation. In the meantime Hubert showed her card tricks to take her mind off the depression. Slowly, Eva began to breathe again without the choking combination of fear and resentment. 'How much longer would she hold together?' she asked herself. It probably depended on one's genes and their tenacity. Some made it, some didn't. 'It's all a matter of luck.' She looked gratefully at Else and Hubert.

'You have no idea how often you have saved my life,' Eva said between bites.

'Nobody is threatening it,' insisted Else. 'It's all in your imagination. You always anticipate the worst.'

'Because the worst always happens.'

Monday started as usual with Miss Ehrlich and the ledger, a view on to the canal and the houses across, the church tower, the seagulls, passing barges and motorboats. Only this morning the sky was blue and the air warm. She opened the window a little. Perhaps it would be a friendly day, one that passed by unnoticed, a day pulled from the calendar as if it had never existed at all. Those were the best days.

When she arrived at Darling's with a big package under her arm, she found the old people sitting around the table, drinking coffee and talking in subdued voices. No cards were spread out. Darling had opened the door with moist, swollen eyes and had gone back into the living room immediately without explanation. Eva put the package in the kitchen and joined the others, who were talking about food, about eating or not eating.

'Why aren't you playing bridge?' asked Eva.

'We got our deportation notices,' said Mr Kuhn in a calm voice.

'No more bridge for us,' commented Mrs Lowenstein. Darling sobbed.

'Where to?' asked Eva.

'Theresienstadt. But we are not going,' said Mr Kuhn.

'When did you decide?' Eva felt like a reporter questioning people who were planning to move away.

'A long time ago. We've all got our sleeping pills. It's going to be tonight.'

'I told them to eat something,' Darling was able to say between sobs. 'Do you remember how faint you felt last *Yom Kippur* during the fast?' She addressed Mrs Levy. 'Don't upset your stomach.'

'No,' said Mrs Lowenstein, 'we can't risk throwing up.'

'We all have ten pills. Six should be sufficient but we're taking ten, just to be on the safe side.'

'If they stay down,' warned Mr Kuhn.

'I think Mrs Meyer is right. We should eat now. It will be digested by the time we take the pills.'

They all agreed and dutifully ate the food set before them like medicine prescribed by a doctor to get them well. They were preparing carefully for their trip into eternity.

Eva was stunned. She sat there frozen; only her eyes watched the old lips chewing, the refusal to show emotion, the effort to make some sort of peace with fate.

'We knew it would come one day,' explained Mr Kuhn. 'From the reports we receive, our age-group gets sent to extermination camps right away. We've decided to die in a more dignified way.'

They gave Darling addresses: names of children, grandchildren, relatives. 'Write to them when the war is over. Tell them what happened,' said Mrs Levy.

'Write them down,' begged Darling and handed the list over to Eva. But Eva couldn't lift a finger. The list lay on her empty plate.

'My dear,' said Mr Kuhn, 'it's not that hard once you've reached our age.' Eva stared at him. She couldn't speak. 'It is not the first time Jews have been slaughtered,' Mr Kuhn continued. Eva heard only the word 'slaughtered' and she realised that she was in a terrible place.

'You two are a big help,' objected Mrs Levy.

'It shows that we're loved,' said Mrs Lowenstein.

'Yes, we lose wonderful friends,' said Mr Kuhn.

'We are losing you,' sobbed Darling.

'Then we are losing each other. Other than that, I'm glad to go,' said Mrs Lowenstein who had always started an argument when she was not winning a bridge game.

They were getting into their coats, displaying the Star of David emblazoned with the word 'Jude'.

'No scenes, please,' warned Mr Kuhn. 'We're only human.' Darling pressed each friend's hand firmly and wiped her eyes. Eva insisted on taking them home.

'Please let me! I won't cry,' she pleaded.

In the street Mrs Levy remarked that one really didn't need a coat, it was still quite warm.

'Cancer is worse,' Mrs Lowenstein told herself. 'Paralysing strokes or senility, all worse.'

Eva felt her own forehead. 'One hundred and ten, minimum,' she estimated. Cancer is worse, of course. This is just an hygienic mass suicide with pills from the pharmacy and jugs of water. The only problem was the stomach. Stomachs were unreliable, especially Jewish stomachs. They had had to swallow too much through the ages. Well, one always had to take chances in life. Nobody was allowed to die neatly without taking a risk.

The remaining Jews of Hamburg lived in a row of houses in the ghetto. Most were old and infirm, existing on a starvation diet without medical care.

'We are not alone,' explained Mr Kuhn. 'There are thirty people on our floor alone joining us tonight. Tell Mrs Meyer not to come here before tomorrow evening. I forgot to mention it.'

'It's better than dying of cancer,' repeated Mrs Lowenstein.'

'Just don't talk about it,' begged Mrs Levy. 'I'll take the pills and think of something unimportant.'

In front of their house Mr Kuhn warned Eva. 'No scenes, my pet. We all know how we feel. Stay dignified and proud. Tonight we'll pray for you.'

'No scenes,' echoed Mrs Levy. 'I'll think of something unimportant.'

They shook hands as though exchanging condolences before the funeral. Then Eva embraced the two women and Mr Kuhn, turned around and ran down the street. She ran for a long time without noticing where she was going. Finally she was out of breath and kept on walking towards the golden three-quarter moon until she reached the river. She hoped to find Arlen at the theatre restaurant, as if he possessed the power to make the horror disappear. She had the feeling she was slowly drowning, being deprived of air.

Eva arrived at the restaurant before the final curtain came down, looked at the board and saw that Arlen wasn't scheduled. She went inside to check the table – it stood empty, the 'Reserved' sign in a silver frame in the middle. She left and walked towards his house. Her legs felt tired. She could hardly make it up the stairs; music from some trashy record was all around her. She called out but nobody answered. She stood in the dark hallway numb and hot, having reached her goal, no longer knowing why she had bothered. The record can't play for ever, she told herself. When it stopped she heard Arlen's voice talking to someone.

'Arlen, it's me!' she called through the door.

'I have company,' he yelled back.

'Let me in!' she cried, banging on the door.

'Damn!' said Arlen as he let her in.

Renate was sitting on the sofa looking at Eva with rage. 'A sob story,' she predicted. 'It'd better be a good one.'

Eva tried to report rationally but the more factual she became, the harder it was to keep her emotions in check. 'There will be hundreds of suicides tonight. Mr Kuhn is praying for me.'

'Give her a brandy,' suggested Arlen.

'I don't need a brandy!' screamed Eva. 'I want this insanity to stop.'

'It will, one day,' said Arlen.

'When it's too late. It has to stop now.'

Eva pulled out a cigarette and began to smoke; she couldn't keep still.

'They're old,' said Renate.

'Don't!' yelled Eva. 'They are alive.'

'In the long run we are the victims,' said Renate as if in apology. 'We carry the guilt.'

'Do you expect me to feel sorry for you?' asked Eva.

'No,' answered Renate.

'Drink the brandy!' ordered Arlen.

'All right, here!' Eva drank the brandy. 'Satisfied?'

'I want you to calm down. There's nothing you can do. Imagine having to fight now at the Russian frontier, or being in a camp.'

'Or dying of cancer? It doesn't make this execution any less horrible.' She drank another brandy. Her head began to spin. She hadn't eaten since lunch time. 'May I sleep here tonight?' she asked.

'Of course, my pet. You can have the bedroom.'

'Hope you don't mind.' Eva smoked another cigarette and focused her eyes on Renate. 'I won't get in your way.'

'You usually manage it quite successfully.'

'Only in emergencies, believe me. I'm not playing games.'
She drank another brandy as if she were determined to block
out her mind. 'I think I'm ready to go to bed.' She wasn't
quite steady on her feet, so Arlen led her into the bedroom,
made her lie down, took off her shoes and kissed her on her
swollen eyes.

'You'll manage, my pet, I know you will. Tomorrow
you'll feel less pain.' She didn't reply. The room spun slowly.
She closed her eyes and began to count outstretched hands
with pills in their palms, disembodied hands. Then she saw
bodies lying neatly in rows on the floor. One said: 'It's better
than dying of cancer.' My God! Eva realised they hadn't taken
their pills yet. She began to search for the disembodied hands
but they were gone. Then she looked again at the bodies lying
on the floor in red and golden robes, only this time she knew
they were corpses. Amazing, she thought, how fast it all
went. It must have been easy, nobody threw up.

She was at the office before Miss Ehrlich arrived – tired,
hungry, with a headache.

Darling called early. 'I haven't slept a wink all night. I even
tried to pray towards morning. It seemed like a godly hour,
when the sun rose. But the praying didn't improve anything.
When will we know the outcome of, of – ?'

'Don't go there before nightfall. Mr Kuhn forgot to
mention it to you.'

'All right, I'll sit it out.'

'Call me as soon as you know.'

Eva couldn't work. She looked out of the window, felt her
depression and almost envied the old people who, hopefully,
had made it by now. She called Arlen.

'I planned to phone you later,' said Arlen a little embarrassed because he had forgotten about her.

'Don't hand out charity. I want you to have time for me
tonight.'

'I'll try to keep the evening free.'

'I need the whole night!' she shouted down the telephone.

'I understand what you mean,' he said calmly. 'I'll call you back around five.'

'Thanks for last night,' said Eva and hung up.

Arlen was the only person who responded to her unreasonable demands as if they were legitimate requests. Both expected to spend the night together like two derelicts who had taken up, for the moment, the same stretch of bench, sharing their few belongings. Neither enquired into the other's downfall. Downfall was obvious. What they discussed and practised was their method of survival, dismissing pretence or goals. In the end they felt some form of freedom which created the illusion of relief.

At lunch time Eva walked over to Else to pick up her sandwich. The store was crowded as usual and Else looked puzzled at Eva's swollen face.

'The bridge party decided to go on a journey of no return,' whispered Eva.

'Tell me later. I'll cook something good.' Else smiled and Eva wasn't sure that she understood what had happened.

When she returned to the office she heard the Ehrlichs talking to each other, saying the same things they always did. Today Eva couldn't face them. She sat in her office, looking at the canal, chewing her sandwich and drinking her coffee. In the afternoon she made a few entries in the ledger. At five Arlen called and asked her to meet him at eleven-thirty at his house.

'The key is under the flower pot. You can go in.'

'See you,' said Eva. 'Nothing yet from the travellers. I'm waiting for Darling's call.'

At six the phone rang. Darling reported that the house was surrounded by police with trucks standing about. Bodies, wrapped in white sheets, were carried out and dumped into the covered lorries.

'I told them I wanted to see my friends but they just pushed me aside to make room for the bodies. They were piling them one on top of the other; there must have been hundreds. It was so ghastly and unreal. They're taking them to the mortuary. When I asked a policeman what had happened he said: "Killed themselves. That's all they were good for." I asked whether there had been any survivors but he said not

51

that he knew of. Apparently nobody threw up. It's a blessing.'

'Thank heavens,' answered Eva as if something great had been achieved.

'When will I see you?' asked Darling.

'Not tonight, but I'll come right after work tomorrow.'

'I'll feed you,' promised Darling.

'They made it!' said Eva triumphantly.

Chapter Five

1943

After another grey, cold and rainy spring, summer promised to become warm and sunny.

Sometimes after dinner with Else and Hubert, Eva would return to Mr Lindner's office and work on the ledger, reducing the backlog by a considerable amount. She could hardly account for the strength she suddenly felt at tackling the pile of typed and printed sheets of paper, transporting figures and text into straight lines in wide books, adding columns in her head twice to make sure, drawing lines, turning to a new page, sighing with relief when another month had been closed and was balancing.

Once every week she visited Darling and played, with little enthusiasm, a two-handed bridge game that Darling had taught her. They never talked of the old Jewish friends but to Eva they were always present.

Once Werner called and asked her with old-world charm to an elaborate dinner, though the old world had lost credit and value in the underworld. To Werner, however, the past kept him protected from the downfall that he feared and he always found another surprise, an even better set of dishes, finer decorations, softer linens. He dressed in evening clothes and played the gracious host, the giver of parties without guests. He opened the door like a butler, helped her off with her coat as if it were a mink cape, accompanied her to the drawing room where he bowed and kissed her hand. All evening they would play their part like actors sitting on a stage, each one prepared with the script of a different play, neither of them waiting any longer for cues but finishing their own text regardless of the other's inappropriate responses. They didn't suffer during these incomprehensible conversations. They sat too far apart to notice and they were much too involved in their own scenes to give the failure a second thought.

Every morning Miss Ehrlich arrived with the vigour and good cheer of a well-lacquered toy soldier, walking fast across the bridge with mechanical steps, waving at Eva like a wound-up doll. She woke up cheerful and stayed cheerful most of the time, clutching at cheerfulness with a strong grip. Only when Mother, the prison warden, showed her head on the bridge, did Miss Ehrlich permit herself a moment of paleness before she straightened up again, waved her arm and resumed her smile.

Standing in the hallway one day, Eva heard Mrs Ehrlich suggest to her daughter that Eva should be sent to a concentration camp instead of being allowed to sit in an office, having an easy life and taking a job away from a German girl.

'I'm glad to have her,' Miss Ehrlich had told her mother. 'You can't find employees.'

Eva felt frightened. The assaults came from all sides. She ran over to Else and Hubert, sat for longer hours after dinner in the small kitchen behind the store and felt protected. Hubert would stretch out and relax in his chair while they prepared sandwich fillings and herring salad for the next day. They always had a cup of strong coffee by their side, plenty of cigarettes and an even-tempered, unhurried flow of conversation. Else might give her a tip on how to remove the herring bones more efficiently or show her a way to cut cucumbers thinly. Else would praise the ripeness of her nice, plump tomatoes while the beetroot for the herring salad boiled on the stove. Hubert would grunt his approval of life into the conversation, catching fire from Else's sense of well being and adding to the satisfaction that hung in the air.

'What would I do without you?' Eva exclaimed every time.

'Don't get overexcited,' laughed Hubert.

'But I mean it,' Eva persisted.

'We enjoy ourselves.' Else was cutting the herring into tiny bits.

When the advance warning wailed through the city Eva would run back to the office, both because she was often on air-raid duty, and also because she preferred the office shelter to the rickety little shop. Else and Hubert preferred to remain in the store, persisting in their logic that no one would want to bomb a little place like theirs.

Then summer set in with a vengeance. Suddenly it became unbearably hot. Werner suggested a Sunday walk by the river. He would bring a picnic basket. They met at the station. He stood under the clock, staring at his wrist watch every few seconds until Eva arrived.

'You're late, as usual.' He lost his temper.

'It's Sunday. We can take the next train and still find the river where it always flows.'

'Hurry.' He began to run towards the platform, holding the picnic bag under one arm like an attaché case.

'For heaven's sake, relax!' Eva looked at the big clock on the platform. 'We're five minutes early.'

'That clock is late; the train should arrive any moment.'

'I hope we find some wild flowers.' Eva preferred to change the subject.

'Why can't you ever be on time?'

She looked at his strained face. 'There should be red clover, daisies, Queen Anne's lace, buttercups, forget-me-nots and what else?'

'I've never picked wild flowers,' he grumbled.

'There'll be lovely grasses too.'

During the train ride they looked out the window. Later they walked through woods and across fields. Werner was still sulking and Eva wanted to find wild flowers. The air was hot. Werner had taken off his jacket. They sat in the shade under a tree right by the river, ate their sandwiches and drank strong coffee. They stretched out and looked at each other.

'Still angry?' she asked.

'Long forgotten,' he smiled.

'Did you hear of the air raids at the Ruhr?'

'Rumours,' remarked Werner. 'They talk of ghastly fires that can't be extinguished, that burn right through the skin. The cities are supposed to look like infernos, people dying by the thousand in one raid.'

'If it's true.' Eva fell asleep for a while. When she woke up she wondered if she was feeling anything at all except perhaps some little spark for the already wilted bunch of wild flowers that she would now have to lug around all day.

'It's a lazy day,' Eva remarked. 'Did you sleep?'

'I think so.'

'Let's walk towards the woods. Perhaps we'll find some mushrooms,' suggested Eva.

'I know nothing about mushrooms.'

'Neither do I. But they're pretty and we can admire them.'

On their way Eva picked up a piece of dirty, weather-stained paper with faded but still legible print, surrounded by a black border. *To the inhabitants of Hamburg*, it read. 'That's for us,' said Eva. It advised everyone to leave Hamburg immediately because of an impending destructive air attack. Warnings to the authorities had remained unheeded, so now they asked anyone who found a leaflet to spread the news, to warn mothers and children in particular, etc., etc.

'Do they want to ease their own conscience?' asked Eva.

'Probably. "See how humane we are – ",' Werner laughed sardonically.

'Who could leave the city without being considered a traitor?'

'Very few. I get my vacation in September. Too late in the season.'

'I could leave now and join the actors at the Baltic who are on holiday later this month, but somehow I feel like sticking it out here.'

'I don't believe a word,' said Werner. 'It's just scare tactics.'

Eva was sure they would come with their new fire bombs. 'You'd better get ready and save your treasures.'

'Hamburg is not an industrial town,' he protested.

'No, it's only the largest port in Germany. That's all.' She looked at his neck, stiff as though he were wearing a starched collar with a tight button. She recognised his intractability.

'I'll help you. Let's just put the pictures and the most valuable treasures into a safe place.'

'I'll think it over.' He left it in the air, as usual.

Eva warned Else and Hubert. 'Store some of your goods in our back office and come to our shelter. It's eight storeys down,' she begged, but they wouldn't listen. 'They have new fire bombs.' No, absolutely not, they wouldn't abandon the store. 'You're hopeless,' said Eva. 'If anything happens to you, don't blame me.'

'We would hardly be in a position to,' laughed Else.

'Can't you see that it's serious?' Eva's voice rose.

'All right,' said Else. 'If it sounds very bad, we'll come over to your shelter.' But Eva knew they wouldn't.

Eva heard Marion's customer breathing heavily at the other end of the hallway. It had to be over soon. She waited behind her door until his boots echoed through the empty building. Then she called out to Marion.

'In a minute,' Marion disappeared into one of the toilets. Afterwards they sat in Mr Lindner's office and smoked a cigarette.

'Can I have the key for the back office?' asked Marion.

'Certainly.' Eva handed it to her. 'But bring it back. I stole it from Miss Ehrlich.'

'For me?' asked Marion.

'Who else is using it?'

'You're wonderful.'

'Thanks. Now listen.' Marion always had the blank expression of a doll. 'Are you listening?' asked Eva.

'Of course.'

'Don't stay in your apartment from now on during air raids. Always come down right away, either to the hallway or, even better, to the shelter. Is that clear? We're going to be bombed badly.'

'How do you know?'

'I found a leaflet in the woods.'

'Oh, my God!' Marion paled. 'Don't leave me alone.'

'Just stick around,' said Eva. 'Keep the news to yourself, do you hear? Otherwise we'll both get into trouble.'

'You wouldn't tell Miss Ehrlich?'

'Of course not. You can be arrested for spreading enemy rumours. But stick around, hear?'

Nothing happened. The raids continued to be severe, long, exhausting, and to rob everyone of much-needed sleep. However that was an old story. Every night many houses were destroyed, many died or were injured but nobody wanted to know figures and none were released. People sat in their shelters like animals in traps. It was a matter of luck who got hit and who would live another day.

The weather was glorious, the nights were light and soft. 'Velvety,' she thought, 'like Werner's orchid.' One evening, instead of sitting in the stuffy office she walked through the city towards the theatre. The restaurant was overcrowded, the show over. It had been the last one of the season. Audience and actors occupied the tables, ate their supper, drank their wine. The hum of voices rose and fell at irregular intervals. At times it grew to a frightening roar, then people calmed down again. Eva greeted Arlen with her casual 'Hi' and looked at the girl next to him.

'This is Olga,' said Arlen.

Eva was suspicious of strangers. Every restaurant was frequented by the Gestapo. Olga had a cat-like face with slanted eyes, pronounced cheekbones, a broad short nose and wide lips that didn't curve but sat there straight and flat. Her hair was brown and thick, hanging upon her shoulders in a wave.

'Where did you meet?' asked Eva.

'Olga came to my dressing room, asking for an autograph.'

'Really? How flattering.'

'I saw him in the play.' Olga had a Slavic accent. 'He's so good looking, I had to meet him.'

'How did you get past Bill's desk? He won't let anybody through,' said Eva because she felt that something was not right.

'Well, he let me pass – ' Olga smiled. 'I know a few tricks.'

'Could you show us your little tricks?' Eva became frightened. Olga began to scrabble in her untidy handbag.

'Oh, here it is!' She pulled out a small identification card with her photograph on one side. 'I belong to the Gestapo,' she said casually. She might just as well have said that she belonged to the River Tennis Club.

'But you're not German,' said Eva, feeling herself grow hot.

'No, I'm Russian. I was a medical student in Kiev when I met Ilo and we fell madly in love. He's a German officer. My whole family cried but I was so happy, in love all the time. And Ilo said things would be all right, he could get me to Germany and we would marry. But my parents still cried though I was happy. Then my papers came and I left. I cried too but I was very, very happy. I lived with Ilo's parents. He's fighting in Russia and we wait for a marriage permit which doesn't come. Then one day the answer comes: officers can't marry Russians, out of the question. We still hope to marry after the war but meantime they send me to work in a hospital. I work and then Gestapo comes and says either they ship me back to Kiev or I am going to work for them. Now what would you do in my place? You know how they treat Russians, eh, do you know?'

'Yes Olga, we know very well,' Arlen tried to calm her down.

'But do you know what Russians do with enemy collaborators?' She didn't wait for an answer. 'It's bang – finished! Now here I am, waiting to marry, being madly in love, working in hospital and then the Gestapo comes. So I said yes and will see what I am expected to do. I think they are putting me into a Russian labour camp to spy. But I've no assignment yet, still work at hospital. Now tell me, Arlen, what would you do?'

'Don't ask me,' said Arlen rather uncomfortably. 'I think I wouldn't have left Russia.'

'But I love Ilo! You know love?'

'Come on, there are many men you could have loved,' said Thomas, who sat very close to Inge.

'I think I fall in love with Arlen,' Olga laughed.

Eva wasn't sure whether Olga was naive and honest or whether it was a very clever game she was playing. 'I think

I'm going home,' she said. 'Let me know when the quarantine is over.' She got up.

'You think I am stupid and you can talk over my head. I know what you mean.' Olga seemed determined to defend herself. 'Never will I denounce a person.'

'But you've denounced yourself already,' Thomas said. 'The next step is unavoidable.'

'We'll see. I can play games like cat and mouse for a long time. Gestapo is easy. With Russians you can't play games, they don't ask questions, they shoot.'

Everyone was silent. Apparently she considered the Gestapo a bunch of Country Club boys, rather mild and congenial. Or the entire thing was a pretence and she was trying to lure them into her net.

'We're all off to the Baltic, to Ahrenshoop for the summer,' Arlen said suddenly.

'Good luck,' Eva said to everybody. 'You need it.' And she hurried out.

On the way home Eva thought with envy of Arlen at the Baltic, lying on the hilly dunes, swimming in the sea, taking walks in the woods. Eva knew that Ahrenshoop was different from every other place on earth and she longed to be there yet she could not give up the city. She kept on waiting for the promised air raid.

It came one night during the last week of July. Eva had spent the evening with Else and Hubert, playing cards, drinking coffee and wine. The place was veiled with cigarette smoke which danced and curled around the single bulb. Their mood had been cheerful, the cards smashed on the table with occasional outbreaks of emotion.

'How do you do it?' asked Hubert as Else smiled.

'My secret.'

'Come on, let us in on it,' protested Eva.

'I like to do some wheeling and dealing myself.' Else enjoyed her winnings. They were a little tipsy.

Advance warning was given at the usual hour. Eva said good night and walked slowly over to the office. The air was warm, the sky moonlit and clear, the city bathed in a silver light. 'Gone for ever,' thought Eva. 'Every day is like a funeral.' She met Marion in the hallway.

'Could I get the key again?' she asked nervously. 'Everybody's coming down now and I have a customer waiting.'

'You'd better come down yourself,' warned Eva while handing her the key.

In the basement Eva met the people for that night's shift. They greeted each other like old friends, sat down and waited for the sirens to announce the attack. Cannon began to fire far away, the usual rumble that drew nearer until every anti-aircraft gun inside and outside the city was shooting uninterruptedly. The first bombs fell in rows. The building vibrated in an even rhythm, then it shook. The noise became deafening, worse than ever. They sat huddled in the dark, isolated, frightened, holding on to their chairs during uninterrupted, earsplitting explosions. 'A house of cards,' thought Eva into the noise, not knowing how much time had passed since the beginning of the raid. 'This is it!' she thought, 'this is what they announced in the leaflet.' She smelled smoke. 'It's burning!' she screamed into the dark space but nobody answered. She got up and began to search for the door with its iron handles. It had to be nearby. She touched a soft, warm arm. 'Marion?' she asked. 'My God!' cried Marion holding on to the door handle. 'Let's go! Follow me!' shouted Eva. They were out in a few seconds, running up the stairs, reaching the front door. The city was burning all around them. As far as they could see flames were soaring towards the sky, merging with other flames, creating a huge bonfire. The air was unbearably hot, bombs still fell, the anti-aircraft guns shot from all directions, shrapnel flew through the air like a hail storm. Eva didn't think. She wouldn't have known what to think. Then the images of Else and Hubert came into her mind. The narrow street stood in flames.

'We have to get to the store,' she shouted.

'I'm afraid,' cried Marion.

'Then wait here.'

'No, don't leave me alone.' She clung to Eva's arm.

'Hurry, if we run we might make it.'

They ran as fast as they could. Breathing became difficult,

the heat was scorching. Eva banged at the store's glass door with one of her shoes.

'Damn it, they can't be asleep!' Eva picked up a stone and threw it at the glass which broke as if in silence, the noise of the air raid drowning the smash of the shatter.

'Else!' screamed Eva. Else appeared, sleepy-eyed.

'Jesus Christ!' she exclaimed.

'Hurry!' Eva and Marion let themselves into the store where it was cooler. 'For heaven's sake hurry up!' she yelled at her friends. 'I don't know if we'll ever get out of here.'

Hubert appeared with a seaman's bag over one shoulder. 'To the harbour!' he said.

The end of their street was completely blocked with rubble. 'We can't climb that,' Hubert shouted.

'It's burning everywhere,' reported Eva. 'But the bridge is still standing.'

'Let's cross the bridge and get to the church square. From there we'll have to see.' Behind the bridge every building was in flames.

'We won't be able to make it,' cried Marion. 'I can't breathe, my skin is burning.'

'Shut up and run!' ordered Eva. They made it to the square, which was a little way away from the flames. The nave of the church had been hit and lay like a crumpled elephant below the still looming Gothic tower. Else carried a suitcase, Hubert still held on to his seaman's bag.

'Let's try that short street to the quay. It looks the darkest.' They ran again as fast as they could. Sparks were descending from the sky in glowing flakes. They encountered heaps of rubble, climbed mountains of stone and slid down the other side. Shrapnel clicked on to the ground, though the anti-aircraft guns had diminished in activity.

'I can see the water!' cried Eva. Then bombs began to explode a few streets away. The hum remained in their ears as if the explosion were going to echo inside their heads for ever. Then another, different sound became discernible and increased. Eva looked up at the sky. She could see nothing but fire and smoke but she realised that the steady sound came from planes with their deadly load flying over her head. They reached the quay with sighs of relief. The wide expanse of water provided them with oxygen, the air was much cooler. The buildings along the waterfront had not yet caught fire.

'I think we're safe,' said Hubert, breathing shallowly, 'at least from suffocation.' They all took deep breaths of fresh air. 'Let's get to one of those boats. We'll be safe from shrapnel in the cabin.' They walked down the steps to the docks and climbed on to a small, sturdy vessel with a large cabin.

'Oh my God!' Marion cried out and fell on to a bench.

'Lie on the floor below the bench,' said Hubert, who had also collapsed but was still clinging to his seaman's bag.

'A close call,' gasped Else.

'Not over yet. Anything can hit us here.'

'The smoke is dreadful. My eyes are burning.' Marion was in tears. 'I was afraid we would roast to death.' They just lay there, exhausted and empty.

'People are trying to get out all over the city,' said Else. 'Hardly anyone is going to make it.'

'Jesus Christ!' Marion yelled. 'What about us?'

Just then bombs began to fall all around them. Barges, loaded with coal, caught fire, split open and sank. Flames and debris from a direct hit shot into the air, warehouses on the opposite bank began to smoulder and then glow like cinders. A cargo vessel, hit right in the middle, cracked and went under, leaving its bow and stern sticking out like the tops of two church towers. They lay on the floor of their small boat, bobbing on the turbulent sea, becoming enveloped in smoke. A gas tank exploded with an enormous rush of sound: its flames reached the sky.

'I have cramps in my stomach,' sobbed Marion.

'Pull yourself together,' yelled Hubert.

'It's getting too hot here. Can't we move further out on the water?' Smoke was now covering the entire sky.

'I'm thirsty as hell,' said Hubert suddenly.

'Want a beer?' asked Else.

'Don't tease right now.'

'It's warm, I expect, but here it is.' Else produced a bottle from her suitcase.

'You're really something!' Hubert said with admiration.

'What time is it?' asked Eva.

'A quarter to three,' said Hubert, looking at his watch. The light was bright and unsteady.

'I'll check on the fuel tanks.' Hubert got up. It had grown rather quiet. Only the soaring fire was sighing and screaming, and buildings burst and crumbled like sudden thunder. Here and there anti-aircraft guns were still shooting and bombs falling. It was hard to distinguish between them.

'Hope it's over,' said Eva, following Hubert out of the cabin into the open air. 'We'd better get away from here.' Hubert had already jumped to the next boat and was checking the fuel tanks.

Eva walked around the cabin and saw the houses burning along the quay, a wall of fire behind them as far as she could see. Upstream the warehouses were aflame, the opposite side was a bank of jagged torches. The cloud of smoke closed over them. The sky had vanished. 'Dawn will never come,' she thought.

Hubert reappeared. 'I've found a boat with enough fuel to get us further downstream, beyond the harbour.'

'And then?' asked Else.

'Then we'll have to wait and see. We won't be the only refugees.'

'Do you think the store's still standing?' Else got up from the floor and straightened out her dress, stroking it with outstretched hands.

'No chance,' Hubert said.

'It was when we left.' She couldn't imagine a world without her store.

'Don't hope for a miracle. We may never be able to go back.' Hubert was looking at the burning city.

'What's going to happen to me?' cried Marion.

'You'll stay with us.'

They jumped from boat to boat. Hubert balanced his seaman's bag, Else her suitcase.

Hubert stopped. 'Here we are. No luxury liner but a full tank.'

'Let's get going,' urged Eva. 'The smoke is filling my

lungs.'

'I'm sweating like a . . .' Else didn't finish her sentence. Her plaits of hair had fallen down over her shoulders.

'I'm soaking wet.' Marion tried to wring out the skirt of her dress.

'We all are.'

Hubert was urgently trying to start the ignition. Suddenly the motor began to putter. Eva and Else untied the boat and they began to move slowly, in reverse gear, out of the dock towards the harbour proper, away from the burning city. The water was covered with wreckage and debris. Hubert stood like an experienced captain behind the wheel, watching out for obstacles.

'He's a genius,' said Else. 'I wonder how many got out?' They looked at the city. 'If you hadn't come to get us, we'd be a small heap of ashes now.'

'That's the way it goes,' answered Eva.

'They've stopped bombing,' Marion said.

'Even the sirens must have burnt to cinders.'

'It's utter madness,' said Eva.

'The sun should be rising – ' Eva investigated her wrist watch. Their boat puttered away at a slow pace. Hubert didn't take any chances. The harbour looked endless and deserted. They passed more and more bombed ships. Some had sunk to the bottom with parts of their upper decks still visible. An iron bridge hung twisted like a corkscrew in the air with a huge metal crane hovering over its damaged body like an approaching mortician. Ghost town.

Eva and Else huddled together. 'Nothing makes any sense,' said Eva.

'This could break the camel's back.'

'I wish it would – '

'Marion's asleep.'

'Why isn't the sun rising?'

'I'm proud of Hubert. A real seafaring man.'

They were still going through the harbour but they could see the river widen. On one side stood the city in flames, on the other was the country with fruit trees and thatched houses behind dykes. Hubert steered towards the country.

Slowly the sky changed to orange, then a gigantic sun appeared dark red behind the clouds of ashes. The light remained sombre, as at dusk. Eva lit a cigarette. 'We're getting closer to the shore,' she said. 'What a night!'

'We'll have to look for a place to stay immediately,' said practical Else. 'There'll be thousands of refugees. I don't want to end up in one of those Red Cross tents.'

They came to a stop near the shore. Hubert turned off the engine. 'Here we are. We made it.' He sat down and relaxed. 'Give me a cigarette. I think I deserve one.'

Then Eva, taking off her shoes and dress, slipped into the water. She sank to her hips, the ground felt firm and smooth, levelling off evenly. The water was refreshing. She carried her clothes to the shore.

'Better wake up Marion. She can sleep on the sand.'

They all sat against Hubert's seaman's bag half-asleep, numb, waiting for their skin to dry. Then Else and Hubert set off to look for a place to stay.

'You girls guard the cases,' ordered Hubert.

'We'll put up something so that you can find us again,' said Eva.

'Don't worry, I'm a good scout,' Hubert replied. They staggered through the sand and disappeared behind bushes and trees. Marion closed her eyes.

'Do you have any money with you?' asked Eva.

'It's all here,' Marion patted her breasts.

'Good. I might borrow some.'

'Sure,' said Marion, though she disliked parting from it.

'You know you'll get it back.'

'What do you need it for?' asked Marion.

'To pay my way. And just in case we can't return to the city, I want to be able to get to the Baltic.'

'What for?'

'To visit someone,' said Eva.

'It's not a guy?' Marion enquired.

'A friend. What difference does it make?' Eva was irritated and tired. They both fell asleep. When Else and Hubert returned they woke them up. Else held a tin can with fresh milk, opened her suitcase and provided crackers and cold meat.

'Seems life is starting over again. There were moments when I thought we wouldn't make it.' Hubert had begun to shake.

'My God, was it that bad?' Marion stared at him in disbelief. Men always exaggerated, like her father. 'Did you find somewhere to stay?' She was more interested in finding a bed to sleep in.

'Two very nice rooms in a farmhouse about three kilometres downstream,' said Else. 'The prices are exorbitant but we took them anyway. The first refugees are getting near and we should hurry up and occupy them.'

'How much do I have to pay?' asked Marion.

'One hundred marks per room. Makes fifty for you.'

'Thieves!'

'You'd better behave,' said Else. 'I don't want to be evicted on account of you.'

The farmhouse stood near the river, isolated by dykes. Its roof was gabled and thatched. Their room had a double bed, a washstand, a wooden closet with a built-in faded mirror, two plain wooden chairs. The colour of the wallpaper was undefinable, spotty and splashed round the washstand. A single electric bulb hung unshaded from the ceiling.

Marion lay exhausted on the bed. 'Not even a picture,' she said disappointedly. 'For a hundred marks you would expect a few luxuries.' She fell asleep. The others walked to the nearest village to watch the lines of refugees come crawling in. They were a tired, apathetic and bewildered lot. Everybody was looking for somebody they had lost, perhaps for ever. They came crawling like an endless stream of ants in a strange directionless way, walking on and on. They heard rumours of a Red Cross station erected past the village; they had heard this before but they kept on walking.

'Serves them right,' thought Eva. However, she was too exhausted to feel any triumph.

'Let's get home,' she begged Else and Hubert.

The sun never penetrated the thick dome of smoke that hung over the city. It remained sombre and hot all day, with a menacing red ball crossing the sky.

They lived in luxury compared with other refugees. Hubert began to deal with the farmer's wife, selling his wares for food. They were invited to eat at the family table. Marion enjoyed the country because she discovered that it was populated with young men. Night and day they heard the continued raids on Hamburg, saw more of the city burning, watched the steady flow of refugees searching for safety under the smoke-veiled sky. Eva lay in the grass between peacefully grazing cows and felt a sense of doom. Else and Hubert had a hard time adjusting to idleness. They took long walks and offered their help to the farmer. Marion was on the prowl. She hardly appeared for meals but woke Eva towards morning when she returned, kicking off her shoes and throwing herself on the creaking bed.

'I can't stand it any longer,' complained Eva. 'I want to go to the Baltic.'

'How do you think you'll get there?' Hubert asked.

'She'll get there,' encouraged Else. 'Try to have a real vacation.'

'Keep an eye on Marion. I don't think she knows what she's doing.'

Else filled her own suitcase with coffee, cigarettes and food, put it in Eva's hand and said, 'I'll miss you. Get there safely.'

'How much money do you need?' asked Hubert. They embraced.

'If you move, leave your address with the farmer,' begged Eva. 'I don't want to lose you.' They embraced again.

Eva walked for miles against the stream of refugees still pouring out of the burning city. Then a military car stopped. A man in SS uniform leaned out, grinned and asked: 'Where to?'

'Any station.' Eva was terrified of the man in the black uniform with the skull and crossbones insignia.

'Jump in!' he ordered. 'I'll drive you to a station.'

'For heaven's sake,' thought Eva, but she couldn't think of an excuse. As soon as she was seated next to the man he put his big hand on her leg, high up. He squeezed her thigh and moved higher.

'Keep your hands on the wheel,' said Eva, thinking that

this was worse than the air raid. He smiled with malice. She continued, 'in my family we are not used to vile behaviour. Father is a high-ranking officer – ' The car moved past the main flow of refugees. What else could she tell him? 'Two of my brothers gave their lives for the fatherland – ' Did they really talk like that? Eva wasn't sure. At any moment the angel of death might find her out. ' – two are fighting. My eldest brother is running the estate – ' Why did she keep on talking about a non-existent family? She trembled. How many brothers had she invented? Five altogether, two dead. The man remained silent, keeping her in suspense. He asked no questions. The silence became menacing. 'My name is Jutta von Dona,' continued Eva feverishly.

Suddenly the black uniform stiffened and straightened up. 'Adolf Stifter,' he mumbled.

'It's very kind of you to give me a lift.' Eva's heart was racing. Her hair was wet from perspiration, the refugees were thinning out. They approached a wooded area. 'Do you know your way?' asked Eva. 'More or less,' said Adolf Stifter. They passed three middle-aged ladies going in their direction.

'Stop the car!' called Eva. 'They might need a lift.' Adolf Stifter obeyed without protest. The ladies too wanted to reach a station, got into the back of the car, talked incessantly and seemed to enjoy their ride.

The farewell at Hagenow station was short. The SS man sped off to find a more suitable girl. The ladies queued up at a Red Cross tent for something to drink. Eva disappeared behind a bush, then sat on an embankment that looked down on to the platform and the shining tracks. Hundreds of people sat around, some empty-handed, others holding on to the little they had saved. From where she sat they resembled bees in a hive. They were moving slightly, waiting, trying to get on one of the few trains that were running. Nobody knew whether further trains were expected, least of all the station-master. The system had broken down.

Chapter Six

The sun shone from a clear, blue sky on the waiting refugees at Hagenow station. Eva had moved closer to the tracks just in case a train should arrive. She wanted to make sure she was on it. She began to eat some of her provisions and watched butterflies in their strange, jerky flight. Her pulse started to race again when she thought of the SS man and his hand on her thigh. But the raids had been a decisive victory. According to the news, Germany hardly ever attacked British cities any longer, and the Russians continued to advance. Her pulse calmed down.

For the first time Eva worried about Darling and Werner. Were they safe? She certainly hoped so. She had so much of her own meagre existence invested in Darling that she thought the old lady owed her longevity if nothing else. Eva didn't care if Darling's future was boring, centring round her love for Mr Bertram and her card games, as long as she prolonged her established, third-floor, front-facing, middle-class life. How many hours had Eva spent keeping Mr Bertram in the centre of Darling's heart, bringing him back, celebrating her everlasting affection? How many hours were spent making Darling forget her loneliness by playing cards, by shuffling, cutting, dealing? Eva thought back to the time when Darling's pension was in jeopardy, when Mr Lindner had made up his mind to discontinue payments. He had taken possession of the family's firm with the inherited commitment to pay Darling a monthly pittance until her death. It had been the only request made by the ousted Jewish Meyers. It was so little and a matter of simple decency. They had no reason to doubt the word of that gentle, well-mannered Mr Lindner. But that same man had slowly changed. He was probably not even aware of it at the time. Having yielded to the pressures of the authorities to clean out contaminating Jewish traces from his nest, he had felt obliged to change the company's name. Once his own name had appeared on letter heads and bank statements, the transformation became more obvious. He suddenly felt gratitude towards a government that had given him something which would otherwise have always lain beyond his reach. Now he was the owner of a company. His gratitude made him apply for party membership. 'They expect it of me,' he had apologised to Eva. 'We're still getting short-changed with import permits.' Once he had become a party member it was expected of his staff that they join the Nazi Workers' Guild. Since Eva and Friedrich were both half-Jewish and therefore not eligible for the Guild, Mr Lindner had given them notice, with regret. However, Friedrich had managed to produce membership books and so they were allowed to stay. Once the Swastika button had been fastened to Mr Lindner's lapel, he had begun to identify with the symbol. He didn't change into a ruthless fanatic. He remained basically mild and weak. He was in love with Eva and made no secret of this fact. Every morning Eva would find another love poem on her desk, written in a tiny, neat hand. Each stanza looked like needlepoint, four-line squares going down a straight path for many pages. It was amazing how much sentimentality could be produced day in, day out by a single person. Eva seldom read it. 'It's trash,' she would declare and throw the sheets into Else's rubbish bin behind the counter. That he didn't turn against Eva but kept up his hopeless longing was another of his good qualities. But then he forced Friedrich to disown his father and to apply for a certification of pure Arian blood. 'I knew your father,' said Mr Lindner, 'and he told me himself that you weren't his child, that he married your mother when she was already pregnant. I can testify.' He was now taking Nazi race laws seriously and Friedrich didn't know what to do. 'The authorities won't help half-Jews,' he declared, and he was right. Mr Lindner kept on calling the people in charge but the papers got regularly shifted from one office to the next or couldn't be found at all.

A train arrived going south. People scrambled, pushed and kicked. It was an ugly sight.

One day Mr Lindner had dictated a letter addressed to Darling cancelling the pension. 'I don't see why I should pay,' he had said as if he owed Eva an explanation. 'This is no longer the company I once took over – '

'Who do you think is supposed to take care of Mrs Meyer?' Eva had asked. 'Her family has been chased out of the country, trusting you – '

'It's none of my business,' Mr Lindner had become red in the face. 'Her husband was a Jew. I don't see any reason why I should – '

'It *is* your business. You took over their company.' Eva had been close to tears and even now, thinking back, her eyes became moist.

'That was a long time ago. Things have changed.'

Eva had agreed. 'They certainly have.' They had sat silently for a while.

'Won't you reconsider?' Eva had pleaded. 'You know you're wrong.'

'I would,' he had said, 'if you made love to me.'

Eva still felt the shock. It had not been a silly advance but criminal blackmail. She had to be sacrificed so that poor Darling could get enough money to survive.

'Once,' Eva had said. It was worse than the SS man this afternoon, she decided. 'With a written contract.' So she had written down the conditions for Darling's pension, increasing the monthly payments.

'Don't be surprised if he breaks his word,' Else had warned. But she thought she had to risk it. The act had been ghastly, that much she remembered. The rest, the details, she had blocked out of her memory. 'Nothing happened,' Eva had told herself, dressing and leaving to get into the real world of Else's kitchen. 'No, nothing happened,' she had insisted and from that moment on amnesia about the incident had developed. Darling went on living, using up the hard-earned pension which she thought came from the goodness of Mr Lindner's heart.

Mr Lindner had given up writing love poems. He became distant and shy, called in Miss Ehrlich for dictation. When he passed her in the hall he looked like a beaten dog who begs for forgiveness. But Eva didn't want to forgive. Fortunately, soon afterwards he, Mr Schiller and Friedrich left for Russia to collect skins and hides in that vast, faraway territory. She missed Friedrich, with whom she could talk frankly and openly without having the censoring machine buzz in her brain, translating every word into Nazi-accepted language.

The platform was less crowded. People lined up again at the various tents erected around the station.

'I might get to the Baltic.' The thought crossed her mind suddenly and she began to whistle a song. The sun almost touched the tree tops now where the Red Cross had settled their equipment. 'It's getting late,' she thought when she heard the sound of a train going north. Another scene of pushing, yelling and scrambling followed. Everybody tried to get on, knowing that many would be left behind. They were moving, moving north. The first stop was Lübeck and lots of people got off. Perhaps they thought this was the end of the ride. But after a while the train pulled out of the station and continued on its way north. Eva now had enough room to sit on the floor in the corridor, hugging Else's suitcase. It got darker outside. She tried to read the names of stations they passed. Sometimes the train stood still in the middle of a flat meadow. People got nervous. They wanted to arrive somewhere before more bombs fell. Then the train moved on through the night with stars in the sky and cows lying peacefully against the horizon. 'The Baltic,' thought Eva, and she fell asleep for short stretches, clutching her suitcase. The train stopped and a voice from the dark called 'Wustrow – Wustrow'. Eva pushed her way through the crowd, climbed over trunks, sacks, sleeping people. Wustrow was her station.

Two ladies in Red Cross uniforms greeted the five exhausted travellers with enthusiasm. It seemed as if they had prepared themselves for a long feast of doing good and providing charity. They snatched the tired women with excitement and guided them to the shelter and kitchen. While the refugees lined up in front of the only toilet, the food was heated on a stove and then the dinner was served, accompanied by long reports of the Red Cross helpers' good deeds. Afterwards a man with a torch directed them to the sleeping quarters, which were in a school building. He acquainted them with the facilities, let his light glide briefly, once, over bunk beds and cots in a dark room, then bade them good night. Eva put her suitcase at the end of her bed, so that she could feel it with her feet. She took off only her shoes, put them in the suitcase, shut it tight, fell on the bed and closed her eyes. She was still on the train; the landscape passed by in bright sunlight under her dark eyelids. 'I've reached the Baltic!' she told herself, and fell asleep.

The next day was another hot, blue-skied summer surprise. After a plentiful breakfast, handed out by another two of the ladies, Eva began her walk through the small, ancient town along unpaved roads, shaded by huge, wide-spreading trees and past gabled houses in overgrown gardens where the sun danced on leaves and flowers. She decided to take the narrow sandy path on top of the dyke along the bay, watching through the bulrushes the sparkling light shine on the water. She passed small pastel-coloured cottages with thatched roofs, surrounded by flower gardens and fruit trees. Meadows stretched on either side, interrupted by silver-green willow trees. There wasn't one thing that needed changing. It seemed as though Nazi ugliness could never approach or touch the beauty given to this land. 'It can't last,' she told herself. 'Don't be disappointed, people haven't changed.' Once she rested at the bay, ate from her provisions, stretched her legs. Behind her lay a small cemetery with sand-coloured washed-out stones. Little pink roses were climbing over the graves. No church and no houses were in sight. Nobody seemed to come here any more. She arrived at Ahrenshoop at noon, had to register and get a room and ration coupons.

74

'*Heil* Hitler! What can I do for you?' said a tall, stout woman with an open face. Eva explained her situation. 'Oh my, oh my,' complained the woman, 'another refugee from Hamburg. We're already overcrowded.'

'You have no idea how crowded the places are near the city. They lie on floors, stunned, not quite understanding what has happened to them.'

'Barbarism is hard to understand,' said the woman while counting Eva's ration coupons. 'I know of a beautiful room with a balcony outside the village between wheatfields, near the beach. Price eighty-five marks with breakfast. The only drawback is the owner, a widow Drexler, who so far has refused to let any refugees into her house. "I'll burn it down first," she told me. "I won't have strangers in Mr Drexler's rooms." She talks of her dead husband as if he were still alive. I've never dared to send anybody up, but if you want to try?'

'I hope she won't murder me.'

'If she refuses to take in refugees, I'll have her arrested,' said the woman. 'Show your paper and tell her that you come directly from Nellie, wanting that room with the balcony for eighty-five marks with breakfast.'

'And if she refuses?'

'Then you come back.' She looked at the form Eva had filled out for her registration. 'Eva Ehrenfels,' she mused. 'In school I once sat next to a girl by that name. She was Jewish.'

'What happened to her?' asked Eva.

'Don't know,' Nellie confessed. 'She went on to university and we lost contact.' Eva stood by the door. 'Good luck,' Nellie called. She had forgotten the '*Heil* Hitler'.

Mrs Drexler looked middle-aged with dark, long hair, held back at the neck in a ribbon. Her eyes were deep and black. She did not greet Eva, but looked at the paper Nellie had written out and immediately became hostile, ready to defend her privacy.

'How dare that woman – ' she shouted.

'I promise I won't disturb you. I'll be quiet as a mouse. I can make my own breakfast and we don't ever have to meet. How is that for an arrangement?'

'You understand about privacy,' Mrs Drexler half-smiled.

75

'Of course.' They walked up the stairs to her room with the balcony overlooking the sea, the village and the wheatfields.

'My God!' said Eva.

'I live over there.' Mrs Drexler pointed to a small building with a studio in the garden. 'If you need me, just call.'

When Eva arrived at the beach in the afternoon she found the entire cast of the theatre there, except for Eduard. For years Ahrenshoop had been a painters' colony only, then other artists had come. Now they all enjoyed the wide, sandy beaches that stretched for miles, the flat land surrounded by the sea, the small cottages invisible behind the trees and flowers, the wild woods, the colours and the endless sky. They could seek total privacy or they could join the different groups congregating on the beaches, always awaiting new adventures, excitement, fun.

The sun was still hot and brilliant. There were people coming out of the water and dropping on to the sand, others running down to the sea. They looked so happy, suntanned, healthy and beautiful, selected by God to represent his most successful creation. 'What am I doing here?' Eva asked herself, and suddenly all the joy of being in Ahrenshoop vanished. Her pulse began to race, her temperature rose. She felt that she was already extinct. Nobody noticed her and, even if they had, they would have looked away from the girl in wrinkled, ill-fitting clothes. Arlen lay back with outstretched arms in the sand. She walked away. A Jew would remind them of murder and death, of hatred and crimes. It was such a liability to share a Jew's burden. There were very few who were able to afford it. She walked towards the woods thinking of Arlen. Gradually, she calmed down again. She was in the woods, between tall ferns, under Scotch firs, stepping on grass and wild flowers. Birds sang from every direction, deer leaped through the thicket. Something always rustled nearby. Raspberries and blueberries were ripe and grew in abundance. She would go berry picking tomorrow.

The actors had left the beach when Eva returned. From a previous vacation spent in Ahrenshoop, she knew that they were having their dinner at the small hotel on top of the hill. Eva would not join them. She ate at another restaurant by herself. Afterwards she forgot what she had eaten. It didn't matter. She was depressed. As soon as she got in touch with people, she felt threatened, isolated and alone. She would have liked to be with Arlen but knew he didn't want to be torn away from his gaiety.

Summer nights do not get dark in the north. The sky was like the sea, sprinkled with faint stars. The landscape remained visible in undetailed outlines. Eva walked down to the sea. Laughter broke through the stillness. She sat in the fold of a sand dune, listened to the even, short splashes of rippling water reaching the shore and felt the gentle breeze touch her face, felt her hair lifted and allowed to fall as if by a caressing hand. 'Tomorrow I'll go berry picking and I'll write to Else,' she told herself. 'No more ledger. It's summer time in Ahrenshoop.' She wanted to ignore Arlen's presence nearby. Without him she didn't have to chart emotional reactions, statistics of pain, joy, restlessness, drunkenness and boredom. Emptiness would mark the lowest point, the base line, and Eva was afraid they might reach it quickly. 'I'll ask Mrs Drexler for a container,' Eva smiled, standing on her balcony with a last glance at the sea and the wheatfields. Then she threw her dress into the air and fell on her bed. 'Berry picking,' she thought and was asleep.

She woke up to another sunny day. The air was still cool. She stood outside, above the land wrapped in a faint vapour. 'It's going to be beautiful,' she thought. She took a bag with coffee from Else's suitcase and walked down the stairs. Mrs Drexler sat in the kitchen, pointed at a tray and told her: 'You can take it up.'

'Wouldn't it be nice to start the day with a cup of really strong coffee?' Mrs Drexler suddenly laughed, and looked much younger. So they sat in the kitchen together and enjoyed their breakfast. They discussed the berry picking and Mrs Drexler promised to produce some pancakes or a farina pudding to go with them. It was a good beginning. Eva stepped outside with two pails, provisions for lunch and a bottle of leftover coffee. Once in the woods she lost herself in picking berries. It was amazing how everything became timeless, how thoughts vanished and peace reigned. The fuller the pails the more fulfilled she felt. As if all her goals had finally been reached.

She put the berries on the kitchen table with a smile. She and Mrs Drexler sat opposite one another, reaching across the table and pouring more berries on to the pancakes. Their lips were purple-red. 'What a wonderful night,' one of them said. Then they moved up on to the balcony and watched the sea and the silver moon. They hardly talked.

Eva went berry picking almost every day. There was such an abundance in the woods. At night she would stand with Mrs Drexler in the kitchen and make preserves. Afterwards they would eat dinner together and then go their different ways. Eva never found out whether Mrs Drexler had friends or saw other people, or what she did all day in her studio. She didn't ask. She had promised to keep her distance.

One night she was sitting on the balcony, drinking a cup of coffee, smoking, looking at the sea, when a voice called from below. It was Arlen. She closed her eyes. She didn't want to face the real world here. He called again.

'Why don't you answer? I can see you sitting there.'

'I'll be down, wait.'

She led him up the dark staircase on to the balcony.

'Why didn't you come to see me? I was worried to death – and here you were all this time – '

'I walked down to the beach immediately when I arrived. You were there with your friends. You all looked so happy. I couldn't come nearer, couldn't spoil your fun.'

'What makes you think I was happy?' he cried out. 'I've been lying on the beach scared and miserable waiting for my draft papers to arrive.'

Eva didn't want to think about Arlen's fears. 'Take it easy. Most of the records have been destroyed in the fire.'

'Are you crazy?' He moved to get a closer look at her face. 'How can I take it easy?'

'I go berry picking every day I can,' said Eva. Arlen produced a bottle of wine from the inside of his jacket.

'Do you have glasses?'

'In the kitchen.'

'Never mind.' He drank from the bottle. 'Same effect.' He

wiped the top with the palm of his hand. 'Tell me about the raid! Was it ghastly?'

'We almost roasted to death. But death isn't so bad, I think. Life is the difficult part.'

'I thought you were content now, with your berry picking.'

'I am, Arlen. That is, I think I am. If you're not in despair, you're lucky.'

'Are you able to share your luck?' he asked, offering her the bottle.

'How can I share?' she questioned. 'You get one half of my sandwich, I get the other – is that how you want to share?'

'We're able to share our unhappiness, aren't we?'

'I don't know,' she pondered. 'Somehow we get stuck in it together.' She drank from the bottle. 'It's sour,' she commented. She could feel the night breeze on her hair. The stars flickered on a steel-blue sky. The moon hung misshapen over the sea, creating an alley of light. 'I do love you,' she said. 'I wish you wouldn't drown your sorrows in wine. It might kill you faster than the war.'

'May I stay here tonight?'

They put the mattress on the floor in front of the open balcony door and watched the sky for shooting stars. From time to time there were showers of them, passing silently like a far-off firework display. 'We *are* lucky,' Eva said. 'Only lucky people see so many shooting stars.' Arlen calmed down and became gentle. They couldn't close their eyes, always waiting for another shooting star to appear. Just as the sun was rising they fell asleep.

'It's a miracle,' thought Eva, watching the crimson sunset from a hollow in the dunes. She had slept for hours. After dinner she had walked along the grassy dyke towards Nellie's small, thatched, pink cottage. She had been invited to a party. Nellie entertained her guests outside on the meadow between the dyke and the bay, on folding chairs with a folding table in the middle. Apparently they had just finished dinner because Nellie appeared from the house with two pails of steaming hot water for the dishes. A middle-aged man with light blond hair rushed to her aid.

'I didn't know they were ready,' he said reproachfully. 'You shouldn't carry such a heavy load.'

'I am still a little stronger than you are,' said Nellie and then laughed into the night. She put the pails down and declared: 'If you want to do something, my dear Alfred, clean the dishes.'

'Bruny!' he called his wife. 'I suppose it's our turn.' Bruny, in a simple, expensive dress, got up with dignity. Her hair was pinned on top of her head. Alfred and Bruny belonged to the aristocracy of traders, merchants who had been wealthy long enough to allow their children to venture into other fields, though they didn't allow any nonsense. They owned the largest mansions in the most expensive suburbs. They possessed wealth, education and arrogance, topped by fervent patriotism. And yet they looked rather unassuming. Bruny could have been a schoolteacher of an earlier vintage and Alfred the head waiter in a hotel.

'More company's arriving!' Alfred called when he saw Eva crossing the meadow in their direction.

'Well,' said Nellie, 'nice of you to come. Did Mrs Drexler warn you of my wagging tongue?'

'She hardly ever talks,' answered Eva.

'I told you she's a queer person, a kind of recluse.'

Eva was introduced to two sisters, Anna and Bertha, whose round faces looked alike.

'People usually think we're twins,' one explained, glad to have something to say, 'but we're not. I am two years older.'

A retired sea captain and a blonde woman with lots of make-up were introduced as neighbours. Several young people, whose names Eva immediately forgot, were the talented artists whose works were exhibited at the village art gallery. Eva sat down. She watched the oddly-shaped willow trees in the dark, the gentle sway of the bulrushes, and the silver moon reflected on the water, its light shining through a filigree of stems and leaves. Alfred and Bruny were splashing in a big basin, trying to clean the plates of grease. They were squatting on the grass like natives of a faraway country. Snatches of conversation drifted through the night air.

'I sold four watercolours yesterday . . .'

'We've lost all our belongings . . .'

'Always know what to do with a troublemaker in my classes.' This was from one of the sisters. Apparently she was a teacher.

Bruny poured the dirty dishwater on to the meadow.

'We're finished,' announced Alfred. Now they all sat in a circle. Words dropped like rain. They talked about the war.

'I should be with Arlen,' thought Eva.

'What do they need concentration camps for?' asked Alfred into the night air. 'If they intend to kill the Jews why not shoot them right away?'

'You can't mean that!' Nellie cried out.

'Tell me what you were trying to say,' said Bruny in some agitation. 'He sometimes says things he doesn't mean.'

'Well, if they're going to be killed, why not right away?' questioned Alfred, as if it were a matter of shipping cargo from one country to another. 'I don't see the point in prolonging their suffering.'

'You are a true humanitarian,' said the over-made-up neighbour who had come with the sea captain.

'Then you feel sorry for them, Alfred?' asked Bruny. 'The trouble is you always express yourself so clumsily.'

'You're scaring me,' said Nellie. 'I've never heard you say anything like that before.'

'Did you see the signs the British put up after the First World War in African harbours?' asked Alfred.

'No,' said Nellie, 'and I don't know what it has to do with the Jews.'

'Because the Jews were behind it, nobody else. The signs said: "No dogs and Germans allowed here". What would *you* say to such insults?'

'If you lose a war you are not very popular with your former enemies,' said one of the young artists. 'That's an old story.'

'A poster has never killed anyone yet,' murmured the sea captain.

'They've insulted us long enough,' explained Alfred.

'Do you think that was worth another war?' asked the

made-up neighbour. Eva's vitality drained out of her with every word. 'It's better than dying of cancer,' she repeated Mrs Lowenstein's words. Then she got up.

Nellie tried to persuade her to stay. 'Let's change the subject,' she begged. But Eva turned and simply ran away. She realised that how she felt now would just go on and on. Perhaps she should carry a bottle around her neck like Arlen in case she required immediate medicine. After a while she slowed her pace and then she kept on walking, as if life were an endurance test, a weighing of strength, a pressure chamber. She would go berry picking. She was determined not to go under this time.

Arlen was waiting for her on the balcony. 'Where have you been? I'm going crazy with anxiety. I can't stand the old gang any longer. They're so complacent – '

'That's all we're going to get, my dear pet,' said Eva. 'I've just had a taste of public opinion that made me sick.'

'I can't get any sicker.'

'Put your head under a cold shower. You've had too much to drink.'

'I prefer to stay in a fog,' Arlen insisted. 'Nobody can find me there. Besides, my ulcers may start bleeding from the wine. Do you think they draft people with bleeding ulcers?'

'I doubt it.' Eva tried to console him.

'They'll make me shoot people, they might even make me shoot Jews.'

'Why make them suffer,' it hammered in Eva's head. 'Kill them right away!' And here was Arlen drunk and miserable. How could she get rid of him? Now he began to cry, his body shook and he sobbed loudly, sitting there alone on his chair above the sea, below the sky, sobbing, sighing, howling. 'Why make them suffer?' She went over to caress him.

'Sh-sh-sh, calm down, my pet. Nothing is going to happen to you, just calm down, come on.' Arlen clung to her. She stroked his hair, she kissed his wet face, she did all the things he had done so often for her. It came like a prescribed formula from inside, like a mother calming a frightened child. 'I'll put down the mattress again and we'll look at the stars. I'll stay with you, my pet. Nothing is going to happen.' They trusted each other's voice.

They lay on the mattress, Eva holding his head. 'Don't think,' she recommended. 'Listen to the wind.'

Then the moon appeared, silvery white behind trees, rising until its light swept over the wheatfields and the church steeple to the far right, outlined against the sea.

'We're going to the woods tomorrow blackberry picking,' said Eva.

'Berlin is burning,' he said. 'I heard it on the radio.'

'Let it burn,' Eva replied. 'Serves them right.' When she turned round, Arlen was asleep.

She walked out on to the balcony where light and shadows changed with the rising moon. A bright shooting star swept across the sky. 'That's a good omen,' thought Eva. 'Only I don't believe in omens.' She felt Arlen's presence intensely. She could find him in complete darkness. More shooting stars rushed across the sky like long distance runners trying to reach a goal, trying to melt together, creating a new planet.

When Eva opened her eyes the room was flooded with an orange light that cast crimson-tinted shadows over the walls. Arlen opened his eyes for a second and fell asleep again. Mrs Drexler began to stir in the house. A door opened and closed.

Later Eva and Arlen sat on the balcony separated by the table and their own worlds. They drank coffee and swallowed bread with blueberry jam.

'I'm going to the woods,' said Eva.

'Let's stop at the hotel,' he suggested. 'I want to change my clothes.'

'You hate the woods. Why can't you say so? Why do you have to lie?'

'It's easier.'

'You're right, we all do it.'

Afterwards, as Eva was walking along the dyke towards the woods, she was sure they had escaped something dangerous, something that could have set the house on fire. She thought back to the morning, the breakfast table where they had sat, chewing, bending heads to reach the cups, smoothing jam over bread, biting into it, chewing, drinking, saying a few words, looking about, doing the things people did in life, playing the game, ping-pong, ping-pong, back and forth, never exactly the same but always the same. She was glad she had escaped. 'Berries,' she thought and looked up at the blue sky shining through the trees.

Next day Eva got her first letter from Else. Hubert had been to Hamburg and back. Like a miracle, the store and Eva's office building were still standing in the middle of a wasteland of ruins. But the air raids continued. For the time being nobody was allowed to return. There was no water or electricity. The dead had not been buried. It stank, Hubert had assured her. There were rats everywhere. But the store was standing and the house next door. In the countryside Marion was keeping the farmhands content. 'I can't make that girl out,' Else had written. Otherwise nothing was new. The weather was still beautiful. It must seem an irony to those who had lost everything. 'But that's the way it goes,' Else had added.

Eva was leaving the house. A slight smell of autumn mingled with the ripening fruits and flowers. A breeze rippled the bay into thousands of light-embroidered folds. There were no clouds in the sky. The blackberry harvest was over but she still found some here and there. They tasted sweet. The ferns had grown far above her head, fox-red squirrels sat in the oaks and threw acorns to the ground.

Eva sat on top of a dune, naked after a swim in the sea. Below, the waves came rushing forward with the rhythm of the hour, splash, splash, splash, like a lullaby. From the woods the air filled with bird song to the accompaniment of the wind whistling through dying leaves. The sand ran soundlessly through her fingers. It wasn't hot any more, the wind felt cool. Summer was passing. She was on holiday and she was taking it in, storing it for a sad day. Splash, splash, splash. Time was ticking in her blood.

She saw Arlen again a few days later. Mrs Drexler had shown Eva some of her paintings.

'You have to see them, Arlen!' Eva shouted with excitement. 'They are amazingly good and original.'

'So what!' said Arlen, who needed attention. 'May I say something?'

'Of course.'

'At the moment art is a bit beyond me, Eva. You know, I think I'm past the stage of fearing death. What haunts me now is mutilation. Spending my life in a wheelchair, coming back blind or limbless. I can see myself deserted, being pushed round in inaccessible houses to the end of my days.'

'I know, you can be sure, I know. I've been on a thousand trains, arrived at a thousand concentration camps. I've been murdered so often that when the time comes, I think I will be well prepared.'

'But you are allowed to die. Imagine a life without arms and legs, being blind. You lack the means to commit suicide, you have to go on living – ' Arlen began to sob.

'Don't torture yourself with the worst, my pet. It's not going to happen. You'll fail the physical. I am sure they'll never send you on active duty, never.' Eva hugged his body and stroked his hair. She noticed that he didn't smell of alcohol. 'You're making yourself sick for nothing,' she assured him. Arlen clung to her, sobbing still. They lay there, Eva thought, like people in a film. Her next line should be: 'Everyone has to find his own solution. I can't be crippled *for* you.' That was cruel. How could she get away from this mess?

'Shall we go for a walk?' she asked. No, he wanted to stay safe in her arms, lie on the mattress and rest.

'I'm exhausted,' he cried. 'You have no idea how tired I feel.'

'You'll rest, my pet. Just help me carry the mattress.'

Eva lay motionless. Now she had become paralysed, unable to react. How did one respond to another's torments? Splash, splash, splash. All the old worries rushed against her brain. 'I'm tired too. You are putting your weight on me,' she complained silently. This is a variation on a theme. Splash, splash, splash. Her office room with its piles of unrecorded invoices flashed through her mind. She saw the band of murky water in the canal rise and fall with the tides, the church tower behind those pitted, mutilated office buildings and warehouses. Now they stood there, burnt out, skeletons, amputated. It stank, Hubert had reported. The plague stank.

'Don't get ill,' said Eva, stroking his skin.

'Hold me,' he begged. 'Just hold me.'

It was very little he wanted but Eva felt no satisfaction in giving it. She felt his weight. Rock, rock, rock the cradle. She wasn't a mother, she didn't want to hear the crying, whining voice, not from him, not from herself, she had heard it enough. Splash, splash, splash, always the same words, the same scenes and the fake reaction. Was it fake? She wondered. Just keep it up until he's asleep. Her body hurt. She scanned the sky for shooting stars but the season for the spectacle was over. Now the stars stood fixed, while Arlen and Eva whirled through the universe like an inexplicable phenomenon, a sudden light burning for just one night, melting into one beam for a fraction of a moment.

'Don't ever leave me,' he begged her. 'Don't leave me alone.'

'Stop worrying, we'll be fine, both of us, you'll see.' The cradle rocked, the waves splashed. Was this all she could say, all she could do with her life? Couldn't she mix some paint like Mrs Drexler and create the world she wanted to inhabit? Apparently not. At least not in an habitual state of despair.

'You're not holding me!' cried Arlen. Eva sighed.

'Don't you feel better, my pet? Nothing is going to happen.' She wasn't conscious of what she was saying. She was watching the horizon get lighter as if day were breaking through, though it couldn't be later than eleven o'clock. 'Another city burning,' she thought, 'or some cosmic light.' She put her arm tighter around Arlen and kissed his neck. How well she knew him. Or was it all conjecture?

'Are you all right?' she asked Arlen.

'I'm slowly vanishing. I think it's a relief.'

The horizon was definitely getting lighter in a white band. She had answered Else's letter with an account of berry picking and jam making in her landlady's kitchen. She had asked for news. Were people returning to the city, was their district already habitable? Eva was willing to stay as long as possible in Ahrenshoop but she couldn't stay much longer than the others. Abandonment of work was considered treason and she didn't want to get into trouble. Besides, she owed Hubert a lot of money. She had to repay it. They each slept for a while. One or other of them kept waking up. They were restless. The horizon still showed its band of light as if a new planet were about to rise. Then they slept again. Eva dreamt that she was a girl in one of Mrs Drexler's paintings. Once or twice Arlen complained because she wasn't holding him. They were glad when the night was over.

A sudden rain changed the weather to that of a cold, windy autumn. Eva sat at night in her dark room by closed windows and looked out into the shadowy world. She would return next week to Hamburg. Everybody else had already gone. But she couldn't tear herself away from the walks in the woods where gales tore at the fiery leaves and tossed them through the air like drunken shooting stars. Once more flowers were in bloom, goldenrod and lilac daisies. Heavy clouds chased across the sky, sand flew hard and prickly, creating blinding storms. Dead leaves shot up high, rolled over and landed on the ground, then skipped on and on. Animals were more visible and less hurried.

That night the wind howled round the house and the rain hit against the windowpanes. Eva lay under a heavy blanket and listened to the sounds. The wind came in sporadic gusts without warning or rhythm. For a while she heard only the raindrops on the glass then the wind whistled and howled for a few seconds and was gone. Or it circled around the house like an angry animal, rattling and shaking the structure in an attempt to destroy it. Eva's heart beat fast at the sudden onslaught. 'I should be down by the sea,' she told herself, hugging her warm blanket.

The next day the sun came out and it felt almost like summer again. Eva put on a dress and headed for the woods, another day of freedom. The village streets were deserted, the ground covered with dead leaves from the huge poplars which stood stripped and empty in straight lines between the gardens and small houses. Children's voices shouted behind fences.

'I'll stay another week,' she announced that night in the kitchen while Mrs Drexler was clearing away the dishes.

'You are very welcome,' said Mrs Drexler.

Chapter Seven

Eva received another letter from Else, this time postmarked 'Hamburg'. She and Hubert were back at the store, cleaning and clearing away the debris. They had had to find wood to board up the front window and door, leaving just a small glass opening for light. Cleaning was difficult. Everything had to be scrubbed from ceiling to floor. Drinking water was still distributed by trucks and they had to queue up with pails. The store was operating again but hardly a customer came. The district stood in ruins. Else had gone to Eva's office and had found Mrs and Miss Ehrlich there, both mellowed and subdued, perhaps a little bewildered, sitting alone in the desolate landscape. The mother looked rather sick and Miss Ehrlich had said she wanted her to stay at home and rest. The office too had boarded windows and the light had to be on all day. Darling and Werner had telephoned her.

Eva read this with a sigh of relief though she wasn't sure how much it really meant to her or whether it meant anything at all. Miss Ehrlich had given an office key to Else in case Eva should arrive at night and find the door locked. 'Aren't they considerate?' Then the men were expected back soon. The territories they had plundered for so long had finally been recaptured by the Russians. Everyone was in retreat. 'What an admission.' The Gothic tower had survived, the rest of the church lay in ruins. Well, Eva had seen that. The air raids continued night after night and even during the day. 'I don't know what they're after. Do you think they want to hit the church tower?' Marion had come back with them and was up to her old tricks. 'She drops in regularly and misses her old friend Eva.'

At any rate nothing seemed very urgent. Miss Ehrlich had not insisted on her returning at once. Eva was not anxious to sit at her desk, nor did she want to see the men arrive, though she liked Friedrich.

Eva had come down to the kitchen early in her old slacks and blouse. Else's suitcase was almost empty. She looked through the window at the light blue sky between the pine trees and wondered if Mrs Drexler would wake in time to say good-bye. But here she was, coming in the front door. They faced each other on this late September day in the morning sun.

'Let's have breakfast.'

'You can't imagine what it's like doing accounting all day, every day. I wonder how I managed to survive all those years? Here I am a different person.'

'Come back to Ahrenshoop.' Mrs Drexler put her hand on Eva's. 'You're always welcome.'

Eva looked out of the train window and watched the land-scape rush by. Fields, cattle, trees, villages. Then they stopped. Someone called out a name nobody understood, the train was set in motion again and they were off to the next village. Healthy looking peasants with round, dull faces rode short distances, carrying heavy loads. When she changed trains in Lübeck she realised that she would arrive early in Hamburg. It wouldn't pay to go to the office, so she decided not to cross the bridge but to reach Else's store by walking through the ruined backstreets. The destruction was im-mense. The burned and bombed-out houses looked like a vast cemetery hit by an earthquake. Empty windows in half-demolished walls stared like blind eyes over the wasteland. The church tower guided her through a city without streets or sign posts.

The store was empty, like the ruined town. Else stood in the kitchen tasting something that was boiling on the stove. Hubert lay stretched out in his easy chair with closed eyes.

Both seemed unchanged. Else's apron sat tight and white around her hips, her blond hair was neatly piled high on top of her head. Hubert's clothes hung unwrinkled, tailor-made around his body, though without elegance. Else suddenly threw down her spoon and cried: 'Eva!' at the same time as tears started down her face. Hubert woke up from his nap and smiled at Else's reaction.

'All that hugging and kissing. Girls like to do that,' he said good humouredly.

'You'd better get up from your chair and hug and kiss her yourself,' Else scolded and Hubert pulled himself up from his chair.

'Isn't it good to see her again?' exclaimed Else. 'Come, sit down. Tell me about yourself.' Else tasted the food in the pot, added this and that, closed the lid and sat beside Eva.

The evening passed pleasantly and felt full of surprises though little had changed in their lives. Somehow they realised that a new era had begun, that the wind had shifted into a different direction.

'The men are back,' reported Else. 'Mr Lindner came to the store the other day, asking for your address. Don't worry, I didn't give it to him. Said I had no idea where you were living at the moment.'

'Is he still wearing his Party button?'

'Of course, right smack staring you in the eye,' Else laughed.

'The underworld,' Eva shuddered. 'You can't escape it.'

After dinner Eva called Darling who wept over the phone. 'I'm so happy,' she sobbed. Nothing had happened to her home, not even a window broken. They made a date.

Werner's number was out of order. Else listened to the hum in the phone and declared: 'Bombed out. You'll find a message from him at the office. Miss Ehrlich told me he'd called.'

Arlen wasn't home. She called Renate but she didn't answer either.

'You'll see Marion later. She insisted on returning with us though everybody on the farm wanted her to stay. Poor thing! Nothing will change her but old age.'

'That's a long way off,' Hubert added.

'So you really had a good time?' Else enquired. 'We got terribly bored and depressed on the farm – nowhere to go, refugees everywhere. At night, mosquitoes. Then Marion was a real embarrassment. People thought she belonged to us.'

The evening stretched leisurely from moment to moment. Eva sat in anticipation of that vague event that was about to happen, expecting, but anticipating what? She didn't know. It only happened in Else's little kitchen where every move could be foreseen with certainty. They sat lazily drinking, smoking, talking without revelations. Cards and coins were distributed. Else would win. Cards were shuffled, always the same. And yet Eva sat in the tiny kitchen, expecting that revelation which hung in the air like a decisive move in a game of chess. Nothing ever happened. But the tension was delicious. Now it's coming, the expectation sang in the smoke-filled little space: now it's coming!

The sirens had just sounded their advance warning when Eva walked over to the office; Marion and Friedrich greeted her. They sat and talked. Friedrich spoke of the atrocities witnessed in Russia, of the revenge awaiting the Germans. He mentioned the fear that paralysed every Russian, the fear of the enemy, the fear of their own secret police. He spoke of the terrible nights in God-forsaken places where the stench of the slaughtered cattle made him throw up and the fear of being murdered turned him into an insomniac.

'We sometimes worked for sixteen hours a day and still I couldn't sleep.' He looked haggard and changed.

'You've lost weight,' remarked Marion. 'Should have been on the farm, the other side of the river. We had everything and I was the star of the show.'

'The holidays are over,' remarked Eva.

'I never had one,' complained Friedrich.

'Men must love wars,' concluded Marion. 'Otherwise we wouldn't have that many.'

'Who has a choice?' asked Friedrich.

Eva was back in the underworld. She watched Friedrich's hand move slowly over Marion's neck, down her arm.

Marion sat like a stone-carved statue. The raid was still on, cannon fired from all sides, bombs crashed, houses crumbled, ruins fell on ruins. They were inhuman sounds.

'Too many planes and bombs,' decided Eva. 'First they had none and now they have too many.' Somewhere, very far away, lay Ahrenshoop. She imagined herself standing on the balcony, looking up at the sky, listening to the wild onslaught of the waves. The wind would tear the last leaves down, bend the branches, howl past her face, rush around the house, whirl up fears and summer memories.

Friedrich suddenly grabbed her arm and began to tremble. His face wore an expression of pain.

'What's the matter?' she shouted. But he had got up and was feeling his way through the dark office, out, towards the toilets.

'He must be ill,' concluded Eva.

'Yeah, he got sick in Russia. They gave him morphine to ease the pain and he got hooked. He found a way to get at the stuff. He still does, stealing and forging prescriptions just for another fix. Mr Lindner wants him to go to a hospital but he refuses. He wants his fix or death. He's crazy. I expect his father beat the shit out of him. He can sleep in my apartment tonight; you probably want the couch.'

'I can't believe it!' was all Eva could say. 'And I counted on his support against the others.'

'Don't mention the drug,' begged Marion.

The raid was over. They smoked another cigarette each. Friedrich had still not returned.

'I wonder what's keeping him?' asked Eva. 'Do you think we should have a look?'

'He's probably waiting until the shakes stop.'

'I'm dead tired,' declared Eva, who didn't want to hear more about Friedrich's addiction.

'What took you so long?' asked Marion, when Friedrich returned. 'You can sleep upstairs. Eva is tired.' Eva lifted the air-raid curtains at the corner and saw the ruins in flames.

'All right, little moonface,' said Friedrich, slick and smooth. 'I promise you some star-spangled joy with fireworks against a moonlit sky.' He was rather euphoric.

'There's enough fire outside,' grumbled Marion. 'But you're going to have a good time anyway!'

The two left to climb the eight flights of stairs. Eva sat back paralysed. That was it: the underworld in full swing with every possible mode of horror. Arlen had vanished. Either he had been drafted – she looked at the flames consuming the burnt-out houses – or he too was full of fear. 'At least I still have Else,' she sighed, though at the moment this didn't provide enough comfort to change her mood.

'Just get up!' she told herself the following morning. 'Don't make a fuss.' She folded the blanket, opened the curtains and discovered that the ruins were still smouldering. The outside world was clouded in vapour. She went over to her own office and looked at the neatly arranged piles of papers. They meant uninterrupted work for weeks. At the edge lay a few private letters. One was from Darling. Eva didn't open it since she had spoken to her the night before. The next was written by Werner. The house with its irreplaceable treasures had gone up in smoke. He had grabbed a few unimportant objects. He was living now with Dr and Mrs Kromer, who were old friends of his parents. He would call her soon. 'Please don't say "I told you so",' he had added as a postscript, 'because I could not have parted from my world voluntarily.' Eva found a later message from him with a Hamburg number. 'We don't make sense,' sighed Eva. The third letter was from Arlen.

'My pet, it happened immediately after my return from Ahrenshoop. Forty-eight hours were enough to make me break down. I almost died, partly from a bleeding ulcer, partly from a kicking inflicted by the sergeant's boots. I am lying in hospital and will be discharged when I can walk again. I've heard that they'll train me in electronics for some factory assembly line. My apartment is badly damaged but I'm sure I can fix it before winter. Will call you at the first possible opportunity. You are all right, my pet, aren't you?'

It was seven. Time to go to Else for breakfast. The store smelled of soap. Hubert sang in the bathroom, shaving.

'You're going to cut yourself again,' warned Else. But Hubert kept up his song in fits and starts.

The breakfast table was set. 'Can I start the eggs?' asked Else, but got no answer. 'He only hears his own voice,' she commented.

'Most people do,' agreed Eva.

'They're not all singing.' She started to boil the eggs. 'Four minutes is perfect. Don't you have any other clothes to wear? You look a mess. You haven't combed your hair.'

'I know. But I left my suitcase here last night. May I use your bathroom after breakfast?'

'Of course. Never ask. You can keep the suitcase if it's of any use to you. Hubert can always . . . four minutes!' She removed the eggs from the stove and poured cold water over them. 'Hubert,' she shouted, 'breakfast is ready.'

'Coming, my sweetie.' Hubert appeared patting his chin with a damp towel. Then he slipped on a fresh shirt. Still buttoning it, he sat down and inspected the food. 'Have we finished the ham?' he asked. 'Always gives me such a solid foundation for the day.'

'Plenty left.' Else got up and put the sliced ham on a plate. They started to eat. 'Nothing like a soft-boiled egg,' mused Else, 'if it's properly done.' She sprinkled on some salt.

'I have to get my ration cards today,' said Eva.

'You'd better,' agreed Hubert.

Eva told them about Friedrich, and Hubert became rather excited. 'They'll catch him. Drugs are one field in which you can't escape for long.'

'He told Marion it's morphine or death. I understand his need for relief.' Eva stared at the wall. 'Having to face the men again, the Ehrlichs, office work – I really can't see that it's worth fighting for.'

'Don't talk like that,' said Else. 'It's only the first day. You'll see. Slowly you'll get used to things again.'

'Doubt it. Poor Friedrich is on skid row.' Eva chewed her bread. 'Arlen will be released from the army. His sergeant almost kicked him to death with hobnailed boots.'

'Fine outfit, our army,' commented Hubert, putting several slices of ham on his bread.

'Werner is bombed out and he's lost all his treasures. I almost think he enjoys his loss though I can't work out why.'

'Perhaps he's getting sympathy instead.'

'He doesn't care for people. He only loves his mother and they took her away.'

'Have another cup of coffee,' offered Else.

'Thanks, I will. I have to face Mr Lindner and the rest.'

Eva washed and changed in the bathroom, then turned to Else for inspection. 'Off to work, see you later.'

Miss Ehrlich was crossing the bridge as Eva reached the front steps. She stopped and waited, Miss Ehrlich smiled and waved one hand with little jerks back and forth through the air as if Eva's appearance actually excited her. 'I'd better wave back,' thought Eva and they each swung their arms back and forth. They sat for a while in Miss Ehrlich's office, which was dark because of the boarding. The Ehrlichs had not been bombed out, luckily.

'It's good to have you back,' said Miss Ehrlich. 'Lots of work has piled up.'

'We'd better talk at lunch time,' suggested Eva, 'though I must get my ration cards today.' They parted. Eva's office had the same dim light. The window was drastically reduced, allowing only for a narrow view of the ruins opposite the canal. She began to sort out papers, putting them on different piles, then arranging each pile according to date. July had not been completely entered and now it was October. Mr Lindner called on the intercom: would she please come to his office. Of course. She had no choice. He greeted her with an uneasy cordiality, begging for something. Eva wasn't sure whether he wanted love or forgiveness. Perhaps he still waited, like a dog, for punishment. Then suddenly he lifted his head, straightened up and looked quite ordinary.

'How was your holiday?' he asked.

'How was Russia?' enquired Eva. She wouldn't tell him a word about Ahrenshoop.

'You read our letters, I suppose.'

'No, they always ended up on Miss Ehrlich's desk.'

'Never mind. You'd better catch up with your work, we're far behind.'

'I know,' agreed Eva.

'Have you seen Friedrich?'

'Last night during the air raid. He got quite ill and Marion took him to her apartment.'

'He should be seen by a doctor again. Perhaps he needs an operation.'

'You'd better talk to him. He looked ghastly last night.'

'Could you go up and find out how he feels?'

'Of course.' She was glad to escape.

In the hallway she collided with Mr Schiller, also back from Russia.

'Hi, ho, girlie! Glad to see you. Had a good time by the sea, eh?' He laughed from his belly, patted her on the behind and was about to disappear when Eva stopped him.

'Don't you ever touch me again!' she shouted. 'Anywhere!'

Mr Schiller's laughter continued from inside the office. Eva shrugged her shoulders. He was made of cement, a block-head, an imbecile.

Marion's rosy round face appeared at the half-opened door. Her eyes were slightly puffy and sleepy.

'Am I glad to see you.' She pulled Eva into the room. 'He refuses to get up. I can't keep him here all day.' Eva went into the bedroom.

'Listen,' she said, 'if you don't appear in the office, Mr Lindner is going to send for a doctor who will get you into a hospital. He's just told me so.'

'What time is it?' Friedrich was scared.

'After nine.'

'My God, not a hospital.' He sat up dazed and shaky.

'Do you want a cup of coffee?' asked Marion.

'Nothing! Leave me alone, damn it!' He walked like a drunken sailor to the bathroom. 'The light's not working.' He sounded desperate.

'Use the kitchen.' He shut the door, came back, got his clothes and told them not to bother him.

'He seems so unpredictable,' said Eva.

'You're telling me! I was scared all night.'

Eva knew she should be downstairs at work. Instead she sat next to the apprehensive Marion and waited for Friedrich to reappear. Time dragged on. Eva became edgy, paced up and down the living room, looked over the ruins towards the bright sunlight on the river, the harbour like a chiselled ornament in polished gold. Friedrich entered, dressed and ready for work with a clown's smile.

'I'm the only man who knows the truth,' he declared.

'All right,' Eva was impatient. 'Tell us another time. Mr Lindner is waiting downstairs.'

'Who cares? Aren't you anxious to know the truth, the only truth?'

'Of course, but not now.'

'When, my dear Eva, was the pursuit of truth more important than right now? Will you kindly answer my question?'

'So come out with it. We want to hear,' said Marion.

'Life is nothing but an illusion,' he said solemnly.

'You don't say!' Marion exclaimed.

'There are only two points of reality. One is your moment of birth, the other your moment of death. What lies between is perceived by an inaccurate, arbitrary machine that reflects illusions. It's called life.'

'Rather an interesting observation.' Eva was desperate. 'We must talk about it tonight. Now off to the office.'

'Off to illusory times and places,' sang Friedrich as they finally proceeded towards the lift.

A nice beginning, Eva told herself, making entry after entry into her ledger, sitting hunched over the illusion of life. But she preferred her hell to Friedrich's. She entered one invoice for goatskins and wondered which department was selling chicken feathers. Unfortunately, her pile of unentered invoices did not confirm Friedrich's theory of illusion. Invoices and expenses got entered factually, one after the other with an endless amount of boredom. Before lunch she had finished the last of July's records. During the afternoon she could add up the pages and see if they balanced. She looked out of the small piece of glass in the middle of the wooden board and saw only the ruins opposite. The water in the canal was gone, the tow pole stood empty. She couldn't see the bridge or the looming church tower. 'It's all diminishing,' she thought.

Mr Lindner and Mr Schiller left for their meal at a

restaurant. Friedrich poked his head through the door and said that he had an appointment with the doctor.

'What for?'

'Trying to get hold of a prescription pad or at least of some pages. Helps me along.'

'Those prescriptions'll end up at the Narcotics Bureau. One day they'll catch up with you.'

'Possibly.' He grinned and left.

Eva went to pick up her ration cards. She had to stand in a queue. People looked tired and poorly dressed. 'The first signs of mortality,' thought Eva. 'Their sickness is taking its course. I only wish mine would improve as theirs worsens. But it doesn't work that way! Irreparable damage,' she diagnosed, feeling her pulse, which was too fast for this time of day. Then she ran to Else's store hoping for a few words with her friend, but business had picked up. Else stood behind the counter serving customers. People were digging inside ruins, finding rooms that could be repaired and made habitable. They became cave dwellers and Eva thought that it served them right.

Then she sat in Miss Ehrlich's office and ate her lunch there. She observed the pale face and concluded that Miss Ehrlich had not profited from the involuntary summer vacation. She looked unkempt, ungroomed. Her hair seemed in need of washing. The pins in her greasy bun reflected the dim light that shone through the narrow window.

'How is your mother?' Eva knew she had to enquire.

'Not very well. The raid was too much for her. The doctor thinks she strained her heart. You see, after we made it out of the city that night she was totally exhausted, lay in bed for weeks. And we had such primitive quarters. The toilets were a disgrace! But she's slowly gaining strength. Only I won't permit her to come to town yet to pick me up. That has to wait until she's her old self again.'

'Hope that will be soon,' lied Eva.

'She has an iron will.' Miss Ehrlich laughed.

'Did you find nice people among the refugees?'

'Some very helpful, others were troublemakers. I suppose that's what you have to expect in a crowd.'

'Probably,' agreed Eva.

'I also met such a brave soldier with an amputated leg, wheeling himself around in a chair at record speed and cheering everybody up. Mother was crazy about him. We became really close friends.' Eva thought she detected some blood flowing into Miss Ehrlich's pale face but wasn't sure. 'He explained the strategy behind our apparent retreat, how Hitler is luring the Russians into a trap and will destroy them with his new secret weapon.'

'Oh, I see. The retreat will be the victory.'

'Yes, that's what he thinks. Of course, everyone's hoping.'

'Of course.'

'Friedrich has changed since he came back from Russia,' Miss Ehrlich said after a pause, trying to change the subject.

'He's not feeling well. He's gone to the doctor. Something wrong with his gall bladder.' Eva didn't want to discuss Friedrich with Miss Ehrlich.

'At times he behaves like a madman.'

'In what way?' Eva asked politely.

'Well – as if he were mad. You have to experience it yourself. Next time he goes crazy I'll call you. I think Mr Lindner should get in touch with the doctor and find out what's wrong.'

Eva changed the subject. 'I'm going to close July today even if it takes all night.'

'We are behind.'

'July was the month of the raids,' Eva reminded Miss Ehrlich. 'Very few people still have an office, let alone their ledgers.' She went back to her office with a half-empty cup of coffee. Today she was in the perfect mood for adding figures. Number after number got registered, recorded without effort or mistake. There were other days when her brain seemed blocked by steady interferences. Her brain on those days seemed as murky as the water that flowed through the canal with the tides. But today, fortunately, she hardly looked at the figures before the total appeared at the bottom of the page.

Friedrich dropped in for a moment, showing her a prescription pad that he had swiped from the doctor's desk. He laughed like an idiot.

'They'll catch you quickly this way. It's a question of a few more weeks.' Eva hoped to scare him into reason.

'Any time is okay with me.' He gazed at her from a distant world. 'Either I stay on a little longer in a state of freedom or I face the other reality – death. I'm not opposed to either of those possibilities. What I can't endure is the futility of illusions.' He stared into the void.

'But that illusory span of time between two points of reality is all we've got. For heaven's sake don't throw it away,' said Eva.

'It throws me up, I throw it up. Isn't it revolting? There's music – music is like a magic potion, like dope, good dope, but it can't be sustained. It will be thrown up like everything else. Ah, you know about the arts, don't you? And people who water their plants. You have to shave every morning, brush your teeth, eat your food – I throw it all up. I'm not even speaking of the war and the mass slaughter – '

'Stop it!' shouted Eva. 'You've made your point. Don't get carried away.'

'Well, then have fun.' He grinned and left.

Did it really matter how he would end his life? Was there anything that mattered? Eva asked herself. He had certainly depressed her. She took another sip of Else's strong, aromatic coffee. That was her dope. Later she turned on the electric light. The ruins across the canal remained dark and ominous.

Around seven she heard voices in the hallway. Everyone was getting ready to leave. Miss Ehrlich entered to say good night.

'It balances,' said Eva with triumph. Mr Lindner joined them and looked at the figures.

'Looks good,' he said. 'Russia has put us into a high profit bracket.'

'Remember that the fourth quarter of the year will slacken,' warned Mr Schiller, whose head had appeared, peering over their shoulders.

'I'm taking it into account. Still, we'll have had an excellent year.'

'What a year!' thought Eva. 'The city in ruins, the army

retreating – but the profits are good. What does he think he can do with his paper money once the war is over? The mindlessness behind that bloody money! Stolen cattle and starving Russians made his pockets swell with paper.' She drew two lines under the final figures.

Friedrich was the only one now left in the office. Eva went to his room. He was busy sorting out papers and putting them into files.

'Follow-up stuff, you know,' he explained.

'Do you have a place to stay?'

'I'm still living with my aunt. We weren't bombed out.'

'Good. What happened to Jutta?'

'Got fed up with my addiction.'

'I don't blame her. It seems a bad foundation for a love affair.'

'Stop preaching. I don't care what anybody says. I throw it all up. It's dope or death with me. A simple equation.'

'Yes, dope equals death,' Eva replied.

'Are you trying to scare me?' he laughed. 'You see, I am a step ahead of you. I'm not afraid of death any more.'

'Since you are so advanced – ' Eva didn't know any more what she wanted to say. 'Ah, so it's no use talking to you. Only remember, I won't go to your funeral.'

'You're going to miss a great event – it's your loss. But, of course, nobody is going to my funeral. Why should they? I wouldn't either. What a hoax!' He laughed.

'Good night. I'm going over to Else.'

It was a mild autumn night with a slight breeze coming in from the sea, blowing dust and ashes into the air. The universe appeared through empty windows in crumbling walls. Several stars shone in the sky, then were gone behind jagged ruins. 'Air-raid night,' thought Eva. 'It's always air-raid night nowadays.' Else stood behind the stove, Hubert lay stretched out in his easy chair. The air smelled of spices and fruit. Else was testing, tasting, testing again. She put one finger to her forehead, paused, chased some thoughts, reached for a jar of spices and sprinkled a dash into the simmering brew. She stirred slowly and carefully with a long wooden spoon. Else would repeat the same procedure several times, until she was satisfied with the result.

Eva sat in her chair, watching her friends, feeling her dependence on this small shelter behind a store that resisted destruction.

'How much longer?' asked Hubert, getting impatient.

Else looked at the clock. 'Ten more minutes.' Hubert sighed but didn't stir. Eva lit another cigarette and watched Else move gracefully in the tiny space between the table and stove.

They all ate too much of Else's stew. Afterwards they felt full and lazy.

'Let's have a brandy,' suggested Else. 'It was a good stew, if I say so myself.' She laughed. Hubert poured brandy into ordinary glasses. Eva handed the milk around for their coffee.

'It was the best stew I've ever eaten,' said Eva.

'Not bad,' came from Hubert with a smile.

'High praise from high places,' said Else, tossing her head back. They lit cigarettes. The smoke curled in thin veils around the light bulb. Eva had discovered that Else held her cigarette in an artificial Marlene Dietrich fashion. Somehow the fanned-out hand created a crack in Else's solid personality.

They discussed the people at Eva's office. Eventually someone said: 'Shall we have a game of cards?' Someone would say it first.

'A penny, not more,' insisted Else.

Now they would be safe for a while from the world outside. Hubert shuffled the cards: Eva and Else picked them up one by one and began to sort out their hands. Afterwards they had to wait for Hubert to catch up. They played with attention, leisurely drinking coffee, lighting cigarettes, laughing, feeling content.

'Rummy!' said Else, putting her cards down.

'Darn it! I got stuck with nothing but high ones,' complained Hubert. But he liked it when Else won. 'Forty-seven,' he counted.

'Fourteen,' said Eva. They put their pfennige in the till. Else eyed the heap of coins with pleasure.

'May I have another glass of brandy?' asked Eva. 'It's getting interesting.'

Hubert too got animated and filled their glasses. Eva enjoyed Else's gambling fever. They picked up the cards a little faster and got impatient if someone stalled too long. The race-track atmosphere began to show its head. Suddenly they all wanted to win.

'Rummy!' announced Else.

'Just eight, my dear. I hope you're not disappointed,' said Hubert.

'Eight is better than nothing. Eight kisses are better than none.'

'Isn't she something?' rejoiced Hubert while shuffling the cards.

'I think it's past air-raid time,' mentioned Eva.

'That would be a blessing.'

'They're concentrating on Berlin nowadays.'

They played until half-past midnight. Else had won two marks and eighty-four pfennige which she put into her cash register.

'Small change always comes in handy,' she smiled.

'Small change!' Hubert protested.

They decided to take a walk along the quay before going to bed. The air was still mild, the wind blowing. Clouds were sailing across the sky now. For a moment it looked as if the stars and the crescent moon were shooting through the universe, they seemed to move so fast. Then the illusion became obvious as another set of clouds came into view.

'Feels good to catch a breath of fresh air,' said Else. And suddenly Eva realised that nothing felt good. Perhaps it had been the banality of Else's remark that cut through her state of mind. She remembered the flower pot which had stood for years on the outer window sill of the office below hers, a flower pot filled with dirt but no flowers. Nothing grew there. It balanced on a white saucer with a silver rim, surviving the raids, bombs, fire, shrapnel and even the carpenter who put in wooden boards afterwards. The pot still stood there on its saucer, useless, stubborn, purposeless. She felt like that flower pot.

'Hope you enjoyed your evening,' said Else cheerfully.

'You know I loved it. What would I do without you?' Eva

knew that she was telling the truth yet at that moment truth in itself seemed a lie. She waved good night to the friends, standing on the steps of an office building, depleted, alone, without prospect of any sprouting life. Nothing would grow. She had to be grateful for the night air, for getting hand-outs, wearing hand-me-downs, shaking a few hands. Eva watched the friends walk towards their store and disappear. She glanced at the lonely pot on the windowsill. Then she entered Mr Lindner's office and sat behind his desk, smoking another cigarette. 'Come on,' she told herself, 'snap out of it. Your balance sheet really doesn't look as bad as you make it seem. You are far beyond the turning point.'

Chapter Eight

Eva took a northbound tram from the town hall to visit Darling. It was dark. The wheels shrieked on their rails as the cars came to a stop, then the tram rattled on again with its usual jerks and noises. It was crowded with tired people whose faces looked ghostly in the dim black-out night. 'They're wearing out,' thought Eva with sudden joy. 'Even murderers wear out eventually. I'm glad I don't belong to this dismal lot.'

Eva imagined the details of her meeting with Darling. The door would spring open, the white-haired, round-faced woman would spread her arms out and press her against her bosom, perhaps shedding a few tears, mentioning Benny, her beloved nephew, urging her to come into the living room, to sit down and to tell and tell and tell.

Eva was right! Little that actually took place differed from her preconception. Darling cried a little longer and her hugging was accompanied by more warmth and genuine feeling than Eva had thought possible. 'I always underestimate other people's emotions,' she confessed to herself.

Dinner was ready. Eva put her presents, all provided by Else, on the kitchen table: coffee, tea, cigarettes and ration cards. Darling was again in tears.

'If only Benny could be with us,' she sobbed.

'He would be devastated,' said Eva. Darling wiped away her tears.

After dinner she predicted: 'I give them six more months, being generous. But that is the limit.'

'Who knows?' Eva didn't want to play the guessing game. She really didn't care what Darling thought. It was either the war or Benny they were always discussing. Darling gave her the latest report from the BBC which she listened to at night, holding the radio close to her ear. Listening to foreign news stations carried the death penalty. Darling was risking her life for news reports which hardly told more than the German stations. The difference lay in the trust. She trusted the BBC and she needed the truth. When her speculations on the war were exhausted, Darling would turn again to her favourite subject: Benny. The longer she had not seen her nephew the more gallant he grew, the kinder, the more generous . . . It all cascaded down on Eva who sat drenched in superlatives, smiling politely.

'I can't talk to anyone anymore,' complained Darling. 'You know Mrs Katz and Mrs Rose. I told you about them. I go and play bridge with them. They are first-rate bridge players and I have to use all my wits to stay on their level, but I can't open my mouth, have to be on my guard constantly. Such Nazis!' She sighed. 'It's the same wherever you go. Just stand queuing at a store – the nonsense they talk, the lies they believe – '

'I know, I know.'

'Come back again, come back.'

Eva had to catch the last tram. Darling put her short arms tenderly around Eva's middle.

'What a lovely evening it has been. If only – '

Arlen telephoned on Saturday. He had been released and was staying with Eduard. 'I've just arrived. It will take quite a while before my place is habitable again. Lots of work. When can I meet you?'

'Come any time after two. It's nice if you like ghost towns. We can go out for dinner or eat at Else's. Oh, I have a view of ruins, if you like ruins, and an empty flower pot on the window sill below – '

'My pet, it's good to hear your peculiar way of talking again. I missed it. I've had a ghastly time!'

'I'm sure you have. What about the nurses?'

'I can't leave immediately, you understand. Let's make it six.'

'It's hard to find your way out here. A lot of the streets have still not been cleared. Shouldn't I meet you at the town hall station?'

'Don't worry, I'll get there.'

'Of course,' she said, knowing that he was unreliable, got drunk, forgot his promises and his friends who cared, that he was boastful, a dreamer, an escapist.

Miss Ehrlich walked to the toilet. It must be close to two unless Miss Ehrlich had suddenly become irregular. Friedrich looked in to say goodbye.

'Is it that late already?' Eva was amazed because usually time stood still. 'I haven't done a thing. August will be ready by Christmas.'

'Rode out to some little town last night to get my prescription filled. No trouble. Told them I was a salesman with gall stones. Next week I'll drive to Lübeck.'

'It's a mug's game,' scolded Eva.

'I have felt more happiness in these last months than most people feel during a lifetime. I'll die the richest man in town. Just draw your two lines under the figures, I couldn't care less because I have experienced everything.' He wasn't even euphoric when he spoke, rather calm and collected.

'It's all an illusion,' said Eva sarcastically. 'Nevertheless, have a nice weekend.' After Friedrich had left, Miss Ehrlich came in to say goodbye. She was in a hurry to get back to her mother's tyranny. Eva stepped out with the toilet key, hoping that Mr Lindner and Mr Schiller would be gone when she returned. She took the lift up to Marion's apartment, but she was out. So she rode up and down several times, went to the toilet and finally decided to return to the office. Mr Lindner and Mr Schiller were just leaving, wearing the most extraordinary clothes: shabby overcoats, fishermen's caps, dirty, heavy shoes, baggy trousers. They locked the door hastily and rushed into the street. Obviously they didn't want to be seen. Eva couldn't work out what they were up to. Perhaps they wanted to do the sleazy bars and brothels of St Pauli, unrecognised. She really didn't care as long as they didn't come back to change into their regular clothes while Arlen was with her.

It was dark at six. Eva feared Arlen wouldn't find the office – if he had ever set out to seek it. Else had invited them to come for dinner. She intended to go to the cinema with Hubert afterwards so that Eva could stay at the store with Arlen until they returned. It sounded perfect – if Arlen showed up. But she couldn't rely on him.

She switched off the light and looked out of the small window facing the bridge. The night was clear and bright with a few flashing stars above the ruined landscape which was profiled against a metallic blue sky. Anybody crossing the bridge would be easily spotted. So she stood and stared, listening to the gushing sounds of an outgoing tide and waited in suspense, slowly losing hope. Her expectations began to shake and then to crumble like a house hit by a bomb.

It was at least six-thirty when a figure appeared on the bridge. Eva rushed into the street. For a moment it seemed real when she closed her eyes and felt his tears on her skin, felt their bodies too close to be separated again, felt secure, standing in an ordinary hallway. Then the entire moment vanished, crumbled in the darkness of night.

'Come in,' she said. 'Are you all right?'

'Fine,' he replied or something like it. Eva was not sure. She had run up the stairs and held the door open.

'Can you see? Eight steps up and then a left turn.' Inside the office she took his hand and guided him to Mr Lindner's room. He looked smooth and fuller. His hair was cut too short, the ears stuck out and he reminded her of one of the many soldiers in boots and uniforms who shot from tanks, from behind tanks, who were being shot at, who were playing the deadly game of war.

'It's all behind us,' she said. 'Sit, anywhere. You're late. Else invited us over for dinner.'

'I missed you.'

'Our life is diminishing day by day. Look, Arlen, even the views from the windows have shrunk.'

'The army's changed me,' he told Eva.

'We'll see.' Eva wondered if his stay at the barracks had really altered Arlen's personality. Probably not.

She was anxious to get out of the office. 'Let's walk over to Else.' She told Arlen about Mr Lindner's and Mr Schiller's mysterious expedition and showed him their clothes hanging in the closet.

'You don't believe I have changed.' Arlen was offended. 'You don't even take my suffering seriously.'

'Arlen, please. What was wrong with us before?'

'I thought you expected more – '

'You never let me down, not once.' Eva knew that she was lying. He had let her down on many occasions. But it didn't matter and she saw no reason why she should go into soul-searching subjects when nothing could be solved. Besides, Else was waiting with the dinner.

Else stood in the kitchen, putting the last dash of spice to the food. Hubert had set the table with white damask and holiday china, silver cutlery and wine glasses. He folded the napkins like pointed hats and set them in the middle of each plate. Two candles in china sticks made up the rest of the decoration.

'I never dreamt of having Arlen von Volkhardt to dinner.' Else was excited.

'I'm sure it isn't such a big deal,' said Hubert with some disdain. 'Don't get carried away.'

'But I want to get carried away. Can't you understand?'

'All right, my sweetheart. How far do you want to be carried?'

'Oh, Hubert, it's so exciting!' Else looked at the clock. 'They should be here any minute.'

'It's late. Probably thinks he can make people wait.'

'Don't spoil the evening. That's the way it is, he loses track of time.'

'I bet!' Hubert laughed.

They heard the taps on the door. 'Here they are!' Else stroked nervously over her hair from the neck up. She was not even sure if everything was in place when Hubert returned with Eva and Arlen. She stretched out her hand and

109

waited for him to shake hers before she said rather formally: 'Nice to meet you, Herr von Volkhardt. Really a pleasure. I am Else and this is my friend Hubert.'

'Very kind of you to invite me.' Arlen felt out of place.

'Our quarters are rather small,' said Else without apologising. 'So you better sit down somewhere. Dinner is ready.'

'Please call me Arlen.'

'With pleasure.' Else was delighted to be on intimate terms with Herr von Volkhardt. She had turned her back to them and was filling the dishes. Nobody spoke.

'Say something,' begged Eva.

'You're going to eat,' said Else laughingly. 'That will bridge any embarrassment.'

'It's not embarrassment,' protested Eva. 'It's the wrong expectations.'

'I hope you won't be disappointed.'

'Not with your food, never.' Hubert tasted the wine, then filled the glasses. Else tossed the salad, Arlen sat somewhat uncomfortably on his kitchen chair.

'I only got released from the army a few hours ago,' Arlen said as if life had become incomprehensible. 'Then I moved into the household of my overpedantic friend. Just met Eva at her office and saw the wasteland. Do you know that her boss is on a strange mission masquerading as a dockworker?' He sighed several times.

'A bit of good food and fine wine will solve your confusion,' promised Hubert, who thought that Arlen talked too much like Eva, in all sorts of riddles, creating complications. 'They're one of a kind,' he thought. They began to praise Else's food, all three, and she accepted their praises as if they were beautiful flowers.

'I don't know,' she said, a little flushed. 'I think the stew needs a little more flavour – something's missing.' They all protested and continued to eat. Hubert opened a second bottle of wine. Slowly they became more relaxed with each other and began to speculate on Mr Lindner's strange mission.

'They went to a brothel, if you ask me,' declared Hubert.

'Quite likely,' agreed Else, who looked at Arlen for approval.

110

'I'm not sure. Why did they leave the clues behind for Eva to see?' asked Arlen.

'They don't care a damn about Eva as long as she is there to do the book-keeping,' said Else.

'I'm not that sure,' repeated Arlen. 'Your wine is excellent, just perfect.'

'Thanks,' said Else. 'Hubert is the expert. He does the buying.'

'I drink it every day,' boasted Eva.

'We try to keep her in good shape. She lives in a constant pressure chamber. Not that we're not pressured, but it seems she's more exposed than any of us.'

'Being in the army was worse,' insisted Arlen.

'Have another glass of wine.' Hubert was trying to please.

'I thought you'd stopped drinking,' said Eva.

'But we're celebrating, aren't we? Besides, I never resolved not to drink again. I simply had no chance to drink.'

'You told me a different story.'

'Did I? Well, then I must have changed my mind.' Nothing seemed to matter. Else and Hubert decided to skip the film and put coffee and brandy on the table. Arlen began to tell them of his brief experience in the army. He became euphoric, because everybody listened and nobody interrupted. He remembered so vividly the brutality of the place, his breakdown and the punishment of being beaten and kicked, his long recuperation in the hospital barracks. 'At one point I didn't care any more,' he reported and a few tears welled up. 'I was almost unconscious and really wished it could just be over.'

'My poor pet,' said Eva and took his hand.

'Can you imagine what they're doing to their enemies?' asked Hubert. 'Sometimes even I get scared.'

'It was quite different from what I'd imagined,' confessed Arlen. 'In fact, what I lived through was unimaginable before. I simply didn't know a beating and kicking like that existed.'

'This is more exciting than the pictures,' said Else. 'I'm glad we stayed at home.' They hung on Arlen's lips as if he were able to project pictures on to an imaginary screen. The more brandy he consumed the more animated the action got. The number of actors increased, the plot twisted like a corkscrew, turning and turning far into the night.

'He's drunk,' Eva observed. 'It'll help him get over all this quicker.' Air-raid sirens interrupted their show for a moment then Arlen continued to tell stories while the first cannon were heard and the first bombs dropped from the sky. Later the house shook precariously but they hardly noticed.

'Happens all the time,' explained Hubert. 'Like a mild earthquake – means nothing.'

Around one o'clock it quietened down. Eva suddenly realised that Else looked exhausted and aged. Hubert too seemed older than usual. When had they lost their youth?

'Let's go home,' suggested Eva. 'It's getting quiet.' They embraced with emotion and gratitude.

'Breakfast at ten,' reminded Else.

'I'm meeting Werner at noon, main station,' reported Eva as if it was of great importance.

Arlen and Eva stood in the corrugated street with its wasteland view, watching the light beams search the sky, listening to the anti-aircraft guns shooting at invisible targets.

'Perhaps they're coming back.'

'Who cares,' remarked Arlen. At that moment nothing could interfere with the excitement he felt for life. They had reached the office.

'Just wait here in the hallway. I want to make sure we don't run into Mr Lindner.' The office was empty, Mr Lindner's clothes gone. So he must have been back.

'I must get to the bottom of this,' she told Arlen. 'It looks sinister.'

Arlen sat behind Mr Lindner's desk and sighed. 'How can you live here?'

Eva laughed. 'It's luxury. Really very private, hardly a soul around.'

'Hardly a building's standing.'

'Even before. These were all offices, warehouses and factories. You can smell the harbour from here. Are you happy, my pet?'

'I don't have to fear the draft any longer,' he replied. 'Why did they build offices like prisons?'

'That's what they are.'

'Can't you see that I have changed?' Arlen came back to the point.

'It makes no difference to me. I'm not God who sits in judgment.'

'Don't you want me to improve?'

'If it makes you happy – '

He smiled. 'Yes, it does reduce my guilt.'

'We have to sleep on the couch.'

'How about sheets?'

'If I can find any – '

'You sleep without?'

'Yes, in my clothes. It's easiest.' She found some sheets and a blanket.

'You live like a dog.'

'It's my form of freedom.'

They lay in complete darkness like blind people whose sense of touch becomes the entire world. They became engulfed by the sounds of their blood and the few half-understood words.

Chapter Nine

The clouds hung deep and dark. The wind blew in gusts over the wasteland, whirling dust and ashes through empty spaces, past persisting walls, twisting like spirals, carrying along dead and crumbled leaves with a melancholy song, breaking up and starting over again. Eva was returning from breakfast at Else's when it started to drizzle. The drumming of the raindrops would add to the noise of the wind.

Friedrich was already at the office. His young face had aged, the eyes blazed feverishly, yet he greeted her as if his world was without problems.

'What are you so happy about?' asked Eva who hated Mondays.

'Got a new box of supplies.' He had won a decisive battle against despair.

'Lasting how long?'

'We'll see – one day at a time.'

'Mr Lindner asked me if I knew what was wrong with you. He can't understand your bizarre behaviour.'

'What about his bizarre behaviour? Did you give him an answer?'

'Only that he should talk to you.'

'Good.' Friedrich rubbed his hands. 'I'll tell him a long sob story if he wants to hear one.'

'He might fire you.'

'Then death will come a little sooner.'

'How boring. After that nothing is going to happen any more.'

'I can do without it.'

'What about Mr Lindner's bizarre behaviour?' Eva was curious.

'I finally got it out of Mr Schiller. They're spying for the Gestapo in little bars around the harbour, trying to catch subversive elements or organised groups. If they hear someone grumble they're supposed to report them to Party Headquarters which will turn them over to the Gestapo.'

'How low can you sink?'

'They overheard a group of dockworkers who think that the war is lost and that Marxism is going to turn Germany into a paradise. Now Mr Lindner has to write a report to Headquarters and the poor devils will find their end before ever encountering Marx's paradise.'

A big, black umbrella with two heavy bags swinging below appeared on the bridge. The rain had increased, the wind jerked the umbrella back and forth. In a minute Miss Ehrlich would appear with a big smile.

'We have to stop that report from leaving the office,' Eva said with determination.

'Miss Ehrlich might post it herself, registered.'

'If you get it, don't send it out. I'm going to talk to Mr Lindner. What can I lose?'

'Your job,' said Friedrich.

'Good morning,' Miss Ehrlich showed her pale, overworked face, with its big smile. 'Having a conference?'

'Want to join in?' asked Friedrich.

'No time.' She laughed and put her wet clothes over a hanger. She sat at the typewriter to type the report of events which would send several people to their deaths.

'That's how the machine operates. The crimes are divided into such small acts that nobody is aware of participating in a murder plot. I have to be sure that I get hold of the report before it's posted,' said Eva.

'You can count on my help,' assured Friedrich.

Arlen called to tell her that he had slept in his apartment for the first time.

'It was a lot of work,' he explained. 'But worth it. Are you coming for the night?'

'I have a crisis at the office, but I'll come.'

'The front door is broken. You can walk straight up. Nobody else is living in the house.'

Eva sat paralysed. She stared at the grey windowpane with its raindrops running down in different patterns. Miss Ehrlich sat cheerfully typing a report for the Gestapo. Friedrich was definitely going to die, and she was ready to risk her job and her home. Her pulse sank below zero, she was unable to work. Debit, credit. Who cared? Things were weighted too heavily on the liability side. 'I have to save those men from being murdered.' It was of the utmost importance. In case Mr Lindner couldn't be persuaded to change his mind, she at least had to find out the name of the bar and the description of the workers, then go there tonight and warn them.

Around one o'clock Miss Ehrlich walked to the toilet as usual. Eva rushed to her office to find the report, neatly typed, on the desk. She glanced hurriedly through the pages, saw the name 'The White Gull' and vague descriptions of five dockworkers. She was back in her own office long before Miss Ehrlich returned.

The day dragged on in its grey wetness. Why was she sticking her neck out? Why not let people do what they wanted to do? She was in no position to risk her job. Why not go and warn those men? But then, there would be further reports against different people. Would she be able to save them all? Events were pushing her against the wall and there was Friedrich ready to shoot himself.

After lunch Eva knocked at Mr Lindner's door. She was by now so worn out that what she was undertaking seemed distant and divorced from reality. 'I have to appease,' she thought.

'You're not going to post the report, are you?' she asked quietly. Mr Lindner paled, his eyes searched the room for an escape.

'You have no right – ' Mr Lindner stuttered.

'Of course I have no right, but I found out. If the report gets sent, you are condemning those workers to death.'

'Who said the report would be sent out?' He sat uncomfortably in his chair twisting and turning. 'It was Schiller's idea. I never intended to hand it over.'

'Why do you have to go spying?'

'Because I was ordered.'

'Find an excuse, think of one. They can't make you become a murderer.' Mr Lindner blushed.

Then Eva went to Miss Ehrlich's office and told her Mr Lindner wanted the report. 'I'm supposed to bring it now,' Eva added.

'Here.' She handed it to Mr Lindner. 'Throw it away.' He looked at her like a beaten dog, tore the sheets into several pieces and let them drop into the wastepaper basket. 'Never again,' she begged. 'I couldn't stay here.' He didn't say a thing. His eyes were watching his fingers play with a yellow pencil.

'How do you like my apartment?' Arlen was elated.

'It's beautiful! Where did you get those treasures?'

'From bombed-out houses. Look at the Chinese rug. I had to wash it three times before the colours showed.'

'And the wooden chair with the high, carved back?'

'Found it in a house nearby; it's the only one I was able to repair.' Candles were burning in antique candelabra like those on an altar. The iron stove was aglow and gave out heat.

'Do you have something to drink?'

'One bottle between us as a housewarming celebration. I promised myself in the barracks that I would stop drinking if I got out alive.' He filled her glass and Eva drank it down immediately. She held out her glass to have it refilled. 'It's terrible sitting in a room every day being separated only by a thin wall from a Gestapo spy. I have to talk to them as if we were friends, joke and kid because they must, under all circumstances, continue to like me. Am I making any sense?'

'Take it easy, my pet. You're working yourself into a state.'

'Mr Lindner used to be a nice ordinary man. Do you think it's irreversible?'

They were lying on the Chinese rug with pillows propped

under their heads.

'I met Olga in the street. She's back from several weeks in a Russian labour camp where everybody immediately suspected her and nobody talked. Only one woman whispered once into her ear, "You are a disgrace to our country." Olga claims she never complained about or reported anybody. Then the Gestapo called her for an interview and when she explained they took her out of the camp and sent her back to the hospital. Now she's having an affair with a German doctor.'

'And you?'

'I'm not interested in Olga any more. She's too greedy.'

'Still, I feel sorry for her. She's dragged herself into an awful mess.' Eva was feeling better. 'You're lucky to have your own place again. No half-Jew is permitted that much. We're the cave dwellers.' Eva looked up at the lamp hanging from the ceiling, casting its shadow over everything. 'Can you play some music before the air raid?'

'What do you want to hear?'

'Mozart.' Arlen put on a flute concerto. Eva lay very still while her eyes wandered over the strange shapes in the unfamiliar room. The music climbed, searched, jumped. What could be saved? The flute danced on a few happy notes. Marion had little chance to escape her fate. What made her choose it? The orchestra interrupted the flute. Else's apron was white in a soapless world and Hubert polished their shoes. Why do I keep thinking of trivialities? Friedrich's time is running out. Why can't I discover Arlen's true nature? Why put up all those barriers when none are wanted? We're being pushed out to sea, drifting apart. We are not in harmony. Where was the flute now? Werner likes music because his mother loved *Der Rosenkavalier*. Eva's hand was moving through the air with the rhythm of the melody. Darling was baking a cake for their two-handed bridge game. 'I've lost the music,' Eva thought. Arlen was turning the record. She wondered if Werner's mother was still thinking of *Der Rosenkavalier*. The flute was playing a solo. 'Who is Arlen and who am I? At funerals people pull out threads and hold them up: here, see, he was a man of great courage, a man with a

118

need to create, gentle and caressing in manner, words which couldn't come close to reality – there was the orchestra again accompanying the flute – I know the shape of his body but that means nothing. At times we have the same dreams, we have visions beyond the underworld. We're trying to achieve something visible while we're confined to the darkness in the tunnel. That's all I know about Arlen and myself – not much – and the flute sings alone again. The record is slightly scratched, the needle should be changed.'

'Are you thinking?' asked Eva.

'Listening.' He poured the rest of the wine into Eva's glass. 'I don't need any.'

'I've lost the music,' complained Eva.

'I'll start the record again.'

Eva tried to stay with the melody, letting herself be carried back and forth on the waves, out to sea, nearer the shore. When it ended, nothing had been achieved.

'Beautiful,' said Arlen.

'It's wearing.' Eva was rubbing her eyes.

The advance warning howled through the city. They went to the basement.

'Take the torch,' ordered Arlen.

Downstairs the ceiling was low and covered with pipes. In the back stood two boilers, the floor was cemented, the brick walls painted white.

'Basements have their own characteristics,' observed Eva. 'This one is for drowning.'

'We can always get out of the door – '

'If it isn't blocked.'

'Well, there are windows – '

'Iron-barred.' Eva began to laugh. 'It's a shelter for drowning, as I said.'

'If you insist.' He shrugged his shoulders.

The nightly concert started with its drums and percussion, its whistles and crashes, its deafening crescendos. Sometimes it came within close range. Wave after wave flew above the city on its deadly mission.

'You shouldn't smoke in the basement,' said Arlen.

'Afraid of death? You almost sound like Werner.'

119

'Don't compare me with that mouse.'

'He is rather brave in his teddy-bear way.'

'I don't know why I like you at all,' said Arlen angrily.

'I wonder what's in those pipes?' But Arlen wasn't listening: he was whistling a melody from the flute concerto. 'Mr Lindner just crumbled,' said Eva.

'What if the five men were Gestapo agents, testing the loyalty of their spies? What if you've got Mr Lindner into trouble?'

'Then he deserves it . . . spying for the Gestapo – '

A bomb crashed down nearby. Eva was not worried. She worried about Arlen's personality. Another bomb exploded; they held on to each other.

Eva had hardly slept and Else made her an extra strong cup of coffee.

'May I have a bath tonight?' she asked.

'You can have one now.'

'I don't want to be late after what happened yesterday. Do you think they'll stop spying?'

'They will,' assured Hubert.

'I won't get anything done today. I've got the shakes.'

Nobody mentioned the events of the previous day again. Not even Miss Ehrlich asked what had happened to the long report she had typed. Mr Lindner was polite and evasive. Mr Schiller avoided Eva altogether. He probably was angry that she had interfered. Only Friedrich came in at lunch time to congratulate her. Mr Lindner was determined to stop spying and Mr Schiller had agreed reluctantly. It was not what he wanted but he couldn't jeopardise his job.

'Everything you hear these days is filth,' said Friedrich. 'If I weren't taking dope, I would drown in this mess.'

'Instead you're drowning in dope.'

'What a noble way to go – to soar and never to come back. I have a gun and five bullets. I'll shoot through the mouth, up into the brain. I'll leave you my gun and four bullets,' he said solemnly.

'Of course. I'll just take the gun out of your hand and walk away with it.'

'Well, it doesn't really matter. I've gone further than humans are permitted to go. I have seen the unthinkable, felt the unbelievable, I can't go further.' He smiled. 'It's all fulfilled. My only desire now is death.'

'Rubbish!' exclaimed Eva. 'You're in some crazy dope dream. Dope is the great deception.'

'The great truth,' insisted Friedrich.

'It's hopeless.' Eva sighed.

It was a cold, grey December day. Gusts of wind blew tiny snowflakes through the air past the narrow window in front of Eva's desk. It was damp and freezing inside as well. Everybody sat in their overcoats and shivered. Eva's hands felt numb, the skin was rough and cracked. She got up and touched the radiators which were lukewarm. Marion was too lazy to keep the furnace going. It meant shovelling coal, doing dirty work.

The war picture continued to improve. Germany was losing ground steadily. Hubert was elated, making plans for post-war 'operations' in a country plagued with famine. He worked in an underworld beneath the underworld, dealing in out-of-the-way warehouses, in tunnels with secret connections and enormous investments. They were a ruthless lot.

When Eva played cards with Darling she got the impression the war was already won, victories were so overwhelming that the Germans would have to lay down their weapons any minute. Darling's news from the BBC was transmitted to Eva as if the information came directly from God. Otherwise Darling trusted no one. Only the BBC and her nephew Benny were infallible. Eva hardly objected to Darling's dreams. What did it matter? The next day was as dismal as the day before and Eva could see no end in sight. Instead fog, cold and wind turned the decaying city into a place of despair. From time to time she had to run to Arlen, who was now working in a factory making electronic devices and had come back to the wasteland without noticeable improvement.

'Another long, cold winter,' she had complained to him.

'At least we're not in the Russian trenches,' he had said, resembling Werner more and more.

'How they wanted their war!' Eva had replied. Playing the war game, killing Jews while the fate of half-Jews still hung in the balance. Rumours were spreading swiftly from city to city, threatening; nobody was quite sure. The fear became suffocating. The long wait in a cold office, entering assets and liabilities on to neatly lined paper, waiting for lunch and a smile from Else, waiting for Marion to see if she was all right, waiting for Friedrich who might disappear any day, trying not to get noticed by Mr Lindner, restraining herself in the sterile dining room of the Kromers with Werner's meek remarks and everybody's clichés, waiting again for a moment of relief or for nothing to happen, expecting the deportation order, feeling her pulse drop to a record low from lack of heat and love while her heart began to harden throughout its chambers.

The bell rang at the office front door. Miss Ehrlich, who was in charge of visitors, arrived with fast, short steps. Eva heard a voice say 'Narcotics Bureau' and began to wish for escape.

'It all happened so fast,' she told Else, sitting in the kitchen, near the stove. Friedrich had heard the words at the same time and Eva and he had hurried together to Miss Ehrlich's office, away from the entrance hall. There they stood, leaning against the wall. Eva pressed his arm hard as if to hold him back from a foolish move. Miss Ehrlich was coming back in her busybody way, saying: 'They are after you.' Two officers talking to Mr Lindner, one standing guard. 'Don't try to run away.'

'Why should I run away?' Friedrich had asked. His face was pale but he seemed very calm as if he had rehearsed the scene many times before. 'I'm going in here.' He opened the door to the filing room, a long, narrow hallway, leading to the back offices.

'You can't escape through there,' warned Miss Ehrlich. 'The door is locked.'

'Just don't follow me,' he said full of hatred. 'I warn you, don't come after me.' Then he disappeared, closing the door.

For a moment everything remained deadly silent. Miss

122

Ehrlich's teeth were exposed from an over-zealous smile, making her face look like a skull. Then there was a crash in the filing room as if a couple of heavy files had tumbled down.

'He is upsetting our files,' Miss Ehrlich complained, returning to her typewriter.

At that moment Mr Lindner appeared from his office, calling Friedrich.

'He's in the filing room,' said Miss Ehrlich. 'But he warned us not to follow. I think he's armed.'

The men from the Narcotics Bureau joined forces and debated what to do. Mr Lindner just stood there frozen. At this point Eva had left, unnoticed.

'What do you think is going to happen?' asked Else.

'He's dead. So they'll call the undertaker,' Eva sobbed.

'You expected it all along.' Else tried to calm Eva down.

'Yes, intellectually, the safe way. For most of the time you live in fear, fear of the Gestapo, fear of the bombs – but when it happens it's quite different, much worse that what you had expected. He said the gun would be mine. I wish Hubert could get one for me. It's good to know you can choose your own end.'

'He might have missed,' suggested Else.

'Not Friedrich. You don't miss when you're determined to die.'

'Perhaps you should have stayed at the office.'

'Who cares. They got their victim. That's what they came for. May I stay here until the body is removed?'

'Of course, make yourself comfortable.'

'He tumbled over and made a crash. I don't think we heard the shot.'

'You're simply assuming.'

'He's dead all right,' said Eva as if it were a guessing game. 'I'll try to reach Arlen later. I don't want to sleep in the office tonight.'

A customer interrupted their conversation. Else prepared a sandwich with herring salad and pointed out that she was selling a tasty home-made soup. 'Bring the mug back, hear!'

'Of course. Smells delicious.' The news about Else's home-made soup would spread like wildfire around the neighbourhood, from one dismal office to the next. Nobody would care about Friedrich's suicide. Another death – so what? The Narcotics Bureau would close their case, Mr Lindner would have to make the funeral arrangements, probably leaving it to Miss Ehrlich to find something cheap. Friedrich's aunt would have to be informed and Mr Schiller would have to look for a replacement. Friedrich had never believed in Eva's conviction that what she did, what everybody did, mattered in the final analysis. That's why her pulse fluctuated so often, her temperature rose so dangerously high, that's why she held out like a frayed and battered flag during an endlessly losing battle.

'I think I failed Friedrich somewhere,' she accused herself after Else had returned from the store.

'He had a girlfriend, hadn't he?'

'Yes, I'd better call Jutta tonight.'

'Let me run over to the office and see what has happened,' suggested Else. 'If customers come, tell them I'll be right back.'

'I'm not going to the funeral,' Eva decided while waiting for Else to return.

'He is dead,' reported Else. 'I talked to Miss Ehrlich. He must have died instantly according to the police.'

'Through the mouth, through the brain, he told me.'

While Else was busy in the store during the lunch hour, Eva was sitting nervously in the kitchen. She didn't want to return to the office. There would be an investigation, the corpse removed, drawers searched. 'I hope they don't find my dirty sheets,' rushed through her brain. 'It can't feel like much once you hold the muzzle against your palate, just hard and cold. All you think of is how to position the gun properly to achieve the desired end. You don't think of the end, only of the way to achieve it. I'm sure it becomes an end in itself like the last figures on my balance sheet. It is the sum total and requires two black parallel lines. One goes step by step, engraved in time, until one can depart, flawlessly, without pain.'

At nine she finally got through on the telephone to Arlen.

'Where have you been? I've been trying all evening.'

'Well, I wasn't home.' Arlen was annoyed.

'I can't sleep at the office. Friedrich has killed himself, in the filing room, and I don't know if they've removed the corpse yet.'

'Too bad, but I have company.'

'Can't you send her away by eleven or twelve? Sorry to treat you like this but it's an emergency.'

'All right, I'll tell her to come back another night.'

'I'm such a nuisance,' she apologised.

'Don't worry, my pet.'

'Then I'll see you at eleven.'

She hung up. 'I'd better try to reach Jutta.' Jutta came to the phone and took the news very calmly. Perhaps she felt relieved.

'Believe me, it's better this way than the torture he went through by living.'

'Did he torture you?' asked Eva.

'You saw him daily,' Jutta was surprised at Eva's question. 'Why do you ask?'

Eva spent Christmas at the store. Else had decorated a small tree with tinsel and coloured ornaments, had prepared a number of dishes, invited Marion and put presents on everyone's plate. The radio played *Stille Nacht, Heilige Nacht*. Eva had found some trinkets in different stores and was putting them now, gift-wrapped, next to Else's presents. Eva was amazed at the excitement the unwrapping created, how everyone seemed to expect a surprise in spite of the fact that nothing worthwhile could be had in any store. And they were pleased, as if it were a duty to produce Christmas cheer. Hubert handed out cigarettes and biscuits. They had everything, even oranges and nuts, but Eva didn't feel like celebrating.

'If you don't mind,' she said, 'I'm going over to the office. It's not my day for celebration. I feel guilty sitting here.'

'Come on,' encouraged Else, 'most Jews in Germany celebrated Christmas.'

'They had to pay for it dearly.'

'Take the thermos flask with coffee then,' ordered Else.

'Take a bottle of wine,' said Hubert.

'Don't forget your biscuits,' reminded Marion, who was having a holiday.

'Turn on the electric heater, don't catch cold.'

Eva sat with her riches in Mr Lindner's office, feeling the warmth of the heater and counting her blessings. One radio station was playing Beethoven. Perhaps this was her last Christmas. The Germans didn't take defeat gracefully, they would lash out against their enemies with fury. 'Total extermination' meant nothing to them. Murder was a pastime, a game of power, handed down from department to department, nobody feeling responsible. It worked like a well-oiled clock. Every rank added a necessary portion to the execution, then handed it on to someone else. The final act was done behind barbed wire, in secret places. Nobody ever saw those who committed the murders. The men in power had it all figured out.

She drank more of Hubert's wine. Arlen had not called. She tried him but there was no answer. Either he was sitting at Eduard's fireside or he was spending Christmas with Renate. Actors like to congregate and talk about 'The Theatre', each one pointing out his or her particular talents. Arlen wasn't ashamed to proclaim that he was the most admired young lover on stage. Truth didn't matter. They were living in a world of make-believe and magic. Few outsiders could match their style. Most got tired of the constant shoptalk, the inside jokes and gossip.

There was no air raid that night. Then the telephone rang. It was Arlen. He wanted to know how she felt and why she wasn't at Else's.

'Christmas is no holiday of mine,' said Eva.

'Do you really feel that way?'

'Honest.'

'Peace on earth,' he shouted into the receiver and Eva realised that he was drunk.

'Peace unto you,' Eva answered.

'Can I come and visit you?' he laughed.

'Of course, you know the way.' He would never arrive,

never think twice about it.

'Fine, I'll be over soon.' He hung up.

It was nice of him to call, though. She turned off the light and looked out of the window. The sky was clear. Stars were twinkling, the moon looked silver and bright. The landscape of ruins, covered with snow, rose like a ghost town. She put on her coat and ran out into the streets, across the bridge, down to the harbour, the same way they had escaped during the fire. She ran a few steps and then skidded over in the slippery snow. Her steps made crunching noises. Her breath was producing a cloud of white steam like a train engine. The streets were deserted, this was no man's land. She skidded sideways down a hill and wondered if she was unique. Had anyone ever experienced Christmas night in a wintery waste-land, close to death, skidding under the stars, feeling joy? There was the river, going out to sea. The waves splashed and gushed against the hewed stones of the quay. The wind blew from the north. Shadows of barges and small boats danced a wild dance, iron bridges were silhouetted against the sky. She began to run and skid again with outstretched arms to keep her balance. As she returned to the office she met Arlen walking back towards the city.

'I banged at your door for at least fifteen minutes, then gave up.'

'I am sorry, my pet. I didn't believe a word you were saying.'

'Did I sound drunk?' he asked. 'I wasn't. Just desperate. It was the most depressing kind of evening at Eduard's with the entire gang sitting around a tree singing Christmas carols. The birds joined in too. "Be joyful, oh Christmas . . ." I couldn't bear it any longer. Then I called you.'

The office was warm. Eva showed her presents. 'Have some wine,' she suggested.

'No, thanks, the heater will do.'

'Some coffee instead. I'll drink wine to celebrate your coming. I skidded over in the snow and the ruins looked like ancient castles. The wind blew from the north and near the water I thought I was a witch riding a broomstick.'

'You've had too much to drink.' He smiled.

'I am trying to cheer us up. Eat a nut, it's supposed to be healthy.' She peeled an orange and cracked some walnuts by pressing two together. One broke open. 'Eat,' she encouraged. 'I am so glad you're here.'

'1943 was good to us.'

'Nothing is good, my pet, but you. There are too many rumours circulating about the fate the government has in store for people like me. They can't all be inventions, something is going on.'

'Everybody claims to have heard it from a reliable source but nobody wants to reveal the source. I think it's all humbug.'

'But if it were true?'

'I'll hide you in my apartment.'

'Thanks.' Eva pushed the food in Arlen's direction. 'Eat a piece of orange with a nut. Tastes great. We can sleep late tomorrow and have lunch at Else's.'

'I'm sure I have a date with somebody.'

'Perhaps Renate. You can call her.'

'No, it wasn't Renate but I can't remember – '

'Olga perhaps.'

'No, she's occupied with her doctor.'

'You're still in touch with her?'

'Of course. She needs friends. The Gestapo is constantly threatening to send her back to Russia since her fiancé broke off their engagement officially, under pressure.'

'How come she's still around?'

'Don't ask me. She probably goes to bed with the guys. It's better than being shot by your own people.'

'Poor Olga!'

'She's not that sensitive.'

'She can't afford to be touchy. Look what the Nazis made of ordinary people like Mr Lindner. I'm so glad you prefer a non-Christmas too. How burdensome traditions are!'

'But without them, nothing is left.'

'You're healthy, you can fill the void.'

'You'll pull through.'

'With these?' Eva held out her arms as if they were stumps or deformed.

'Witches on broomsticks can hold out.' He didn't want any tragedy.

'Spanish oranges,' Eva studied the wrappers.

'Don't you have any candles?'

She went in search and found some in her own office. She lit three. 'Is that better?' she asked and he nodded. 'Think of all the horrible places we could be tonight.'

'We are lucky, aren't we?'

'Tonight, my pet, yes, tonight we are lucky.'

The office got a replacement for Friedrich, a young, married woman whose husband was stationed in France. She was tall and strong-boned, her hair cut short, wavy and blond. The face looked impish with lack of beauty. Eva couldn't tell whether her constant laughter was an expression of mirth or of nerves. She suspected that it was a mixture of both. Now Miss Ehrlich's quiet cheerfulness seemed threatened by the boisterous, loud laughter resounding through the office from Mrs Richter's merry person. Within a short time she was calling Miss Ehrlich 'Deary', claiming that Deary was over-worked and that she could easily take on some extra work. 'There isn't enough to do in my department,' she claimed, breaking into laughter.

'It's an affliction,' thought Eva, 'worse than eczema. I have to listen to it from morning to night.'

'Deary, I am taking over the dictation,' she announced to Miss Ehrlich whose cheerfulness wore thin under the burden of an ailing mother and a retreating army. 'Cheer up and breathe freely. I have plenty of time.'

Miss Ehrlich complained to Eva because Mrs Richter was taking over. On the other hand she was grateful for the help. However, Mrs Richter knew no enemies, she bulldozed everyone into friendliness with her laughter. 'Good morning, feeling fine?' The laughter echoed from room to room. She showered the world with happiness that came from nowhere and rained down without reason.

'It's the noise of the laughter that's driving me crazy,' Eva complained to Hubert and Else at night. 'When she's silent I'm anxious from anticipation. I'm waiting, listening, waiting, and when it comes it pains me like a toothache or like an unending itch.'

Mrs Richter was unaware of the storm she created. At night, things fell back, violated and disturbed. But during the day she undermined everybody's composure. She received more and more dictation from Mr Lindner. Eva heard them talk through the wall, interrupted by outbreaks of Mrs Richter's laughter. Slowly Mr Lindner began to respond and they laughed together in fits and spurts. Every day Mrs Richter stayed a little longer in Mr Lindner's room. Soon they went to lunch together, Mr Lindner, Mrs Richter and Mr Schiller.

'Would you believe it?' asked Miss Ehrlich.

'They're having a good time. What's wrong with it?'

'Her husband is fighting in France and she runs around with another man.' Miss Ehrlich was hurt too because Mr Lindner had never asked her out for lunch.

'They're sitting in a restaurant being chaperoned by Mr Schiller. Look, it's none of our business anyway.'

Miss Ehrlich, who was not allowed to alter her life or her appearance, consoled herself by agreeing with Eva. It really wasn't their business.

Rumours about the arrests of half-Jews persisted. At times Eva became over-anxious, on other days she would shrug off the idea as something that simply couldn't happen, always realising that it was a likely event. She blamed her fluctuating moods on the appalling climate of the city. How could she not be depressed with dark clouds hanging over ruins and an ice-cold drizzle falling for weeks on to a wasteland? The temperature inside her office was so low that she shivered. However, Mrs Richter seemed unaffected, and even Miss Ehrlich was displaying more cheerfulness since Mrs Richter had begun to sew a dress for her. They had become friends.

Chapter Ten

1944

'When would you advise me to go into hiding?' asked Eva, sitting at the Kromers' dining table, having listened to a mildly boring conversation. Nobody paid any attention to her question. Dr Kromer continued reporting on some clinical case he had cured. Eva watched Werner watch Dr Kromer. He would have liked to imitate the doctor's excellence, his high standards of achievement. Mrs Kromer was docile and colourless but not without authority. She enjoyed pressing the bell during meals and giving orders to the maid in an impersonal, soft-spoken voice. She interrupted her husband's conversation with some gossip from her circle.

'They've moved into their Austrian chalet since Professor Dr Meier retired. It will be a great change for Emily. She is so used to city life.'

'We all have to make sacrifices nowadays,' remarked her husband.

'Of course, of course. And knowing Emily, she will turn her exile into a success.' Eva wondered about the extent of Emily's success but didn't enquire. The macaroni constantly stuck to her teeth and palate as if it were made of glue. She drank too much wine. After the macaroni the maid took the plates away. Nothing else was served.

'May I offer you a cigarette?' asked Eva. 'Werner, I need an ashtray.'

'We smoke only in the drawing room,' said Mrs Kromer.

'Let's go into the drawing room.' Dr Kromer was addressing Eva. 'You see, not even I am allowed to smoke in the dining room.'

'I don't have any rooms,' remarked Eva. 'I sleep in my boss's office.' Later Eva sat in Werner's room and complained about the Kromers. 'If you want to see me in future, you'll have to come to the office.' She laid down the law. Werner objected, asking her who else would take in a half-Jew like a son and invite another half-Jew to dinner?

'In any case, I asked you here to let you know that Dr Kromer has it from a very reliable source,' Werner continued, 'directly connected to the government, that arrests of half-Jews are being planned or are being carried out already. How long it will last, nobody knows.' Werner talked exactly like Dr Kromer. 'Now he suggests that we disappear for a while until the intentions of the government have become clear. I know a small village high up in the Austrian Alps where no Gestapo would look for us. Could you take two weeks' vacation now?'

'And if massive arrests are carried out? How will we get back from the mountains undetected?'

'I don't know, but I think it'd be better to be away for the time being.'

'The escape may turn into a trap,' warned Eva.

'Dr Kromer doesn't think so. Anyway, it's no use worrying too much. Perhaps nothing'll happen. All you need is a skiing outfit. See if you can be ready by next Wednesday. I will make all the arrangements.'

'I don't know if it's doomsday or just rumours,' Eva had said to Mr Lindner, who felt guilty enough to understand her situation.

'By all means, go. I am sure Mrs Richter can handle some of the entries and I will help with the rest.'

Hubert got her a secondhand skiing outfit with boots that were too big. But then he came up with heavy socks and the problem seemed solved.

Eva sat in front of the small office window and felt half frozen, suspended between debit and credit, longing to draw two lines under the columns as a final gesture. The struggle seemed too much for her depleted resources, they had shrunk to a minimum when she needed them most. Only Arlen could make her feel stronger and reliable.

'Once you're there – it's high and beautiful – you forget the things below,' Arlen had said.

'I won't find you there,' Eva had objected.

'You'll find something better,' he had said reassuringly. Then they had parted.

Werner and Eva were taking the night train to Munich. Not in a cattle car, though Eva was aware that cattle cars were standing on other tracks. She was pacing in front of her sleeper on a crowded platform.

'You're lucky, going on a winter vacation,' Mrs Richter had commented. 'Do you know how to ski?'

Else had handed her a small suitcase full of provisions. 'Enjoy yourself, hear!' she had ordered. 'Forget about the future. I always say it's written in the stars, why worry?' She looked radiant in her white, starched apron and her golden crown.

Werner had stood under the clock of the main station viewing the large hands above reproachfully.

'I know I'm late as usual,' Eva had apologised.

'Why do you make me stand waiting every time we meet? It's humiliating.'

'Try to be late yourself. Then perhaps I'll pace under the clock, getting anxious.'

'No time for arguments, we're late as it is.' He had rushed down the hall, leaving Eva to struggle for herself. They had twenty minutes in which to catch their train and had reserved sleepers, so she couldn't understand the rush.

Now he appeared in the corridor rather nervously looking out for her. 'You see how we had to hurry. I think you make it a point to leave me waiting. I have the compartment to myself,' he added triumphantly.

'I'm sharing mine with two middle-aged sisters who can't get into the top berth, which leaves me to occupy it. I had no choice in the matter. The two ladies were already undressed and lying in bed.'

'They're lucky you didn't turn out to be a little old lady.'

The train had left on time and was now heading south, slowly gaining speed. Eva took the provisions and went to Werner's compartment.

'Here,' she said. 'Anything your heart desires.' She poured herself a brandy and ate a slice of cake, then lit a cigarette. 'My sisters are secretaries by profession and their name is Seidel. I could do without them. You're lucky.'

'So far.'

'Well, this could be our last trip,' announced Eva after several glasses of brandy.

'Don't start on that subject. If it's the last, let's make it enjoyable.'

'Sometimes you frighten me with your denseness,' said Eva.

'What have I done?'

'You always look at the clock but you never know what time it is.'

'Didn't you say time was unimportant?'

'It is. You arrived early but as usual you've missed the train.'

'I'm riding in it.' He laughed.

'You don't get it,' said Eva. 'Pretending to be on holiday. I'm going to sleep now. Wake me tomorrow for breakfast.' She kissed him on the cheek. 'Sleep well.'

The light was still burning when she returned to her compartment. The Seidel sisters were asleep. Eva took her time undressing. Hubert had got brand-new pyjamas for her in burgundy with beige piping. She looked in the mirror and was amazed at the elegant picture that appeared – a model in sleepwear. 'I am beautiful,' she told herself. 'I really am.' She climbed up the ladder to the top berth with confidence and then discovered that it required acrobatics to get into bed and under the cover. She turned off the light. The train ran at an even speed, jerking Eva in her bed this way and that. She felt every curve and thought of derailment. Her heart started to beat faster. Then her head began to spin. 'Wanting to go, wanting to go – ' while the wheels filled her ears with ratata-ratata. 'Wanting – ratata – wanting.' She was asleep.

They had breakfast in the dining car. Werner was well-shaven; every hair lay in its proper place. He looked elegant, a man of the world like Dr Kromer. The windows were covered on the outside by a sheet of ice. There was no view; they rode through an invisible landscape.

'The beautiful part begins after Innsbruck,' explained Werner. 'Have you packed your suitcase? We have only a few minutes for our connection.'

Eva became a little excited when the train pulled into the huge station at Munich. The sun shone through broken windows. The steam of the engine puffed and rose to the iron roof. The platform was covered with drab-looking people, the youngsters carrying skis over their shoulders. Everyone seemed in motion. Werner began pushing his way rather ruthlessly through the crowd, heading for platform 23 where the train to Innsbruck stood, ready to depart.

'Hurry,' he yelled at Eva, then ran, without turning round again.

'As long as he's going to make it – ' thought Eva. 'All he cares for is skiing.' Werner stood outside the car, waiting for her. He had reserved two seats in a half-empty train.

'Trains don't wait,' he explained, fumbling nervously with his hands.

'You don't wait either.'

'We have to make our connection. Otherwise we can't get to Obergurgel.'

'I can get there very well without you.' She climbed into the carriage, sat down, opened the provision case and had a sandwich with strong coffee. He looked small and lost on the platform, still waiting for the signal for their departure, after having rushed and run with such anxiety. Then the whistle blew and he joined Eva inside the carriage. They both looked out the window, saw bombed Munich, saw the first woods and snow-covered fields with mountains in the background, here and there a frozen lake. Soon the windows glazed over and the landscape disappeared. They took out the books they had brought along. Werner produced Hoelderlin's *Hyperion* and Plato's *Republic*. Eva had brought Nietzsche's *Untimely Reflections* and an autobiography by an artistic lady which

Renate had recommended. 'It's perfect entertainment,' she had said. Everybody thought she was travelling for pleasure, even Werner was convinced.

'We'll be too tired to read,' he promised. 'Skiing makes you sleepy.'

'I won't be on the slopes all day, I also intend to lie in a deckchair and read.'

'Suit yourself. I'll ski.' He was determined. His eyes flared up, his mouth moved, the nostrils of his fleshy nose quivered. There was definitely something sexual in his desire to ski. Eva watched his face slowly relax again. She began to read the autobiography while Werner opened Plato's *Republic*. A pair of peasant women were gossiping. Neither Eva nor Werner could understand their dialect. An elderly lady in Bavarian garb sat stiffly on her seat, her eyes on her hands which lay folded together in her lap like discarded flowers. Perhaps she was praying. Her features were hard and defiant. The green hat with a hawk's feather on one side certainly didn't soften her expression. Was she praying for forgiveness or for others' sins to be found out? It looked like a frightening battle.

In Innsbruck they had to wait for their train to Oetzthal. Eva walked outside the station, stood under the cloudless sky, close to high snow-covered mountains and ancient roof tops.

'Don't walk away from the station,' warned Werner. 'We have to catch our connection.' He showed signs of nervousness and only calmed down after they had settled in an old-fashioned local train that would stop at every village.

'It's a long stretch at a slow pace,' explained Werner. 'The bus isn't any better. It rolls for hours.'

'When will we arrive?'

'Late. It depends on the weather conditions and whether or not the sleigh can meet the bus on time.'

'Are we going to the end of the world?' asked Eva in despair. She had certainly had enough of train rides by now.

'Almost,' he smiled with his skiing smile. 'Remember, nobody is supposed to find us.'

'That's right. We're on a mission. I just wonder if it's worth it.'

The sun shone through the windows, which didn't freeze

over. They watched the white country with its barren trees and miles of fence poles dotted out in the snow. They saw the square, solid village houses, barns, occasionally a cow or a horse, children on skis waving at the travellers. Mountains drew closer and grew in size, measuring ominously against their small puffing train, against the shape of their hands.

'I wonder what catastrophe created these mountains?' asked Eva.

'You always have to imagine a catastrophe. I happen to like the Alps.'

'I hope we don't have to climb to the top to ski.'

'Not quite,' he laughed. 'But it's a long trip. Why don't you read?'

'I wonder if anything's happened in Hamburg since we left?'

'Forget about Hamburg. We're going to ski.' Werner couldn't hide his annoyance. 'And don't spoil my fun.'

Country people got in and out of the train. They didn't seem to travel far. The landscape changed little, only the mountains came nearer.

'I prefer the Baltic,' said Eva.

'We're better off in an out-of-the-way place in Austria,' explained Werner as if she didn't know.

'I miss my friends.'

'You are lucky to have friends.'

'Yes, I know.'

Finally they reached Oetzthal. The station and the tracks stood out against a white, oppressive world. Eva had given up protesting. She took her suitcase and walked behind Werner to the waiting bus that was to carry them further into these uninhabitable mountains. 'I am not even remotely in tune with Werner,' thought Eva when his face lit up at the sight of the winter landscape. They began to travel through a valley which met a colossal mountain in the far distance. 'This is never going to end. We are the only vehicle on the road. The valley gets narrow and the mountains grow near.' Sometimes they passed a small village or just a single house with a barn. A pile of manure was soiling the snow; everything else looked glaringly white except for dotted fence lines and barren trees. The sun was sinking early, drawing a long shadow over the white land, turning it into a valley of grey and blue.

'It will be dark soon,' said Eva. 'How much longer do we have to travel?'

'Over three hours on the bus. But there'll be a stop at a restaurant soon and we'll get something to eat.'

They had soup and bread in a country inn. Eva opened the thermos flask and they enjoyed Else's coffee.

'That's good,' said Werner appreciatively.

'I wonder if anything has happened in Hamburg?' Eva wondered again.

'We're on holiday. Stop worrying about Hamburg. I hope you didn't tell anybody where you were going. Dr Kromer can get in touch with me if necessary.'

'Sorry, I have my own back-up system. You're making a secret out of everything. I think the entire trip is a mistake. No one is allowed more than two weeks' holiday and what shall we do afterwards?'

'Two weeks' skiing in the Alps can't be a mistake.'

'We have to consider our plans for hiding. Have you counted how often our identification cards have been checked during the train rides? The same will happen on our way back.'

'We might have to resort entirely to local buses.'

'Luckily Hubert provided us with plenty of ration coupons.'

'Let's go skiing first and worry about the rest later,' suggested Werner, holding on to his toy.

Then the bus rolled along the country road again in a dove-grey twilight. Suddenly night arrived without warning. Eva closed her eyes. She was exhausted and cold. The bus moved, wheels turned on white snow, over bumps, jerking the riders slightly. She had no choice but to sit, freeze and endure the ride towards the looming mountains.

'I'm cold,' said Eva. Werner didn't respond, he was asleep.

The road made a sharp left turn and drove parallel to a chain of vast mountains. Then it stopped suddenly in the middle of nowhere. This was the end of the road.

'Everybody out!' called the driver. 'Don't forget your belongings. Have a good time.'

'That's it?' asked Eva in disbelief.

'Of course not. Now comes the best part. The sleigh ride up the pass.'

'In this temperature?'

'They won't make it warmer just for you.'

'Very funny!' Eva had reached her limit yet knew quite well that she had to go on.

Everybody was scrambling to get into one of the three sleighs first. The ground was slippery, the luggage heavy. Eva was so weary that she thought it wouldn't be difficult to give up what was left of her. If this were Auschwitz – 'I am going to ski,' she reminded herself. 'First I'm going to ski and then we'll see. It's life that is difficult; what one makes of it and what effect one has on others.' She shivered, not only because of the sub-zero temperature, but also at the thought of the impression she would leave behind in Werner's lofty personality or in the sand dune of Arlen's. 'It's going to be a big lie no matter how honestly I'm trying to live,' she concluded, lugging her suitcase up the slope, dropping it on a wide, wooden bench.

'On the floor,' ordered the driver. 'Twenty-five marks,' he demanded. 'Plenty of blankets,' he assured.

The wind blew down from the mountains. They huddled together wrapped in blankets, not getting any warmer. The horses pulled with a sudden jerk, they held on to something or each other, then the sleigh turned into a white road leading through pine woods. The wind stopped blowing. Eva felt some warmth come back into her body.

The drivers signalled to each other by whistling through their teeth. The harnesses on the sturdy horses' necks were decorated with bells which rang out in even notes. The snow sighed under the sleighs' runners, leaving imprint upon imprint. None would remain distinct.

'How long?' asked Eva.

'About two hours,' answered Werner.

Eva pulled a flask with brandy from her suitcase, drank, then handed it to Werner.

'Heavens,' she complained, 'we've just begun.'

Then they were in the open again. The wind blew through the blankets, the sleighs moved slowly upwards. Whips cracked through the air. 'Hoi – hui!' cried the drivers. The broad bodies of the horses steamed, the bells rang without vigour or joy. Crack, down came the whip, up and up the horses pulled. Eva handed the brandy to Werner again. The sky was covered with stars as large as dew drops. The moon wrapped the landscape in a silver light. They could see far, they could recognise each other's faces. The moon wasn't a flat disc in the heavens but a round body gliding through the universe attached to earth's orbit. The whip beat through the air: 'Hui – hoi!' yelled the drivers. 'If I fall off the sleigh I'll freeze to death,' thought Eva.

'Tomorrow is our first day's skiing,' said Werner. 'You'll have to enrol in the beginners' class. I'll be gone all day.'

'There's nothing but snow,' complained Eva.

'Fortunately,' said Werner and laughed. 'Would be bad for the skis if it were otherwise.' It was no use talking to Werner. He held on to his little facts. 'I can't take that away from him,' considered Eva, 'or he might hold on to me instead, which I couldn't endure.'

For a while they had to get off and walk uphill beside the sleighs. Eva was glad for the movement after having been cooped up all day in compartments on narrow seats. They blew steam, the horses slipped several times, hooves bent, then jumped up again to the crack of the whip, the hui-hoi, shaking their manes, pulling up, up. The valley widened, the surrounding mountains grew smaller. The sky looked like a display of diamonds. It was splendid and frightening. What if this really turned into a trap? They wouldn't be able to escape. There was only this one pass, leading up and leading down.

When they finally drove into the small village of Obergurgel, the church bells chimed ten times.

'We made it in record time,' commented Werner. 'Just follow me.'

The hotel wasn't far from the sleigh station. It was a wooden structure of some length with a square tower on either end. A lady greeted them and two other guests with natural friendliness.

'First I'll show you your rooms.' She shook hands with every guest. 'Then, in perhaps fifteen minutes, you come down for your supper. I kept it hot. You must be hungry.'

Eva's room was elegant and warm. She had her own bathroom. Everything was decorated in a light sea-green colour, the curtains, bedspread, lampshades, rug, bath. 'Civilisation!' thought Eva in amazement, feeling transported back in time. 'The underworld must have spared this valley.' She thought of Hamburg, of her office existence and looked again at the hotel room with its gilt-framed flower prints hanging on the walls, the sea-green silk curtains, the ruffled silk shades over the lamp at her bedside, the clean, soft rug. She was glad Hubert had given her new pyjamas. 'I am going to take a bath later.' She hung her fur coat and ski jacket in the wardrobe.

'How do you like it?' asked Werner.

'Marvellous!' admitted Eva. 'Would you order a bottle of wine with our dinner?'

Later they had to register at the desk. The lady with the friendly smile and friendly manners collected ration coupons from every guest for their two-week holiday.

'Let's take a short walk through the village,' suggested Werner. 'I have to walk off my food.'

'Wasn't that much.' Eva was at the point of exhaustion.

'You had too much to drink.'

'I feel light, like a balloon,' she laughed. 'You're top heavy, your feet are touching the ground.'

'I am going to ski tomorrow.' He said it like a litany. Then he showed her the route he would take and which peak he would climb.

'Skiing before doom.' Eva couldn't reconcile the two worlds.

'Dr Kromer is going to hide me,' protested Werner.

'I got an offer from Arlen and one from Else. But will we be able to get back? I can't understand why you brought me here.'

'It's great skiing country.'

'I give up.' She smiled because she felt so distant from Werner. He would never think of their innermost feelings.

Their travels together wouldn't bring them a step closer. Werner was cut off from the world without having created another one for himself. There was the secret life with his mother and that urgent need to ski. Perhaps he was mad. Madness had gnawed at everyone for years. How could one know if a seagull, sitting on the anchor pole day in and day out hadn't lost its mind – people looked at it with such queer eyes? Werner's nose shone in the moonlight. His eyes dreamt of mountain tops. His home was at Dr Kromer's and at night he cried for his mother. Why had they come here? Into a winter resort to escape deportation. She thought of her elegant hotel room and longed to sleep in the bed with its sea-green silk cover. 'Wake me for breakfast,' she told Werner. 'I have the feeling that I could jump off this planet if I wanted to and sail straight for the moon.'

'I prefer skiing,' Werner insisted.

He went skiing every day, leaving after an early breakfast, taking along lunch and returning before dark around five o'clock in the afternoon. Eva progressed to the advanced group of skiers after several lessons with the beginners. She climbed up the hill dutifully and skied down with more speed and skill as time went on. They made excursions into the mountains for the purpose of skiing down snowy slopes without falling, becoming more efficient and professional. Eva didn't like the alpine mountain peaks, the endless stretch of snow-covered stones without vegetation. The first view had been overwhelming. Then it began to bore her and finally made her depressed. Everything inaccessible, cold, dangerous. What a place!

In the afternoons she lay in a deckchair near the hotel, wrapped in blankets, lay there with closed eyes or read the books they had brought along. The lady in the autobiography had lost her lover and was terribly despondent. Eva couldn't respond to the book. Werner returned every day full of enthusiasm and vigour. He never talked about his adventures. They were probably unexplainable. He just felt happy. They walked together to some distant hotel and ordered coffee and cake. He smiled and joked. Eva declared the entire life in the alpine village a mad dream and felt like an impostor.

Dr Kromer telephoned on the last day of their holiday and advised them to prolong their stay. Nothing had been settled, the rumours were increasing.

'What shall we do?' asked Eva. 'The hotel will have to turn us out because our holiday permits are up. You know the law.'

'We can't return. I have an idea. I don't know if it's going to work, but we must try. High up in the mountains there's a hut run by an old couple who don't talk. They won't ask questions. If we go there tomorrow and just stay on – I could ask the hotel to store our suitcases until we return.'

'Are you sure the hut is still there?'

'I was there recently. Not many skiers go up that high. I remember the old couple from when I went skiing with my father as a child. They looked the same then and they never uttered a word ten years ago. I know because my father commented on it. The couple interested him. Adaptation to surroundings, you know.'

'Are they fossilised?'

'I doubt it. Just silent, communicating in different ways,' Werner suggested.

'Perhaps they're teaching us something valuable.' Eva was willing to try the silent method.

The weather was beautiful when they set out the next morning. They climbed up all day and got exhausted. They rested on their skis, ate lunch, felt hot from the sun. Then they were off again, up higher and higher. The sun stood between two mountains like a rising moon when they finally reached the hut.

'We just made it in time. Night falls rapidly and unex-pectedly.'

The dining room which they entered was illuminated by an oil lamp standing on a counter. Behind the counter a head was bent over a book. Wooden chairs and tables, set up for guests, were empty. A round iron stove gave off some heat.

'Greetings,' said Werner. The head lifted, glanced at the

newcomers and continued reading. 'May we stay here for a few days?'

The figure put down the book, stood up, small and withered, dressed in a long skirt and woollen top, took the lamp and led the way to a large room with a number of bunk beds along its barren walls. The place was unheated and unadorned. They put down their knapsacks and returned to the dining room, guided by the lamp. The small figure stopped once and opened the door to the toilet. She pointed at a bucket of water next to the bowl. Then they sat by the stove, taking off their ski jackets and asking for food. Eva went over to the counter and showed the woman her ration cards.

Meanwhile, the sun had disappeared. The sky looked greenish-blue like the ocean before nightfall. A well, with a bent pipe, stood in front of the window. Water had turned into a long icicle at the pipe's end.

'I'm tired,' declared Eva. 'The sun looks like the moon. Perhaps the moon will look like the sun.' They drank beer which Werner picked up from the counter. 'I wonder how cold it will get here at night?'

'Far below freezing, inside.'

'I hate the cold,' said Eva, getting tipsy and warm from the beer. 'Do you think we will get dinner?'

'Something for sure.'

'I wish the old woman would reveal something of her life in this barren isolation. It's empty up here.'

The old man came in with a few logs. They greeted him without getting a response. He simply put some of the logs into the stove, dropped the rest on a pile and disappeared while his wife began to clatter with pots and pans.

'At times I wish the story would end,' exclaimed Eva after finishing her pea soup with two sausages. 'How much further do we have to go?'

'Just to our beds,' laughed Werner. 'I'm sleepy. Tomorrow –'

'Don't tell me!' interrupted Eva with anger. 'Your stupid skiing gets on my nerves.'

'No use arguing about taste,' he said, getting up from his chair and paying for his meal at the counter. The withered woman handed them a small lamp and returned to her sink. The moon had risen and shone brightly through the windows, painting distorted shadows over the wooden floors and stone walls. No shutters closed, no blackout curtains. This was forgotten country.

Eva couldn't fall asleep that evening. The blankets lay like a heavy weight on her body and made her bones ache without providing any heat. She shivered and yawned, yawned and shivered. Then Werner began to snore. Eva was ready to cry but didn't. Instead she crept into Werner's bed, slowly feeling the heat from his body warming hers. Then she fell asleep.

Next morning Werner went off skiing, instructing Eva not to wander far. Eva spent the day finding suitable slopes to ski, to look over the immense design of snowy slopes, jagged peaks which some tremendous force must have crushed into their eternally frozen state. The sun got hotter than on a summer's day. She left her jacket and sweater on a bench in front of the hut and skied in her blouse. She ate lunch and then sat on the bench in the sun, trying to read but thinking of Werner instead, of his denseness and immaturity. He had lost the charm of a child and had become a source of annoyance. He didn't respond on equal terms. It had to come with an air of arrogance or with a snub, putting her down because she was late or dressed untidily. How he put one foot forward in his well-fitting suit, trying desperately to be somebody, a personality with recognition and authority. Eva thought that's what he wanted most, to be recognised. Perhaps she liked him best then because he was not posing but pleading in earnest. He reminded her at those moments of a teddy bear propped against a pillow on the drawing-room sofa in polished shoes and neat tie, participating in human interaction with the twinkle of glass-button eyes and a gloss on his imitation fur, knowing that it was all a hoax but one he could not abandon. His mother wouldn't let him.

She started to read the lost woman's autobiography for the third time. Suddenly a soldier with a gun over his shoulder appeared from nowhere and all her fears blew up like a huge balloon.

'Greetings,' he said. 'Here for some skiing?'

'I'm not good at it yet, just started to learn down at the village.'

'Who taught you?' he asked with a smile on his young, suntanned face.

'Joschel.'

'He is a fine teacher.'

'Then you're from the village?' asked Eva.

'Lived there all my life until this damned war started. The army sent me up here to patrol the border.'

'What border?' Eva hoped they might be near Switzerland.

'Austrian–Italian border. Italy starts right behind those ranges.'

'But who would come here?'

'Nobody, fortunately, except a few tourists. We rather enjoy it, praying to God to let us stay until peace is declared. Are you up for the day?'

'No, at least a week. My friend loves to ski. He's out from morning till night.'

'If the heat continues we're in for avalanches. They might come down as soon as tomorrow. Be careful, and tell your friend.' He went inside the hut, the young soldier who hoped to remain forgotten by the authorities until the end of the war. Eva began to relax again but the shock had its aftermath. She put on her skis to walk off the fear.

Werner returned from his skiing expedition tired and satisfied. They had lentil soup with bacon and potatoes. Eva reported her encounter with the border guard and mentioned that they could expect avalanches. They drank brandy, smoked cigarettes, looked out over the silver landscape that appeared like the surface of the moon, silent, uninhabited, dead.

Eva felt restricted and imprisoned after the few extra days in their Alpine paradise. She wandered further and further away from the hut only to realise that the landscape never changed, that the mountain peaks were the same all over, the ice and snow remained the only colour below the blue and sunny sky. The border guard had come again to warn her of avalanches, the books said the same words after every reading, her thoughts returned more and more to the reality of her situation and its future prospect. But nothing yielded, she remained ignorant. She stared at the endless snowy surfaces, she began to hate climbing up slopes for the sake of skiing down them again. It didn't make sense. But nothing did. She wouldn't be better off locked up in Arlen's apartment. Besides, she doubted whether he could carry out his promise. It would be bad for both of them. If she had to go into hiding she'd prefer one of Hubert's underworld pals who knew the ropes, considered it a deal, strictly in the family, for their own profit.

'Let's go back to Hamburg. I'm going out of my mind here,' begged Eva. But during the night it began to thunder. The house shook and snow tumbled down into the valleys. It thundered and echoed from the mountain sides. Werner went skiing as usual the next day, in spite of Eva's warning. She sat on the bench and saw walls of snow crack, break loose, disperse and then cascade like tremendous waterfalls through the air on to the slopes below. First it was exciting, then it began to bore her like the red glow of sunset. She undid some buttons on her shirt, the heat was strong, the sun stood high above the jagged outlines of the Alps. She longed for the grey damp fog of Hamburg, for the ghostly ruins, the shrieks of seagulls, the dirty water of the canal coming in with the tides. She even missed the monotony of her work; at least it took her mind off her worries. She was longing for Arlen and Else, and a little for Darling, Hubert and Marion. In her imagination she wrote long letters to Arlen, telling him about her skiing, her isolation and her disgust with the Alpine world. 'Man is not made to dwell here,' she cried out silently. 'There is not a tree in sight, no animals, just ice and snow and an unchanging view of the universe. I wish you could save me from this place,' she begged Arlen. For hours she continued to vent her grievances against her fate – while she was skiing, while she was sitting on the bench, while she was eating her lunch in silence. It was always the same story. But putting her complaint into words made her more tolerant of Werner's egotism when he returned at sunset, always the same, as if there could be no turning point, no tomorrow. One day resembled the next to such an extent that Eva lost track of time. It was the day for beans or lentils or peas, it was always one of those days. Otherwise the sky remained blue, the sun hot, the landscape frozen. Only the moon changed in shape and one day felt shorter perhaps than the next, one less painful than the one that preceded or might follow.

Then a cold wind began to blow in from the east and the surface of the soft melting snow turned into a sheet of ice. Even Werner had to give up his excursions and remain at the hut. The short walk to the well was difficult. The snow had turned to slippery ice and the wind blew with gale force.

One morning they woke up to a snow storm, in the midst of clouds. The world around them had vanished, only veils of mist passed by, twisted and whirled around by a gusty wind which made the snowflakes dance a wild dance, then settle down again. This went on for days. Werner became restless, both were irritated and began to attack each other's sensitive spots with small bites.

'Dr Kromer probably chased us up the mountains to free himself of your presence,' she said.

'The mountains were my idea. Besides, you didn't have to come along.' He was annoyed.

'I didn't know it would be like this.'

'Your friends can't even provide a place for you to sleep,' he sneered.

'Like a room at the Kromers'? No, thanks. I prefer the office. It's impersonal and without obligations. Darling would want me to move in with her.'

'The office is a disgrace.'

'At night it's mine. I feel extremely rich. At Dr Kromer's you will always be a charity case, forced to live your life according to the rules of your benefactor.'

'At least it's a home,' Werner defended his situation.

'Let's face it: neither of us has a home. We don't belong to any country, any group. We don't belong anywhere.'

'Perhaps that's why I love the mountains. I discovered them with Father.'

'Something's wrong. You don't even realise what they've done to you.'

'You mean the Kromers? They're very nice.'

'The Kromers and the rest. It's all rather brutal.'

'Well, look at your friends – '

They moved, the same attack, back and forth, a little drunk and a little bored with the game. At night the wind howled around the hut like a hungry wolf. Then it abated and sounds like harp strings spun across the valleys from mountain range to mountain range playing their icy songs until the howls became overwhelming again. Eva didn't know any more if getting up was worse than going to bed. Everything had become such a nightmare.

One morning the sun came out behind the dispersing clouds and the torture seemed over. The border guard appeared and told them that they could descend without danger.

'Let's go!' shouted Eva.

'One more day of skiing,' begged Werner.

'I'm leaving,' persisted Eva.

'All right.' His teddy-bear conscience told him that they had already overstayed.

'Back to civilisation,' said Eva.

'Back to what?' Werner asked.

'Oh, my ruins, my office and my fascinating work.' The snow was blinding. They were crossing a wide field.

'You are missing your actor friend,' Werner suddenly said as if he were trying to explain something else.

'Arlen is my security blanket. I often miss that.'

'Can you love him?'

'I love what he gives, but I guess that's not what you mean.'

They made it down in two hours.

They collected their suitcases at the hotel, returned the skis, ate sandwiches on the sleigh which brought them to the afternoon bus. They would spend the night in Oetzthal, take the morning train to Munich and the night train to Hamburg.

'You have to call Dr Kromer,' insisted Eva.

'I know. We have to hear the verdict.'

'Innocent, yet guilty,' pronounced Eva.

Werner learned from Dr Kromer that the scheme had been abandoned. Whether for good or only for the time being, Dr

Kromer's source couldn't tell. Nobody really knew. As always, it depended on whether one of the highest officials was in the mood to bring up the question of half-Jews again. For the moment deportation and extermination had been cancelled.

'That calls for a celebration,' Eva said.

They ordered wine with their dinner and later drank at the bar, surrounded by tourists in skiing outfits.

'I don't mind going back to the city,' said Eva.

'You have Arlen waiting.'

'We haven't waited for each other. We lead different lives.'

'What are you then?' Werner asked with a smile.

'A rescue team. When the alarm sounds we are ready to help each other. When life goes its old bumpy way, we experience it separately, each in our own manner.'

'Why not experience life together?'

'You limit the scope of adventures to those only acceptable to both.' Eva's brain jumped easily from subject to subject, she was so relieved. 'And then,' she continued, 'you cut short your own development or you force the other into unwanted directions. Some people don't mind amputations and sacrifices. We prefer freedom.'

'Love is not a sacrifice,' said Werner, looking at her with his shiny glass eyes.

'Love demands sacrifices and erodes the ground on which it has to grow. It's always self-defeating.' Eva was proud of her analysis.

'You shouldn't drink so much,' warned Werner.

'I am quite sober.' She yawned. 'Love is an exhausting subject.'

The night train was crowded. They couldn't get sleepers so switched from second to first class tickets in the hope of finding empty seats. But even first class was crowded and they were glad to get seats opposite each other at the door. Once the train left the station they were able to sleep for a while. When they woke, the train had stopped somewhere in a moonlit landscape. They stood in the corridor, smoked a cigarette and sighed because it wasn't later than two o'clock.

'An air raid,' suggested Werner.

Throughout the night the pattern continued. They stopped, then rolled along for a while. By morning they found themselves halfway between Munich and Hamburg. They queued up to get something for breakfast, waited for two hours before they were served a meagre meal. Still, they were among the lucky ones, most people were turned back and the dining car closed. No lunch was served and the mood became angry and resigned. Some said things they wouldn't have dared say a year ago. Eva and Werner looked at each other with joy. For them it was part of the process leading to victory. They were hungry too but didn't mind. They triumphed because the others minded.

The train arrived at three in the afternoon, eight hours late. It was a Saturday.

'The office should be empty.' Eva was looking forward to the bleak view. 'But I think I'll go to the store first.'

'I'm going straight home to get something to eat.'

'Where else should you go?' asked Eva.

'That's right. I am going home. See you.'

'Give me a call tonight. Don't forget,' Eva begged.

'Sure.' They parted as if they had returned from a Sunday picnic.

The closer she got to the store the more excited she became, as if it were a homecoming. And from the 'I don't believe it!' to the hugging and tears, Eva was convinced that their bonds were indestructible. So she had been right about her jumping heart and the feeling of coming home. 'I can't believe it,' repeated Else, wiping away her tears and blowing her nose. 'It's so good to see you again.'

'I am glad to be back, believe me!' exclaimed Eva. 'The Alps are just too big and too cold.'

'Let me finish. Then we can sit down and have a nice cup of coffee.' Else was in the middle of her Saturday cleaning. The high shelves with their little drawers, the counter with its scale and cash register, reminded Eva of a toy shop she had once been given for Christmas as a child.

'It's wonderful to have a store,' she said.

'Couldn't you have risked one small letter?' scolded Else.

Eva laughed. 'There was no post. We were caught high up

near the Italian border in a small hut. Indescribable! When is Hubert coming?'

'In an hour perhaps. We're getting a new shipment through the friends who were ready to take you in. Everything had been arranged.'

'I might need it one day.'

'At least you can rely on us,' Else said proudly. Then she wiped her hands dry. 'Finished,' she announced.

'I'm starving. Had nothing since a meagre breakfast.'

'I'll make you something special.'

'May I phone Arlen?' asked Eva.

'Sure.' Eva dialled with apprehension. She was afraid he might have become unavailable. It crossed her mind that she couldn't go on without him, while the phone rang several times.

'Hello,' she said. Arlen remained silent for a moment.

'I can't talk now.' His voice sounded impersonal and business-like. 'But I will keep our appointment for nine o'clock at the usual restaurant. We can discuss your case then in detail. Goodbye.'

'He couldn't talk,' explained Eva. 'Probably had a girl-friend there.'

'If Hubert had a girlfriend I would kill the two of them.'

'I'm not involved.'

'You are not honest,' protested Else. 'Here, sit down and eat.' Eva began to chew with pleasure. The coffee was steaming, she was sitting next to Else.

'I don't believe in getting involved. It doesn't work for me.' She looked at her friend who was waiting for Hubert. 'But I'll never forget you,' Eva added. 'No matter where I am.'

'What a suntan you've got!' said Else.

'You look as if you need a holiday.'

'The air raids don't let me sleep. Bombs drop nearby and wake me up. Hubert sleeps right through the noise. Mr Lindner came over one day to let me know that you wouldn't be back yet.' Else held her coffee cup with the little finger sticking out. 'I was surprised he bothered coming. Marion claims he's started a love affair with Mrs Richter.'

152

'Mr Lindner is one person I would like to forget about but probably never will. He will haunt me to my dying day,' Eva said. 'And Marion?'

'Still up to her old tricks. Something's wrong with that girl. I can't work her out.'

'She was probably beaten too hard and too often.'

Hubert arrived and called out: 'Glad to see you, girlie. We missed you.' Then he discussed the expected shipment with Else. 'Hey,' he said afterwards, 'all those ration cards came in handy, right?'

'They saved our lives,' admitted Eva.

'That's why I'm successful. Always imagine what could go wrong.' He had his moment of glory.

'No more victory music over the radio,' said Else.

'What about the secret weapon?' asked Eva.

'The flying bomb? That's all he has up his sleeve and it won't get him far. No, the game is over, the war lost.'

Else served wine with dinner. Afterwards they had more coffee and filled the little kitchen with cigarette smoke.

'A game of cards?' asked Hubert.

'Arlen is coming to the office at nine.'

'I understand.' Hubert put on a smile.

'What is there to smile about?' Else asked angrily.

'Come now girlie – ' he tried to appease.

'No, I don't like it!' Else made it clear. 'Treating love like a dirty joke.'

'Calm down,' begged Eva. 'Don't start a fight. There's enough of it going on already.'

'I have to live with Hubert,' persisted Else.

'We're expecting a shipment,' said Hubert. 'So drop in at any time. We'll probably be here waiting.'

Eva walked slowly to the office, carrying her suitcase and looking at the familiar ruins. Nothing but destruction and desolation as far as she could see. Well, that was real life. She was far away from the Alpine beauty, the snow-covered mountain peaks, the blue sky, the diamond studded universe. She was back in the underworld where she knew how to behave. She took in the silence of the weekend night, the rising moon over the dead landscape and thought, 'Air-raid weather.'

She drew the curtain in Mr Lindner's office, switched on the light and realised that nothing had changed. She sat in the chair, lit a cigarette, as she had done so often and waited for Arlen. She could hardly believe that she had only arrived a few hours ago. 'I'll take off my skiing outfit,' she decided and began to rummage through the boxes containing her belongings which were stored in the adjoining, unused office. But before she could make up her mind which of the wrinkled garments to wear, she heard a knock at the front door.

They stood in the dark hallway holding each other with the intensity that comes with danger and threat. They were afraid of letting go. It was always in Arlen's presence that she felt her crippled state most.

'I missed you,' she told him.

'You stayed so long – ' He kissed her face. She guided him into Mr Lindner's office.

'You have a new girlfriend,' said Eva.

'Who told you?'

'I pieced things together.'

'Why did you stay so long?' It sounded accusing.

'The elements. Avalanches and snow. Storms too and being caught high up in the mountains. You can't imagine my loneliness and the fear about the future.'

'Poor pet.'

'That hardly covers it,' said Eva with sarcasm. 'Are you honestly in love?'

'I thought so until you called. Then, when I said I was leaving, she made a scene. These affairs do bore me. They hardly ever seem to differ. It's exciting to start with but I soon lose interest. Do you know what I mean?'

'I understand,' said Eva. 'But the girls don't. One moment you're crazy with love, the next you drop them because you get tired. What's supposed to happen to their love?'

'Who knows?' sighed Arlen. 'I'll keep this one a while longer, I expect.'

'Doesn't it feel good to be loved?' Eva asked.

'It's just an illusion. She doesn't know me at all.'

154

'Let's drop the subject. I expect you're right.' She suddenly became very sleepy. Her eyelids dropped like a wet and heavy blanket. She saw Arlen through the narrow spaces of her lashes, sliced and in odd shapes, then she put him together again by opening her eyes. She could have closed her eyes and still seen him. She knew him that well.

'Get some sheets,' he begged but Eva couldn't focus on any of the paraphernalia for lust, she could hardly take in that she was still sitting in Mr Lindner's chair with ski boots on.

'It's too much,' she said. 'I simply can't move a muscle.'

'Do you want me to come back tomorrow?'

'Would you? I don't understand why I got so tired suddenly. Go to your love, my pet.'

'Love is merely a madness!' Arlen waved his hand.

'Sounds like Shakespeare,' she yawned.

'Probably is,' he agreed. 'Go to bed. I'll see you tomorrow at nine.' Eva put her arms around his shoulder, then sank back on the chair and began to untie her bootlaces.

'Can you find your own way out?' she asked while she fell on the couch and pulled up the blanket over her skiing outfit. She was asleep immediately and dreamt of white, furry animals that lived in burrows. They killed each other in an orderly, systematic fashion. The larger killed the smaller and the smaller apparently took it for granted. Eva experienced the total madness of the scheme including the small animals' submission to their fate. It seemed so unavoidable that they lost all urge to resist while the bigger animals busied themselves in a brainless way with the arrangement of the dead. They put them down in rows, then regrouped them, busy as beavers and completely taken up by their task. Death was as much a business as looking for food or digging burrows. It depended on efficiency and proper planning, nothing else.

Chapter Eleven

Eva woke up depressed. 'I can't get up,' she realised. 'I'll never be able to get up.' She searched for her pulse but couldn't find it. Her heart started to race. She had to lie back again and close her eyes. Why hadn't she been wise and joined Friedrich in suicide? Then she wouldn't have to lift the curtains to see that it was only nine o'clock, that she had a long day ahead of her filled with despair. She almost started to cry, then remembered her dream, saw the small, furry animals line up to be killed. 'No, I won't!' she decided. 'I will have a great day!' She pulled at the string of the curtains and let the sun shine into the dismal office. She looked out of the small window, saw the diamonds dance on the murky water of the canal, greeted the church tower against the pale blue sky, saw the destruction and was satisfied. Then she decided on a pair of slacks and a turtleneck sweater, changed clothes and called up Darling.

'I'm back,' she announced.

'How wonderful! I was so worried. If Benny only knew what we are going through – I'm so glad he is where he is.'

'So am I. How have you been?'

'Worried. Any change in the situation?'

'Seems quiet, as before. Always the same wait-and-see tension.'

'I would like to have you today but Mrs Fischer is coming. Can you come Wednesday?'

So it would be Wednesday evening. Darling would listen

for five minutes to her adventures in the mountains and then she would return to her preoccupation with Benny. If Eva hadn't met Mr Bertram before, but only knew him through Darling's description, she certainly would have fallen in love with her Benny. He was such an extraordinary character. Darling drew him with more and more brilliance. 'Once the war is over, Benny is going to take care of me,' she had predicted. Benny could do anything.

Eva ran out into the spring sun and stopped at the bridge. A cool breeze blew through her sweater. April in Hamburg was seldom spring. She went back inside to get her ski jacket, then ran out down the street as if to escape something. Was it still her dream? Else and Hubert were sitting at the breakfast table in their dressing gowns.

'Am I glad to see you!' exclaimed Eva.

'What does that mean?' asked Else.

'Up so early?' Hubert smiled.

'I am glad to see you,' repeated Eva.

'Something happened?' asked Else.

'Only a strange dream.'

'Did Arlen come?' Hubert wanted to know.

'Yes, he is in love with someone but now doubts his feelings. Was charming, as usual. However, I sent him home because I felt too tired to get undressed. He's coming back tonight.'

'And his love?' questioned Else.

'Will suffer, I suppose. He gets involved too easily and doesn't realise the consequences it creates. He lacks foresight.'

'He should take a sensible girl and get married,' suggested Else. 'Actors need practical people.'

'That's the last thing they want,' said Eva with a smile.

'I don't know,' Else shook her head. 'There are too many crazy people on this earth.'

'Sunday breakfast is the nicest meal of the week,' Eva said.

'We're having a bath afterwards. I expect you need one too.'

'Always.' Eva stretched in the comfort of her friends' lives. They were still waiting for the shipment to arrive. Sitting on a volcano didn't frighten them. It had never erupted yet.

They ate and drank their coffee, glanced through the paper, made remarks, looked up, smiled. After the bath they ate again. Then Hubert picked up his crossword puzzle, Else her women's magazine full of sewing instructions and recipes. Eva listened to the radio playing Brahms' First Symphony. Else's hair hung yellow and straight down her back, making her look less prim and constricted but also less desirable. The golden crown was missing. Then the truck arrived and Hubert sent Eva away.

'There's no need for you to get involved,' he said. 'Come back in an hour.' She went to the office and called Werner.

'Why didn't you call?' she scolded.

'I did. There was no answer.'

'Sorry. How have you been?'

'Slept late after the terrible air raid.'

'Was there a raid? I must have slept right through it.'

'I met an interesting lady in the basement. She seems to admire me and got enthusiastic over my tan.'

'Are you interested?' asked Eva.

'She's beautiful and rich.'

'Be serious.' Eva got annoyed.

'I am serious,' he insisted. 'She seems sophisticated and dresses with great taste.'

'Society?'

'I suppose so. She's been married twice and has a daughter, nine years old.'

'How is the daughter?'

'Haven't seen her yet. She's been evacuated to somewhere in Bavaria with her grandparents.'

'Good, then you have her all to yourself,' said Eva.

'She invited me for dinner. Of course, she doesn't know about my mother and she might drop me once she finds out. We'll see. It will be a good test.'

'It certainly would prove a lot one way or the other.'

'Do you think it's right to go? It'll put her on the spot.'

'Come out with it right away. Don't eat at a table where you might not be welcome. But visit, take the chance.' Eva wondered for a moment if he understood what life was all about. Not that she understood it any better but at least she had experienced it, she thought. 'You know, it's a chance,' she went on. 'And could be beautiful.'

'We'll see,' he answered with no trace of his usual stuffiness.

'I just saw a yellow seagull fly by!' exclaimed Eva.

'Yellow?'

'Yes, it looked yellow. Might have been the sun though. I'll take a walk to the harbour now. Weather is brisk but fine. What are you doing?'

'Getting my clothes in order. Have to look presentable for the widow. Have you seen Arlen?'

'Last night for a moment. He's coming back later.'

'Have fun.'

'My God, Werner, we're living in the underworld!'

'All right, have fun on a relative scale then.'

'Thanks. Same to you.'

The air was still cool outside. Grass and weeds grew in patches on the ruins. The place was deserted, not a human being in sight. The harbour had the same desolate look as the destroyed streets around it. Only the splashes of an algae-green water against the stone quay wall reminded Eva of life's dizzy dance. A thin veil of white clouds moved in from the north. Eva walked along the quay towards the dock from where they had departed during the air raid. She ran down the steps and jumped on to a boat, lay on the wooden floor for a moment, listened to the water splash against the hollow body. She got up. The wind pulled at her hair, blew through her clothes. It was not spring yet, not in Hamburg. But she was glad to be back, to be able to jump from boat to boat, to walk for miles along the quay, through bombed-out streets, to sit near Else and feel her warmth, to expect Arlen.

When Eva returned from her walk Else and Hubert were reading the paper. The delivered goods were stored behind hidden doors.

'You took a long walk,' said Else. 'Want a section of the paper?'

'I talked to Werner. He said there'd been a raid last night.'

'Certainly was,' confirmed Else. 'Woke me up several times.'

'I want to catch Marion before it gets dark. I hate to climb up the stairs at night. It always gives me the creeps.'

'Don't stay long. We have cake and coffee.'

Marion had come out of the apartment and was looking down the winding stairs. 'Who's there?' she called.

'Eva! Come down to my office!'

'When did you come back? What a tan! God, I missed you!' Marion said, sitting on Mr Lindner's couch. 'Nobody to talk to. Nothing's changed since you went away. Still reading my novels and working at night. I had a fight with my friend. She wanted to borrow 500 marks for drugs. I wouldn't lend her a penny, not for dope. So we don't see each other any more and it gets very lonely at times. Some guys talk, but others think I'm too stupid because I work as a prostitute. Last week a soldier invited me to a dance. That was fun. I gave him a "free" one afterwards.' The conversation dragged on. Else was waiting with coffee and cake. Marion looked lonely, trying to keep Eva at all cost.

'Else is waiting for me. Want to come along?'

Marion checked her watch. 'It's too late. Have to get ready. But thanks all the same.'

Arlen sat in Mr Lindner's chair and looked at Eva, who dangled her legs from the desk.

'I'm a wreck!' he confessed. 'Such scenes and tears you have never seen. My God, she was taking over my life, trying to mould me into a different shape. Now we had to do this, now that, now I was the hero, now the big bad wolf. I admit, I was amused in the beginning. It felt like a holiday from real life. But then – what a nightmare!' He sighed.

'Rather a sudden discovery,' said Eva with a smile.

'Agreed, I'm easily taken in but something always makes me wake up. This time it was your return. You know how vulnerable I am to influences of the wrong kind. Louisa will cry for a few hours; it can't be helped – then she'll find someone else who will do just as well.'

'It's hard to know what one wants,' said Eva, turning a little matchbox over and over in her hands.

'You mean two people making it together?' he questioned.

'Yes, do you want that?' Eva turned the matchbox.

'When I have it, I begin to resent what it does.'

'What?' Eva turned the matchbox.

'The finality, the end of the search, the end of a vision. It's better not to find it.'

'You always have the theatre.'

'Yes, the theatre. I almost forgot.'

'Is that a love affair?' asked Eva.

'No, it's part of me, I can't lose it.'

The electric light was glaring. They saw each other's faces like familiar landscapes. They would keep up their intimacy without ever putting it to the test.

'Up in the mountains I was yearning for the wasteland, for my desk with its ledger. I began to prefer the office to climbing up snowy slopes and skiing down them again – all that appeared to be the height of lunacy.'

'Got anything to drink?' Eva poured out brandy. He stared at his glass without touching it.

'Louisa is suffering,' said Eva.

'I am sure she is. But is peace of mind a desirable state?'

'If it brings happiness – ' mused Eva.

'I had everything prepared for hiding you.'

'Sure.' Eva smiled. 'While Louisa moved into your apartment. It would never have worked out anyway. We can't live together. I don't want to spoil what we've got.'

'And what is that?' he asked.

'Something I love.'

'Please don't talk of love!' He drank, then poured himself another brandy. 'I can't hear that word any more.'

'All right, I won't rub it in.' Tonight it would have been so easy to find sheets and spread them over the couch. But tonight Arlen bobbed far on the crest of his wave, unreachable.

'I'd better get home before the raid starts. Will I see you tomorrow? Come after work.'

'If I can play a few records.'

'As many as you like. Louisa brought her own. They blared from morning till night, every bit of trash ever recorded. What do you think I did?' he asked her.

'You enjoyed it,' laughed Eva.

'We danced every step, moving in rhythm, nothing was natural any more. There was this constant music, life was lived with a beat, beating the mind, beating the blood.'

'A bad beat?' Eva shook her head with sorrow.

'You should have heard Renate's verdict. We had a row.'

'She'll come round, now Louisa's gone.' Eva walked with Arlen across the bridge up to the square. The sky was covered with a thin layer of clouds. Moonbeams appeared diffused over the ruins. Eva embraced Arlen and watched at the same time their joined shadow on the pavement. It might be the last time, she thought.

'Get home safely, good night, good night.'

Eva kept on walking towards the harbour. 'Don't rush and don't run,' she told herself. 'This is a beautiful night which will never return.' Tomorrow she would have to explain her long absence, endure Miss Ehrlich's jealous and accusing eyes, listen to Mrs Richter's bellowing laughter, play Mr Schiller's status game and submit to Mr Lindner's . . . she was not sure what he would offer her. She anticipated a wide range of possibilities. 'Don't think of tomorrow,' she reminded herself. 'Slow down, take in the moment.' The water splashed – splashed against the stone wall; time was ticking away.

There would be an air raid tonight. She watched the bobbing boats and barges and was grateful they didn't turn into white mountain tops. Had she made a date with Werner? No, he was taken up by his elegant widow who was no doubt looking for another husband. First she had to seduce the teddy bear and turn him into a man. But she seemed to be the right woman with enough experience and drive. And if no labour camp put a stop to the relationship, Eva thought, Werner's future was secured. She smiled because that was what Werner wanted: stability and security. Splash – splash went the river, moving out again or coming in, destroying on its way or giving birth – nothing was secure.

Back at the office she called Arlen. 'Let's make it another evening,' she suggested. 'It wouldn't work. I'll call you.'

'All right,' Arlen sounded slightly offended. 'I'll get Renate to come then.'

'Give her my love.'

'Why do you say these things?' he asked.

'What things?'

'Not coming – '

'Because at the moment I feel I don't belong to anybody's life.'

'How can you say that?'

'Don't talk like everybody else,' she complained. 'You know I'm right. Think of the tensions on the Alpine trip. Then picture your Louisa affair. I can't combine these worlds. Talk it out with Renate. How is Eduard?'

'Still optimistic, but with a growing shadow of a doubt.'

'And Olga?'

'In love with her doctor, working at the hospital. Officials are still debating if she should be in a labour camp or stay at the hospital. She seems to take it all in her stride.'

'Those Russians are remarkably tough. Never expect anything from life but survival. Good night, my pet, sleep well.'

'Don't forget to call. Good night.' He hung up. 'Now he's trying to get hold of Renate,' Eva thought. She smiled with satisfaction as if she had accomplished a difficult task.

Miss Ehrlich's slender figure was crossing the bridge, leaning against the wind, balancing an open umbrella in one hand and carrying a large shopping bag in the other. Eva watched her from the small window, amused with the fight she was having against the wind, clutching the pointed, unsteady umbrella like a frightened fencer. Suddenly the wind subsided and Miss Ehrlich stumbled forward with unexpected speed.

Eva was shocked by the pale, drawn face with its hopeless expression, but her tenacity had not broken down completely, at least not on the surface. Soon there appeared the familiar smile, pretending cheerfulness. 'Whatever dreams she might have harboured,' thought Eva, 'she has not yet given them up.'

'You look absolutely wonderful!' exclaimed Miss Ehrlich. 'I wish I could get away for just one week.'

'Hardly, under my circumstances. I didn't leave for my

pleasure.' Eva wanted to make this clear.

'I think at the moment I would go under any circumstances.' Miss Ehrlich sighed and smiled at the same time.

'Is it your mother?'

'Mother, the air raids, the war, the office – ' She could have gone on with her list.

'The office?' asked Eva.

'Mrs Richter taking liberties – '

'But you are irreplaceable,' assured Eva. 'You're doing Mr Lindner's work and he knows it. Mrs Richter has no experience.'

'I'm not afraid of losing my job,' she said. 'I know what I know. It's her taking over, treating me like a minor office clerk and laughing – laughing – '

'How is your mother?'

Miss Ehrlich had spread her wet clothes and open umbrella over the office, rubbed her hands dry with a pocket handkerchief and sat down in front of her desk to open the mail.

'She's not as bad as she pretends to be. Just wants attention and it wears me down. Of course, I have to be continuously nice otherwise she raises hell.'

'You seem to have a very difficult time.' Eva felt genuinely sorry though she also thought to herself: 'Serves you right!'

'While others enjoy themselves – ' Miss Ehrlich was close to tears. She bent down to take off her galoshes.

'Be glad some people are not suffering,' said Eva.

'It's unfair,' complained Miss Ehrlich, looking through her bag for a clean handkerchief.

'Hope Mr Lindner won't fire me,' said Eva.

'Definitely not. He was very concerned.'

'I can't afford to lose my job,' she sighed.

'What weather!' Miss Ehrlich was trying to get back to her office position. 'And yesterday it smelled of spring.'

Loud laughter came from the adjoining room. 'Go and say hello,' whispered Miss Ehrlich. 'I don't want her in my office.'

Eva dutifully went next door and was overwhelmed by friendliness. Mr Schiller called her 'girlie' and Mrs Richter enquired after her well being and the trip. Laughter interrupted Eva's replies, which she cut short to escape to her own office. She sat at her desk and looked at the ledger. She was two months behind. It would be a dismal task catching up. But she noticed too that there had been fewer transactions. Business had been slack – there was a limit now to animal slaughter, and there were no more victories. Did it finally occur to them that conquest was turning into defeat, that soon Jew-hunting might become unfashionable?

It was clear to her that a change had taken place when Mr Lindner greeted her like an old friend. He spoke of a possible invasion in France by American and British troops, which, if successful, Germany couldn't combat. 'We can't fight a three-frontier war,' he explained. How realistic they suddenly sounded.

'I might be in greater danger when things look bad,' said Eva.

'At the moment all seems quiet,' assured Mr Lindner.

'Yes, but for how long?' She looked him in the eye. 'I'd better get back to work.'

Eva was running up the stairs as Darling, waiting on the landing, called out her name. Darling's white hair, which had fine strands of grey in it, sat smooth and orderly around her head and her short, round figure remained steady in spite of the excitement. She looked down the dark shaft of stairs and realised that she had forgotten to take off her apron. Well, Eva wouldn't mind. They had more important things to talk about.

'How good to see you again!' exclaimed Eva. Of course it was a lie. She had said it for the benefit of the old lady. Darling had been her obligation now for years and somehow she felt responsible for her well being. She sat patiently listening to the complaints, to the daily edges that rubbed against Darling's white and wrinkled skin.

'A few more months,' she promised, 'and my Benny will be here to ring the bell.'

'Don't get carried away,' warned Eva. 'There will still be fighting before it's over.'

They drank coffee. A present from Else, as usual.

'I want to listen to the BBC's ten o'clock news.' Darling turned the volume of her radio down, holding it against her ear. The loudspeaker canvas showed a round smudge. In Italy the fighting continued on an escalated scale, which didn't sound too promising, though Darling insisted that it meant victory. The eastern front was steadily advancing and both acknowledged this with mixed feelings. Darling did not take out the deck of cards that night. They had talked a lot and it would be too late to start a game. Eva wanted to get home before a raid started.

'Next time we'll have a nice game of bridge,' Darling promised as if Eva had been deprived of her pleasure. 'Come and see me soon.' She was almost in tears.

'I will, I will!' Eva ran down the stairs. Outside it rained with gale-force winds. 'Hamburg,' she thought and felt elated because the visit lay behind her, and she didn't have to wake up to white mountain peaks. Walking towards the tram station she thought of Arlen. No, she didn't want to see him and hear about Louisa. This time she would wait until he called. It was the best solution. She stood at the dark street corner, felt the rain touch her skin and smiled. 'Considering our blunders – ' she thought. 'My God, the world is full of blunders!'

Chapter Twelve

Else and Eva were putting the dinner dishes away. Hubert sat stretched out in his easy chair finishing the evening paper. There had been a day raid which had broken all the small windows in Eva's office. One bomb had exploded in the canal and several others had hit the rubble heaps and burnt-out houses. When they had returned from the shelter they saw through the broken windows a man hanging over the bridge, his body split open. Mr Lindner had notified some authority and later a car had come to take the corpse away. Then the workmen had arrived to measure the window frames and promised to have the glass ready the following morning.

Since Eva's return the weather had changed to something like spring. Mrs Richter interrupted her laughter with sentimental songs these days and stayed for hours in Mr Lindner's office taking dictation.

'They're being too nice to me at the office,' Eva said. 'I liked it better when they showed their true colours.'

'They may have changed their minds.' Hubert folded the evening paper. 'Remember, they changed them before.'

'They are the most detestable lot!' declared Eva.

'Have mercy,' said Else.

'Who has mercy on Jews?' asked Eva.

'Don't start on that subject,' insisted Hubert. 'It gives me high blood pressure.'

'You should get married to Else,' said Eva.

'I can't jeopardise her safety,' Hubert defended himself.

'If she were your wife she'd be better protected, at least in law.'

'Stop arguing,' said Else though she shared Eva's opinion. Marriage could easily be postponed until after the war, she thought, stroking her hair from the neck up to feel if everything was in order. She went to the kitchen; Hubert was leaning back in his chair and unfolded another paper. Eva too leaned back, remembering her conversation with Werner.

'We had dinner together last night,' he had reported, 'and before I left it happened.'

'What happened?' Eva had asked, not caring in the least.

'I kissed her,' confessed Werner.

'Is that the truth?' Eva had continued to write entries into the ledger while Werner confessed his love.

'Well, she kissed me first but I kissed her back.'

'Perhaps you've become desirable since the Normandy invasion,' sneered Eva.

'She invited me before.'

'They're too nice to me at the office,' Eva had complained. 'I don't feel comfortable.'

'Helen is very nice and I enjoy it.' Eva had wondered what the widow Helen got out of a stuffed teddy bear but decided that it was not her business. Anyway, he came from a very respectable family and looked sophisticated. Helen came from money, as far as Eva could make out, though nobody in her family knew what to do with it except to buy houses and things. Apparently when they argued they screamed at each other like street traders – Helen had told Werner that they were rather temperamental and vulgar, but Werner thought this was an exaggeration.

After dinner Eva sat over a map and followed the battle lines in France. Hubert was listening to the news on his battery-run short-wave radio. Once the Americans and British had established solid footholds and were gaining ground, they sighed with relief.

Eva reported that the friendliness in the office continued. Only Miss Ehrlich had days of depression when her black mood spilled over.

Mrs Richter had been in Mr Lindner's office taking dictation when Eva clearly overheard him say: 'We'll have to dispose of her before it's too late,' and immediately the situation became obvious to her. They were plotting to get rid of her, being friendly and nice so that she wouldn't suspect anything.

'She mustn't suspect anything,' Mrs Richter was actually telling Mr Schiller when Eva entered their office.

'Who is "she"?' Eva had asked, hardly able to speak. Mrs Richter had paused for an inappropriate length of time before she replied that she was referring to her mother whom she planned to surprise with a visit in the summer.

'Are they plotting against me?' Eva wanted to know with urgency.

'You're crazy,' diagnosed Hubert.

'I am not insane and I don't imagine things,' protested Eva. 'They're in touch with the Gestapo, covering their tracks.'

'The Gestapo would have come in ten minutes,' said Hubert.

'I'm a sitting duck.'

'You're imagining things, but if you want to disappear, I can make arrangements with my friends tomorrow. They'll hide you, you'll be safe.'

Eva was thinking of the Alpine imprisonment and didn't look forward to another one. On the other hand any safe place was preferable to her increased fears at the office.

She went to see Arlen and told him her story. 'Do you think I'm crazy?' she asked.

'You have every reason to be suspicious. Wasn't Lindner a Gestapo spy writing reports to denounce people?'

'One report, as far as I know.'

'That's bad enough.'

'Yes, but he didn't send it out, I persuaded him to throw it –'

'Then he wouldn't dispose of you,' concluded Arlen.

'You can't tell with these people. Who knows what they did in Russia? Perhaps they think Friedrich told me.'

'You have nothing to fear,' Arlen said with conviction

because it made him feel better.

'What did Mr Lindner mean by ". . . before it's too late"?' asked Eva.

'Before the war is over, I guess,' answered Arlen. 'Why didn't you call me?'

'Because I don't want to hang round your neck like a wreath after the funeral. I have to find my own solutions.'

'Then come when you want to come.'

'I'm afraid it would be too often and each time will end with another disappointment.'

'Yes, disappointment,' he agreed. 'That's what it usually amounts to. I miss the theatre.'

'You'll get it back soon,' she promised.

'We talk as if we were lost at night in the woods, pretending not to be frightened.'

'That's what you do when you're lost in the woods,' said Eva.

'Will you stay overnight?' he asked.

'It might be our last chance. Hubert has suggested hiding me with friends.'

'You have nothing to fear,' Arlen repeated.

'Then why do they talk of disposal?' she asked vehemently and clung like a wreath round his neck. The word 'disposal' had unsettled her completely.

Eva sat at her desk facing the small, square window, knowing that the sky was blue, though she couldn't see it. Only the grey burnt-out houses opposite the canal appeared like a framed picture on the spotted glass. She took another sip of Else's coffee and felt her heart beat faster. 'It's the coffee,' she diagnosed. Her system was out of order. She had not slept during the night and had received an ultimatum from Hubert to make up her mind. His friends had to know whether or not she was coming. The empty lines on the ledger sheet became blurred, credit mingled with debit. 'How am I ever going to get through the day?' she thought when Mr Lindner's excited voice next door became audible. Again Eva heard mention of 'disposal', only this time she heard the words 'insurance', 'law suit' and 'court' too. Mr Lindner was talking of a shipment of raw hides and barrels of animal intestines, goods for which he had paid a high price and which had not come up to expectation. Eva suddenly saw the entire picture, understood her previous conclusions. Disposed Jews were like rotten intestines. It was – it was – words failed her. She had better run over to tell Else that she wouldn't have to go into hiding, that the game of pretended friendliness would continue. At least Miss Ehrlich wasn't pretending. Perhaps she felt free of guilt. Her narrow office world, the constant demands from an ailing mother and her patriotism allowed no room for a critical view. Things appeared so simple and clear when the flags were hoisted, the marches sung by heroes. Germany stayed wrapped around her soul like the national anthem, excluding all suspicion of wrongdoing. That the Jewish owners of the company had been chased out of the country didn't disturb her conscience. Jews were foreigners who had taken property away from German people in the first place. It was therefore only fitting that they hand it back to the rightful owners. Eva had listened to all of Miss Ehrlich's contemptible arguments yet couldn't feel contempt for her. Perhaps it was the poverty of her existence that made her pity the pale spinster with the shiny hairpins. Miss Ehrlich's cheerfulness had faded away like her youth. She looked so innocent and indignant. Somehow Eva couldn't feel 'serves you right!' any more towards Miss Ehrlich.

The men and Mrs Richter were on their way to lunch. She looked at her balance sheet. The morning was gone and she hadn't done a thing.

'The crisis is over,' said Eva, standing at the store counter picking up her sandwich.

'Everything all right?' asked Else.

'I suppose so.'

'Next, please,' Else smiled.

'How are you?' asked Eva over the phone.

'Tired. One never gets enough sleep with these nightly raids.'

'I didn't sleep either,' complained Eva. 'Good for nothing. How is your widow?'

'We are both happy,' confessed Werner in his teddy bear voice.

'As long as you enjoy it – ' Eva laughed.

'Don't be such a cynic,' Werner begged. 'Dr Kromer thinks I'm treating you unfairly. He admires your good manners.'

'What a bore! Helen's manners are not impressive?'

'No, she has no class, just money, he claims.'

'But she makes you happy,' insisted Eva.

'He can't see that and I don't talk about it.'

'Teddy bears should be looked after. They can easily get damaged,' said Eva.

'Don't worry, Helen is doing it fine.'

'I'll check with you from time to time. Can't say I feel at all comfortable.'

'You never feel comfortable, that's your trouble.'

'I'm too clear-sighted. Don't let it bother you.'

'Nothing can, not at the moment.'

Eva dialled Darling's number and immediately got pressed into an evening of bridge.

'I'm sick and tired of patience,' Darling confessed.

'Everybody is tired nowadays. Be glad you're not bombed out and evacuated into a village.'

Darling laughed. 'Come one evening for a bridge game,' she begged.

'I'll come, but not for bridge. I too have my needs,' said Eva.

'Not one single game?'

'Not one. You have your daytime friends.'

'Less and less,' complained Darling.

'Well, it's less and less everywhere.'

Hubert shuffled the cards with vigour and put the deck before Eva to cut.

'Hey,' he nudged her, 'stop dreaming. Cut the cards.' Eva made three piles and put them together again. 'Thanks,' said Hubert. 'That was nice of you.'

'Stop teasing,' shouted Else. 'Eva's bored.'

Eva was watching the cigarette smoke curl around the electric bulb. Shapes moved, danced, spread out like soft silky veils and then defused. The air was hot. Kitchen smells, tobacco and alcohol mixed with the perspiration of human bodies.

'After this game we have to open the front door and sit for a while in the dark,' suggested Else.

'Put your money in the till,' ordered Hubert, who hoped to win. He threw the cards on to the table, counting each deal out loud, one – two – three. Else and Eva picked up their cards the moment they were dealt out. Else smiled. Eva forgot what she was doing. She thought of the great victories and of the fact that a wounded animal was more dangerous than a healthy one.

'Hey,' said Hubert, 'do you want the seven?' Eva sat up, startled, glanced at the cards and picked one from the pile, leaving the seven on the table. 'I hope you know what you are doing,' continued Hubert.

'She doesn't mind losing,' said Else. 'Not everyone is a born gambler.'

'Come on, play!' Hubert grew more impatient the longer the game progressed.

'Give me time to think,' said Else. 'You like to rush people.'

'I'm not rushing you. You simply take all evening to make up your mind.' They both laughed. It was their personal game. Eva enjoyed her friends' involvement. She drank more brandy and began to sense the outlines of her body, as if in a picture, comfortably settled on a cushioned bench. She was giving her winning card away because she didn't care and her friends were so eager to win.

'Eva has a gift for losing,' Hubert observed.

'I'm going to beat you tonight.' Else leaned over the table and touched Hubert's face affectionately.

'No, you won't!' He shook his head. 'What's the score? Put your money in the till.'

'Let's open the door for a while,' pleaded Eva. They sat in the dark and waited for a breeze to come from the sea, but little blew their way. Eva got up and walked into the street where the stuffiness was almost as heavy. Nothing stirred. The night was light, like most northern summer nights. She noticed the high weeds on the ruins, thought that it felt as if a thunderstorm was on its way, but could see only a clear, starry sky. Summer, thought Eva, how glorious!

'Summer,' she said, returning to the kitchen.

'What do you expect in June?' asked Hubert. 'Go, close the door and let's finish the game.' He was rather restless.

They were playing again when a knock was heard at the front door. It was a timid knock yet all sat up for a second, frozen with fright.

'It must be Arlen,' said Hubert.

'We should agree on a signal,' added Else, who was trembling.

Eva got up and made her way to the door.

'You scared us to death,' she greeted him. 'We ought to agree on a signal.'

'I'm sorry. I knocked as softly as possible.'

'I know you did. It just scared us for a second. Come in.'

'Can't you come out? I haven't seen you for ages. Why do you hide?'

'You never think of me while you're amused by others,' said Eva.

'They bore me,' he insisted. 'You don't believe me.'

'You're a bad liar.'

'Come on in!' called Hubert from inside. She took his hand and guided him through the store.

'Want to join our card game?' asked Hubert.

'No, thanks. I don't play. Come to elope with Eva.'

'Have a brandy.'

'And a cup of coffee with a ham sandwich,' added Else.

'What luxuries,' said Arlen and sat down.

'It's all a question of risk,' said Hubert as if he were a business tycoon.

'You need talent, that's for sure,' explained Else. 'Hubert is a genius, he considers any potential for error far in advance, then plans his operations accordingly. Nothing ever goes wrong.'

'It's not that difficult. Fortunately Hitler has corrupted the nation. Everybody can be bought.' He poured Arlen another glass of brandy. 'Supplies are diminishing though,' he added.

'The real struggle will come after the war.'

Arlen bit into his ham sandwich. 'They can't let us starve.'

'Why not? We let everybody else starve.'

'Anything is possible,' commented Else, sitting down and smoothing her hair with one hand in an habitual gesture.

'Tastes like Turkish mocha,' Arlen began to enjoy himself. 'And the brandy is first rate.'

'Only the best for us,' Hubert said with satisfaction.

Eva smoked a cigarette and watched the single light bulb through the smoke as it hung over their heads like the moon. It had looked white and silvery before, now it shone golden. She leaned back and realised how much energy she had spent simply playing cards. Living through one day was an exhausting business and now Arlen had come to make further demands on her depleted strength. The bulb had a yellow halo when she squinted her eyes. 'I haven't discovered one ounce of truth yet,' she thought to herself, 'or I'm blind and can't see where it lies.' She got frightened that she was sailing past some truth without realising it. The yellow halo was still there when she squinted her eyes.

'She doesn't think it's funny,' complained Arlen.

'I wasn't listening,' apologised Eva.

'A penny for your thoughts,' said Hubert.

'Puzzles. Trying to solve them.'

'She's always out to find gold,' said Else.

'Truth,' corrected Eva. 'But it doesn't exist.'

'So why keep looking?' asked Hubert.

'That's just the point,' said Eva. 'I can't stop it.'

It was late but Eva insisted on walking to the harbour.

'We'll have an air raid any minute.'

'What's the rush?' They walked slowly, with long shadows stretching ahead of them through the streets. 'I need some air.'

They had reached the harbour and sat on one of the barges moored at the dockside. The air was cooler here, even a slight breeze touched their skin. The water smelled of algae and rotting spoils.

'I had a letter from Olga, smuggled out of a labour camp. She's unhappy,' Arlen said. 'The Gestapo insisted she do her duty and spy. She met a girl there she knew from Kiev who knew that her father had been killed for collaborating with the Germans. Of course, he had been killed for Olga's collaboration. Nobody else in her family ever spoke to a German. They're calling her a traitor and murderer. She's reported the situation to the Gestapo but they haven't answered yet, perhaps never will. All she wants now is to return to the hospital as soon as possible.'

'Do you feel sorry for her?' asked Eva.

'Who wouldn't?' Arlen asked back. 'Being squeezed between two evil powers.'

'I have the feeling she's quite their equal, always out for her best interest.'

'What other choice does she have?'

'Very little. If the Russians get her she's signing her death warrant. She has to pacify the Gestapo for the time being and later turn to the Americans for help.'

The sirens howled through the night and they walked back through the empty streets towards her office building which stood like a liner between broken tug boats and barges.

'Leave the door open,' suggested Eva. 'You can't breathe inside.'

'Anybody can walk right in.'

'Nobody does, they're downstairs in the shelter.'

'People from the street – '

'Nobody lives here and nobody comes except Marion's customers,' replied Eva.

'There you are, they might walk in.'

'Then lock the door.' Eva had no strength left to argue.

'Your friends are very nice,' said Arlen.

'Without them I'd be lost,' replied Eva, thinking of sheets. Where had she put them? She wasn't at all in the mood for sheets. 'I have to look for sheets,' she said. 'Else is particularly nice,' she added, thinking that they were all castaways after a shipwreck, having to compromise and make believe in order to survive.

'Life seems simple and uncomplicated with them,' reflected Arlen.

Eva was pulling a crumpled, stored-away sheet from a

drawer. Anti-aircraft guns were heard far away, sirens howled the warning signal. Then the shooting came nearer and intensified. Bombs exploded, the ground shook, shrapnel hit the pavement outside the closed window.

'It's getting close,' commented Arlen.

'It's always close around the harbour.'

'I should have left the door open,' said Arlen. Their skin was wet and slippery.

'Not now.'

'No, not now.'

Chapter Thirteen

It was a hot July evening when Eva walked over to the delicatessen. Else stood in the kitchen stirring something in a pot, whistling a tune which didn't remind Eva of anything she knew. Else had her own repertoire.

'Hello,' said Eva. 'What makes you so cheerful?'

'Not cheerful, just excited. Haven't you heard?'

'No, what?'

'The assassination attempt on Hitler by a resistance group. Apparently military and political people – high ranking. They failed, not a scratch on him! Now they've started to round up the conspirators – mass arrests. Hitler's like a mad dog, wants to hang them all.' Else switched on the radio. They were still reporting on the events, on new arrests and mass executions. Nobody would be spared. Eva switched off the radio.

'I can't bear it,' she said with a frightened voice. 'Do you think they're going to arrest us now?'

'Anything is possible,' said Else while attending to the simmering food. 'If I were you I wouldn't return to the office, take no chances. Perhaps you can stay with Arlen for a few days. Then if necessary Hubert's friends will certainly hide you. Just let us know.'

Eva felt paralysed just at a time when she should be alert. 'I can't eat,' was all she could say.

'Of course you can. Now call Arlen and ask if you can go round after dinner.'

Eva got up automatically, dialled the number and waited

for Arlen's voice. 'Can I come after dinner?' she asked. 'I think it's important.'

'I know,' answered Arlen. 'Don't worry, just come.'

Eva was sitting in Arlen's apartment. It had always been her sanctuary, but tonight it felt exposed to the elements just like any other place in the city.

'You have to hold me through the night, otherwise I might crumble. One moment I feel nothing and then I get tossed into a horrible pit. No, it's much worse. I can't describe it.'

'You're safe here for the time being and if it becomes necessary, Else's friends will hide you.'

'How can I find out?' Eva couldn't imagine anything any more.

'You call your boss.'

'He'll be waiting for me tomorrow.'

'I'll give him a call from a public telephone.'

'Not a scratch on Hitler – '

'He's madder than ever.'

'Hold me.' Eva clung to Arlen like a drowning woman. Her nerves were taut. She didn't let him sleep but demanded his attention with a frenzy. In the morning, after he'd gone to work, she finally slept.

Arlen was exhausted when he came home. Eva cooked dinner and they discussed her situation while they ate and drank wine.

'Call your boss early tomorrow morning at his house. Get him out of bed. There's the telephone book, look up the number.' Arlen felt euphoric from the wine and the plan he was developing. Eva rose slowly from her pit. She had to act, to plan, to save her life. She wrote down Mr Lindner's home number.

'I've set the alarm for six-thirty. You have to catch him before he leaves.'

'Then everything is settled.' Eva was amazed. 'Either I stay here or Hubert will send me into hiding.'

'He offered it before, didn't he?' asked Arlen.

'Yes, he means what he says. However, one never knows, not even with best friends. They might get scared. You might throw me out under certain pressures. I wouldn't blame you.'

'Don't think it hasn't entered my mind,' said Arlen. 'But really, either we join the rats or we're on your side.'

'You can also stay neutral.'

'No, you can't.'

Arlen yawned, said he was tired and fell asleep. Eva lit a cigarette. 'I have to stay up and think about the plan,' she told herself. 'What should I ask Mr Lindner tomorrow morning? Have you received any visitors for me lately? Or, Has anyone come to ask for me? Have men come – ? No, the visitors sounded best.' She stretched out on the sofa, put a pillow under her head and fell asleep.

When the alarm woke her she had become herself again, Eva Ehrenfels, a half-Jew, who had to make an important telephone call. Her pulse was racing. She tried to count her heartbeat. 'I should be in an emergency ward,' she thought.

'Don't chicken out, call the number,' insisted Arlen.

'Do you know that the most perfect days are those when a blue sky has tinges of purple in it?' she asked her friend.

'For heaven's sake, call him!' he shouted.

'Hello Mr Lindner. Have any visitors come to see me?' she asked.

'You haven't even dialled the number.' Arlen got annoyed.

'I'm just rehearsing.' Eva checked her pulse.

'This is no joke. And I have to get to the factory on time.'

Eva was dialling. The telephone rang.

'Would you mind feeling my pulse?'

'It will pass,' said Arlen.

'Of course,' thought Eva, 'it will stop.' There was Mr Lindner on the line.

'Sorry to disturb you so early but – ' she repeated her rehearsed question.

'Yes,' answered Mr Lindner, 'and they promised to return today.'

'How nice. Tell them you have heard I've gone away. And look for a new book-keeper.'

'I understand,' said Mr Lindner with a smooth, gentle voice. 'Don't worry about us. Good luck.'

She put down the receiver. 'I hope nobody was listening in.'

'Doubt it. They can only spot check. Now call Hubert.'
She dialled again.

'Hello,' she said. 'Could you get me a place somewhere?'

'Everything's already arranged. Heard from Marion. Now
don't worry about a thing, not a thing, hear? Else went and
collected your clothes in the knapsack. Come tonight at ten to
the dock below the quay we left from during the raid. A truck
will arrive to pick you up on the dot.'

'Can my friend take me there?' asked Eva. Hubert didn't
answer immediately. Apparently he was contemplating the
move.

'All right,' he said finally. 'A couple is less conspicuous
than a girl on her own at the quay. But make him leave before
ten. And understand: no worries, none. We'll come and visit
you one of these days. The rest you will hear from my friend
in the truck. Do you want to talk to my better half?'

'No,' said Eva nervously. 'Only my love and thanks to
both of you.' She hung up.

'Tell me,' urged Arlen. 'I can't be late.'

Eva reported. 'I'll go with you,' he said because he knew it
was expected of him. 'Take it easy.' He ran into the bathroom.

'It's only my heart beating,' she explained, but Arlen was
already under the shower.

'I need hot water to shave,' called Arlen.

Later they sat at a kitchen table spread with crumpled,
greasy papers containing cold meats and pieces of bread. Eva
had heated last night's coffee.

'Will you buy our dinner?' she asked. 'Let me get the ration
cards.' She handed him the coupons.

'My God, it's late! Try not to worry.' He dashed to the
door. 'Lock it from the inside.' 'Don't make yourself visible
or audible,' Eva added in her mind, realising that it wasn't a
joke, no game, that the Gestapo might be busy combing
houses for hidden conspirators. She cleaned up their mess in
the kitchen, then called the Kromers.

'Where's Werner?' she asked without giving her name.

'Oh, I am so glad to hear from you,' exclaimed Mrs
Kromer. 'My husband and I have been worried. Werner is in

181

a barrack camp outside the city, cleaning streets, clearing rubble. I don't like the idea but I doubt it's alarming yet.'

'Have you tried to intervene?'

'We tried but it's no use, not right now, nobody is listening.'

'I'm leaving for the country on holiday. Won't be able to get in touch with you. But say hello to your husband and give my love to Werner if you have a chance.'

'Not much of a chance but we keep on trying.'

Eva was lying on the couch and thought of the poor teddy bear in prison garb, sweeping the streets, hungry, exhausted, not knowing how to deal with the underworld. Another string pulled blindly to destroy the defenceless. Should she call Darling? She wished so much for a human voice. But was it wise? She had now made three incriminating phone calls. If they'd been listening in someone would have been here by now to arrest her. On the other hand – if they had listened in – they had her already in the bag, could easily afford to wait, record more incriminating calls and catch her tonight at the quay, together with Arlen and the truck driver. To hell with it! she concluded. If anything happened it was her own fault, she should have called from a phone box. However, that didn't make any difference. If they listened in they knew she was being picked up at ten tonight somewhere along the quay, in the neighbourhood of her office. 'Don't worry.' Hubert must have been joking! She looked at the alarm clock; the hands had hardly moved since Arlen left. If things went all right and she should be picked up without interference, he would sigh with relief because she'd been taken off his hands and he could live again, carefree. She understood. It was terrible to be involved. Poor Werner. Imprisoned just when he had found love, and probably for the first time in his life. He had been so full of optimism and illusions. 'I'm wise to keep detached,' she told herself without pride. Hubert always says, first things first. Mrs Richter would do the book-keeping and laugh louder and louder while the war was coming to an end.

The day seemed endless. She fell asleep for a while and was glad that the clock showed half-past one. She went to the kitchen and ate more bread and cold meats, then drank another warmed-up cup of coffee. Why had she made a whole pot of coffee when only two cups were needed? It wasn't a disaster. But if she was careless with a move of importance she might get herself and others into trouble. Was she more scared than she'd been yesterday now that she knew they were looking for her? Yes, definitely. Everything depended on the moves of others, on Hubert's underworld and the Gestapo. She was just a ball in the middle that someone would catch and put away. If she should die soon she hadn't done more in her life than fly up and down a windowpane like a poor, dumb insect, insisting on doing the same thing over and over again, getting her wings and body bruised in an attempt to reach the lit room that lay behind the glass. She could have turned round and flown back into the garden but her fascination with the lit room had been such that she hadn't cared about the bruises. She'd been lying on the windowsill sick and exhausted most of the time. An invalid insect on a narrow ledge, hoping against all reason to reach the unreachable. Well, that had been her life. Nothing to show for it but failure from buzzing in one direction. Apparently she hadn't been able to help it during her lifetime and she couldn't help it now, it was too late.

She smoked another cigarette and detected a film of dirt on her teeth. She remembered that she hadn't washed. 'I am exempt,' she told herself, lying back on the sofa inhaling the smoke deep into her lungs. 'I wish it were ten.' But time was particularly slow today. She suddenly realised that she no longer knew how to approach Arlen. What kind of relationship did they have? Would they mourn or would Arlen just feel relief? 'I am going to miss him,' she thought, 'if life goes on. If it doesn't, I'll miss him too.' She couldn't imagine a situation in which he was dispensable. 'Have I put the cold meats away?' entered her mind. She was getting careless and forgetful. She went back to the kitchen and saw the mess. 'I'm going to make myself a fresh cup of coffee,' she decided, cleaning up the table. The coffee grinder made a noise but it wasn't for long, not like playing music or taking a shower. But she was frightened none the less. Else wouldn't be frightened. She also probably wouldn't grind coffee in this situation. She always did the right and sensible thing, made everybody happy. In the long run the entire struggle became a bore. Lying on the windowsill, panting, gathering strength for another attempt – she started to laugh and found she had hiccups. 'Insects die easily,' she thought, still fighting the hiccups. She wouldn't ask Arlen to accompany her to the quay. It was too risky. He'd protest a little at first, then he'd plan his evening with Renate or another girl. She lit a cigarette and watched the grey smoke screen which reminded her of her own fragility. 'That's me,' she thought, 'a smoke screen.' She noticed a hole in her slacks and poked it with a finger. Another hole. 'I'm glad I went to the dentist last month.' She looked again at the clock, which had miraculously advanced an hour. 'I'm going to lose this room.' It came closest to the lit room she was trying to reach in her futile attempts to get through the windowpane. But why was it here and what was it? It wasn't protection from the memories, nor was it protection from death by machine guns. Perhaps it was beauty. No miracles. Miracles were out. Is nobody ever going to grow up? Look at me! She almost cried, bruised, with holes in her wings from foolish, senseless attempts to reach some goal.

Arlen came home with steaks and tomatoes. 'Wasn't it an awfully long day?' he asked, taking her in his arms.

'Yes.' She didn't want to get into a discussion. 'Who will do the cooking?'

'I will,' he said.

'Make mine medium rare.'

'Are you hungry?'

'I don't want you to come to the quay tonight. It's too risky.'

'Don't let's discuss it,' he said as if they were still talking about cooking. 'I'll be right there until the truck picks you up.'

'I don't want you further involved,' she argued with a tired voice.

'I have to know what happens to you.'

'Hubert can tell you over the phone.'

'I want to be there with you,' he insisted.

'Does it matter? You'll only get into trouble.'

'We won't.' He was sure.

'Do you want a drink?'

'Not tonight. We have to be sober.' He talked like a detective.

'Why sober if nothing's at risk?'

'One never can tell. Don't dramatise it. You want your steak medium rare?'

'Yes, please.'

'You must have had an awful day,' he said again.

'What shall we do until nine o'clock? We can't even talk to each other like normal people any more, you treat me as if I had terminal cancer and I – well, I think, I feel like a sick person when there's nothing wrong with me. Perhaps you should put the potatoes on now.'

'Good idea.' Arlen was glad to get away.

'You'll feel much better tomorrow,' Eva promised.

'I doubt it,' he said, annoyed because she never trusted the sincerity of his intentions.

'You made a date with Renate,' she called from the living room. Arlen was rattling the pots and pans.

'I have to talk to somebody – ' he defended himself.

'Of course,' said Eva in a low voice so that Arlen couldn't hear. 'You can't be alone.'

They left much too early. After dinner they'd washed the dishes and stayed for a while in the living room, restless, pacing up and down until they decided to walk to the quay and wait there in the open. Once in the streets they felt more composed. They walked along the river towards the centre of the city. The sun had disappeared behind the horizon but the sky was still light and the visibility good.

'Another hour before dusk,' judged Arlen.

'We'd better not get to the quay too early.'

'Either it's safe or it isn't.'

'We don't know,' Eva stated flatly. The sky began to change into a purple-grey. The outlines of the ruins looked like an immense excavation site. 'Let's stay in the inner city as long as possible and go to the harbour from there.'

'Makes no difference,' said Arlen.

'Perhaps not.' They were quiet again, watching their immediate surroundings, too distracted for reflection.

'We shouldn't sit where Hubert said,' Eva suddenly decided. 'We must hide in the ruins opposite and wait for the truck from there.'

'All right. Perhaps it's safer.' The inner city was one vast wasteland.

'It's eerie. Something's in the air.'

The sky got darker, one star became visible. They were walking along the quay, carefully scanning corners as if playing a children's game. Once they had reached the assigned spot they began to search in the ruins on the opposite side for a convenient hiding place, discovered a number of possibilities but decided on one that gave them a view over the quay in both directions. They carried bricks and built themselves seats side by side. Eva looked at Arlen's watch which showed ten minutes to nine; she rolled her eyes and sighed.

'It will pass,' he whispered.

'Yes, everything does.' She was angry, particularly angry at Arlen who would see Renate later while she . . . men's egotism had no bounds, always conducting events to their own advantage. But here was Arlen risking his life to see her off, not liking it one bit but doing it nonetheless, counting the minutes, feeling tension and fear.

Visibility diminished. Her legs became numb, her pulse had reached almost zero. She felt tossed between anger and remorse. Arlen was quite still, sitting it out with her at the risk of his life. There were probably bodies buried below them, people who had lived on the upper floor before the raids. They always had flower pots in front of their ugly cheap apartments without comfort or facilities – working-class apartments. She wondered what time it was.

'What's the time?'

Arlen put his hand over her mouth and pulled her to the ground. Now she could hear it too: footsteps, military style, probably in jackboots, coming nearer. Her pulse rate increased, raced thumping through her head, her ears. A pair of uniformed men marched by, one saying: 'They must come this way, we can't miss them.' They walked calmly and steadily, there was nothing threatening in the voice, nothing bloodthirsty or taunting in the words. Were they bored with hunting people down or were they perhaps just out to meet friends? In this wasteland, down by the quay at this hour? No, they were looking for them, Eva and Arlen. It seemed ages before the echoes of those boots became inaudible.

'They're looking for us,' whispered Eva.

'Perhaps, who knows?' They stayed on the ground for another few minutes. 'Most unlikely,' added Arlen.

' "They have to come this way," they said,' Eva insisted. 'They're looking for us.'

'Who knows.' They sat down on their brick seats again. Suddenly a man appeared from behind and whispered: 'Hurry. Follow me. The street is patrolled.' They walked quietly after the stranger who turned into the next side street.

'The truck is parked round the bend,' he explained. 'Young man, you'd better run and get home for an alibi in case you need one. Or stay with a friend.' They had reached the truck. 'Jump in,' he ordered. Eva climbed up, found her knapsack on the seat and put it on the floor. The driver closed her door noiselessly, ran to the driver's seat and switched on the engine. Arlen was standing below, opening and closing his lips, saying something she couldn't hear. The wheels began to turn, they moved forward, leaving Arlen in the empty, narrow street with his mouth open.

'Thanks for picking me up,' said Eva. The man didn't react.

'Have to watch out,' he explained after a while. 'It's getting dark and the dogs are sniffing everywhere. The highway's covered with road blocks. We'll have to sneak out by some back streets.'

They drove through deserted narrow lanes, smoothly turning curve after curve as if they were on a race course. 'He's a smooth operator,' thought Eva, 'competent.' Fred was his name, Hubert had said. Slowly her pulse adapted to the ride. Was she really safe? Of course not, but Fred created an illusion of security. She looked at his muscular arms, at his bulging shoulders, the thick neck. She couldn't make out his face, it was too dark now, but she saw the profile of a man with a short nose and a round chin. Arlen would be at Renate's by now and she would lie for him if it became necessary. Should the truck ever reach its destination, Fred had to find out via Hubert what had happened to Arlen. Arlen suddenly seemed of great importance since she now felt cut off from part of her own existence. 'I'm not attached,' she revolted. 'I can't afford to have Arlen invade my privacy.' But he seemed to stay with her whether she liked it or not. She had invited him in once too often. Contact has its consequences.

'I can't afford it!' thought Eva, as the truck rolled and swerved through the streets.

The truck rode along a sandy path with a long stretch of pine woods on one side and wide, flat fields on the other. Fred finally opened his mouth.

'All clear,' he said and readjusted his seating position.

'What could have happened?' asked Eva.

'Too many checks and road blocks. My truck is loaded,' he laughed heartily.

'Then you weren't afraid on account of me?'

'No! Just gave you a lift. But the stuff in my truck I'd have to explain. Of course I have papers and authorisations but the inventory doesn't always check with the contents. Some snoop might have taken the trouble to check. Here we're safe, no one comes this way, it's off the beaten track. My wife Anna will look after you. She's quite a close friend of Else's, they went to school together. That's how we met, my wife and I, when I visited Hubert and the girls had a reunion. Anna will be glad of the company. It's lonely out in the woods and she really likes to talk. Once I'm home her tongue keeps wagging until she falls asleep. I can't get a word in sideways.' He laughed. 'She does sewing. I provide the material, she designs the dresses. Brings in a fortune.'

'I'm glad your wife is a friend of Else's,' remarked Eva.

'Anna is special,' he admitted. 'I'm a lucky man.'

'Else is special too,' added Eva.

'Quite!'

It occurred to Eva that Fred and Anna were going to make her the loneliest person in the world. They would talk all right, but without ever saying anything.

'Don't expect any luxuries,' Fred was saying. 'The house is a long way from any village. We have running water but no electricity.' He laughed again. 'Don't have to search on a cold winter night for the outhouse.' He seemed amused by his own description and chuckled from the belly. 'Of course, it gets cold in the winter but Anna will provide hot bricks for your bed. The kitchen is always cosy, you'll see.'

'What does Anna think of my coming?' asked Eva.

'We should have done something like this long ago,' he said. 'It's her nature, always kind, always cheerful.'

'Like Else,' commented Eva. 'It's a long way out.'

'For a safe place you have to travel far.'

Fred switched on the headlights. For a moment two narrow beacons hit the sandy path. He switched them off again. 'Just checking,' he explained. 'The night is clear enough.'

'You can see without lights?'

'Yes.'

Eva was afraid that in her condition she would get sick of Fred's chatter. Together with Anna he'd drive her up the wall.

'Could drive the truck home with my eyes closed,' announced Fred.

'You and Hubert are old friends?'

'Met when we were kids in an orphanage and decided to run away together. Learned the smuggling trade from scratch. Now we're big wheels in the trade. Not at the top, but big, real big.' He moved on his seat with pride and embarrassment.

'Does Anna know?'

'Would I tell you if Anna didn't know? We have no secrets.'

'People without secrets are the dullest in the world,' Eva's thoughts echoed to Fred's revelations.

'Ever got caught?' she asked Fred.

'Just once, when I was green. I rescued a drowning man off the Swedish coast who was an agent. We took him on board and once in harbour we were arrested.'

'Now he's the world's greatest big wheel.' Eva was annoyed at her own thoughts, over which she no longer seemed to have any control. It was a lie. Fred had never said any such thing. 'I'm not going mad,' she assured herself, 'I'm rational, I know what's going on.'

She suddenly remembered the sticky yellow cake on her father's plate in the little coffee house on Kurfuerstendamm with its sign at the entrance, 'Jews not allowed'. It made her terribly frightened.

Fred was driving through the woods. He had switched on the headlights and reduced speed.

'Have to be easy on the truck,' he explained.

'No rush unless you're hungry.'

'I had dinner with Else and Hubert before I came to pick you up. Hubert told me your parents had plenty of cash.'

'It didn't stop my father from being killed.'

'Having a good wife is more than enough for me,' said Fred. 'But in order to keep her happy you need cash.'

'You're making it,' said Eva.

'Quite a bit,' he laughed, 'quite a bit.'

They kept on driving at a slow, uneven pace. 'Another ten minutes or so,' announced Fred. 'I think we made good time in spite of the detour.'

'Hope Anna isn't worried.'

'Never is, has the right attitude.'

'What a perfect little *hausfrau*,' Eva thought, against her own wishes. 'Please stop!' she begged herself, 'They are trying to save your life.'

Chapter Fourteen

The cottage stood in a clearing surrounded by pine trees. Eva could see its outline against the sky. When the truck drew nearer the outlines mingled with the darkness of the trees. The engine stopped. Fred jumped from his seat and called, 'Anna, I'm home!' The door opened and a figure appeared in the door holding a small lamp which blinded their eyes.

'I didn't expect you yet,' she said in a matter-of-fact voice. 'Must have raced all the way.'

'Got an early start,' explained Fred.

'Come on in,' said Anna to Eva. 'I'm so excited you're coming to stay with us. It's been lonely these last few years at times but I'm never bored. Too much to do, isn't there, Fred?' She held the door open for Fred and Eva to enter.

'Enough work for a dozen strong men,' admitted Fred, taking Eva's knapsack and hanging it on a hook in the entrance hall.

'Let's have a snack.' He steered them towards the lit kitchen.

'Of course we don't expect you to work,' mentioned Anna. 'However, after a while you'll welcome it. I'm a hard worker, aren't I, Fred?'

'You are,' he agreed, inspecting the sandwiches that stood on the table. 'Also a hard talker.' He laughed.

'Two hours at night. I can't talk to myself during the day.'

'She'll drive me up the wall!' Eva was trembling with despair.

'Here we are,' exclaimed Anna, showing off her kitchen with pride, putting the lamp on a chest near the curtained windows. Another lamp was hanging from the ceiling above the kitchen table.

'Have a good look at my wife,' said Fred. 'Isn't she the prettiest thing in the world?' Anna's face possessed real beauty though the individual features were neither spectacular nor regular. It was the way they fitted together, the violet colour of her eyes, the almost steady smile around her mouth, that made her so attractive. She was suntanned, wore a floral-printed summer dress with a low neckline and puffed sleeves. Her feet were bare, indicating that she didn't stand on ceremony.

'You're a lucky man,' agreed Eva.

'I told you so.' He smiled at Anna who was carrying a pot of hot coffee from the stove.

'Help yourself,' she said.

Fred began to tell Anna about the patrol that had almost caught him red-handed picking up Eva, how it would have succeeded but for his having spotted her and Arlen hiding among the ruins.

'You would have made a first-rate detective,' Anna said with admiration.

'I'm doing fine the way things are.'

'Always on the wrong side of the law. Always hiding.'

'I like it. Was brought up this way.' Fred laughed. 'Once the war is over we can move to the city. You can see your friends again, live a normal life.'

'But you'll always be on the wrong side of the law.'

'That's how I make our living, my sweetie. Do you want me to become an officer in the Salvation Army?'

'Isn't he impossible?' asked Anna and smiled.

Before they went to bed Fred showed Eva how to light and extinguish a lamp. Then he guided her through the house, pointing out the toilet, and a bathroom on the second floor.

'The curtains are already drawn,' called out Anna from below. 'She can just jump into bed.' They climbed another flight to an attic room with slanted walls. On a table stood a vase with flowers, next to it lay a stack of old magazines. It smelled of pine and fresh air.

'We have screens on all the windows. In case you can't sleep right away, Anna left some magazines.'

'Thanks,' said Eva.

'I know how you must feel,' said Fred. 'But you'll get used to it. The beginning is the hardest. Well, sleep tight.'

'I hope you know how grateful I am.' She felt obliged to say something.

'It's all right, girlie, don't mention it.'

Then the house became quiet. Outside insects were buzzing and singing. An owl hooted. Eva smoked a cigarette and flicked through several magazines. 'It's nice out here,' she thought, looking at the bunch of flowers. 'It's really very pretty.' She rubbed her eyes. Had she really thought that? Why, when she knew she hated it and the trashy magazines full of last year's fashions?

Was she already thinking like Anna? 'It's nice here.' Who had said it? It sounded like some voice separated from herself and from reality, some form of madness. No, it wasn't madness, she knew quite well where she was: in exile, in utmost isolation, where nothing private or personal would grow. The end of the line. Here she had to forget about the warm and friendly hours in Else's room behind the store, here she had to forget that Arlen's caresses could make her ignore her fears.

From now on human closeness no longer existed; she was alone. Parting from the past would be painful and sad. But in order to survive on this small plot in the woods she had to find an exile's mind, one that didn't feel and didn't long for anything other than what it found.

She had to accept Fred and Anna as her friendly keepers, work from morning till night, unthinking and unfeeling, adapt to a mentality which would see her through and make her survive.

She turned off the lamp, opened the blackout curtains and let the cool night air come in. She wouldn't cry. Not any more.

It was getting cold. Eva stooped in the garden, harvesting

potatoes. Afternoon approached early, the sky was dark grey with the atoms of winter in the air. She pushed one basket with earth-covered large potatoes towards the path and fetched an empty one for the next load.

It had been her idea to work in the garden, to be outdoors, alone, not bothered by Anna's constant chit-chat. Eva had tried simply to work hard and recuperate from her fears. But she still was afraid out here, in her loneliness, surrounded by those tall pine woods.

'I want you to come in now!' called Anna from the house. 'Leave the baskets for Fred to put away.'

Eva took off her shoes at the back door and entered the hallway in socks. She washed her hands in the kitchen sink and sat down at the table opposite Anna. They always sat opposite each other, always used the same mugs and ate the same sort of sandwiches. After the first sip of coffee they always said something like 'delicious', 'that feels good', 'nice', 'just what I needed'. After that they ate the food slowly and Anna would talk about dinner or her sewing. At times her mind would wander to the past and she might come up with a small incident from home or school that sounded as colourless as her present life, but for her it had the exotic quality of faraway countries.

It took Eva months to become aware of her surroundings. All that time she had lived on an untouchable plane, isolated, as though in a cocoon. Now, after several months of living and working with Anna and Fred, she was able to recognise grudgingly for the first time the courage of their personal lives, the courage of the outlaw. She observed their mutual love and dependence, their determination to live or die together.

Since the ground was frozen now, Eva polished every day either the ugly dining-room furniture or the furniture in the living room with a special wax which gave the wood a high gloss and shine. She knew how Anna cherished and admired these pieces, so she polished them with special care. Eva had returned from cleaning the living room when Anna told her that she should do the buttonholes next. 'The buttons are in a little box on the table.'

They had gone together, a few days earlier, in search of a Christmas tree. Anna had sized the trees up with the eye of an expert dressmaker. 'It's perfect!' she had said as she approached one tree among all the others, walking round it, standing back to check the crown. 'Just perfect!' Eva felt sad because Fred would fell it and Anna would decorate it with awful ornaments, putting it between her ugly furniture. The perfect tree would have to die for such a misconception. Buttonholes and the Christmas tree were Eva's present occupations.

'Next week we start Christmas baking,' Anna had announced with glee as if the creation of Christmas cookies would stop the horrors.

Eva held the gilded, star-like ornament for the top of the tree in one hand as she climbed the ladder. 'God-awful, like the rest of the decorations. It's all God-awful,' she was thinking.

'Turn it a bit to the right,' shouted Anna as if Eva were far away, 'just a fraction more.' She stepped back and squinted her eyes. 'I'm afraid I got carried away. It's too far to the right now. Just give it a twist left.' She paused. 'Another twist. Hold it! I think we've got it this time. Perfect. Come down and see for yourself. Isn't it a beautiful tree?'

Eva stood silent before the garish, tinselled triangle which hid a perfect pine tree. Red, green, blue, gold and silver ornaments hung in abundance from invisible branches. Silver tinsel chains wound themselves around its outer shape like a spiral. Multicoloured birds with long, silvery tails sat motionless, half-hidden between sparkling balls. Angels dangled in the air on thin threads, slowly turning. Tinsel hung like curtains from every possible spot.

'Fred will like it.'

'It's perfect. Now to the kitchen.'

From the amount of food they were preparing Eva guessed that Hubert and Else were invited, but since nobody said a word, Eva didn't bring up the subject. She knew it was supposed to be a surprise. Anna worked herself into a frenzy towards the big day and Eva wanted nothing but privacy and quiet.

'Stir the red cabbage a bit,' ordered Anna. The goose was roasting in the oven. Stirring the cabbage, Eva wondered if Mrs Richter had found the dirty linen in the filing cabinets by now. 'That's enough.' Why was she afraid of meeting Else and Hubert here as guests when she had loved their company in that tiny kitchen behind the delicatessen? Would Else behave like a guest here? Would Else show another self, or would these four friends exclude her, creating loneliness but still no privacy? Christmas was not a day to celebrate, not for a Jew.

'See if the Brussels sprouts are done,' ordered Anna. They weren't.

'The cranberries go in the saucepan over there.' Anna was trying to be organised but finding it difficult to keep the big secret from Eva. If only the guests would arrive.

The light was slowly fading. The sky hung full of clouds. If it got colder overnight they might have a white Christmas . . . Then Fred was holding the door. Else and Hubert had arrived. They came in unhurried and a little stiff from the long ride. Else stood erect like a display doll, golden-haired, wrapped in a mink stole, showing her evening gown, made for a queen. 'Do you have the presents?' she asked Hubert. Anna came rushing from the kitchen.

'Finally! I thought you'd never come. Hello Else, hello Hubert. Good to see you and merry Christmas! Take off your coats and make yourselves comfortable in the living room. Fred still has to change. Here is Eva. Look who's here! – my God, I have to watch the food.'

It was all wrong, Eva judged immediately. Else and Hubert were masquerading while in reality they belonged to the devastated city, the crumbling stones and decayed houses, the quay and the harbour. They looked odd and ridiculous, dressed up in tinsel, standing between the ugly furniture and the over-decorated Christmas tree. She wanted to embrace Else but didn't dare to approach the pretty doll.

Everybody helped with the dinner. Fred was carving the goose, putting slices of meat on every plate. Hubert opened a bottle of red wine and filled the glasses. The dishes were handed round fast, as if they were playing a game.

196

'Try the stuffing,' Anna urged.

'So much food, how did you manage?'

'I had a helper,' Anna smiled at Eva.

'Did we find you a good home?' asked Hubert.

'The best,' answered Eva. 'Let's all drink to Anna and Fred.'

'To Anna and Fred!' They lifted their glasses. Anna glowed in her home-made party dress.

'It's a fine wine,' pronounced Fred.

'You are fine people,' replied Hubert.

'Gone through a lot together.' Fred drank some more of the wine.

'Is Eva behaving or does she have her moods?'

'I never give her the time!' exclaimed Anna.

'We can move to the city, you know, once it's over,' said Fred.

'It'll be over soon.'

'Let's drink to that!' suggested Eva.

'What a beautiful Christmas tree,' said Else.

'We'll light the candles later when we exchange our presents. That's the best part of Christmas,' announced Anna.

'Let's drink to that,' said Eva.

'Delicious,' said Hubert. 'Else couldn't have done any better.'

'We can count our blessings,' agreed Fred.

'Let's drink to that,' laughed Eva.

'Don't get drunk now,' warned Hubert. 'It's heady stuff.'

'She has her moods.'

'We understand. We've all served time one way or another.'

'I haven't,' said Else. 'And I am not going to.'

'No, you are the queen.' Hubert said it with a certain amount of sarcasm.

'She's wearing a golden crown.'

'Selling herring salad day in, day out!' Else flung her head back and burst into laughter.

'Soon you won't have to sell anything any more. Soon the world will be wonderful,' said Eva.

'Times will be tough,' warned Fred. 'Have to face facts. We

should start stockpiling now.'

'Not tonight unless you do it in your stomach.' They all laughed. Knives and forks clinked against the Sunday china. Laughter rang through the air.

'Tell us about Hamburg,' begged Eva. 'Nothing ever happens here.'

'We might send you a few air raids,' laughed Hubert.

'Do people from the office come to the store?'

'Mostly Mrs Richter,' said Else. 'She asks whether we've heard from you and I shake my head and say "Nothing". The Gestapo still enquires from time to time, she says.'

'Mr Lindner is on Eva's side now,' remarked Hubert.

'The Christmas tree is a beaut,' said Fred.

'I let Eva put up the crown,' said Anna proudly.

They slowed down the chewing, the picking up of food. They leaned back more, became lazy and content. Little sparks would burst up to the surface and someone would exclaim: 'Delicious, what a glorious dinner!' or: 'It couldn't be better. Life is good.'

'How is Arlen?' Eva wanted to shout, shaking Else so that she might remember everything, but she didn't ask.

'Who wants dessert now or later?' Anna asked. 'I couldn't eat another bite.' They opted for coffee now and decided on dessert later.

'I made strong coffee for demi-tasses,' explained Anna.

'That's for ladies, my love,' said Fred. 'Give us real men's cups.' Anna was disappointed.

'If you wish –' she mumbled. 'Why did we ever get them?'

'Beats me,' said Fred. 'They look pretty though.'

'Don't they?' Anna smiled again.

'Is it really all that easy for them?' Eva asked herself. The pride of those God-awful possessions, the life they've chosen and now must lead, must, every day, without complaint, without annoyance, without vengeance. They were jumping the hurdles together, hand in hand, swinging arms in the right direction, never faltering, always synchronised. The perfect survivors. But what were they surviving? Hurdles, millions of hurdles. Eva saw them lined up far into the future. One day they wouldn't be able to jump them any more. Then they would sit on the side, holding hands, contemplating the number of hurdles jumped during their life together. Was it a record? Eva watched the imaginary course and concluded that after another glass of wine she would be able to endure the Christmas tree and the exchanging of gifts. She wondered how she had ever got through life so far, being an invalid who couldn't run or jump. Somebody always had to come along, had to carry her part of the way and drop her over the next hurdle. At the moment it was Anna's and Fred's turn. Before that Else and Hubert had assisted.

They all got up to have coffee in the living room next to the God-awful Christmas tree and the ugly, polished furniture. Fred lit the candles, Else poured out coffee with skill and ease, Anna wound up the gramophone and put the needle down on *Stille Nacht, Heilige Nacht*. They sat quietly, listening to the music which had so little to do with their lives and yet was dear and familiar to them all.

Later they exchanged presents. Eva had knitted sweaters for the women and jackets for the men. Fred had brought the yarn, Anna had decided on style and colour. Else handed Eva a big heavy package with a peevish smile. 'You won't guess what it is,' she said. Out came four volumes of Rilke's *Letters*. 'It's wonderful,' exclaimed Eva. 'It might carry me through.'

'Do you know who suggested it?'

'Arlen,' said Eva. 'How is – '

'Oh, always the same,' said Else with a chuckle. 'Arriving in despair and leaving elated.'

'Is he drinking a lot?'

'When he has a chance,' Else said calmly. 'Who doesn't?'

'The books are beautiful.' Eva hugged the volumes.

Else admired the lavender sweater Eva had knitted. 'Anna chose the colour,' Eva explained.

They ate walnut cake with whipped cream and had more coffee. The room rocked like a cradle with the melodies of Christmas songs. All burdens had vanished. They sat in their security, proud, complacent and happy, slowing down for the moment on an even stretch between hurdles. 'They are carrying me along,' thought Eva. 'I am safe.'

'How about a game of cards?' asked Hubert. They settled

down quickly round the dining-room table, arranging coffee cups, brandy glasses and ashtrays, listened to the shuffling of cards and smiled with excitement at their special treat.

'We'll always remember this Christmas,' said Eva. 'The last Christmas of the war.'

'Can't go on much longer,' said Hubert reassuringly.

'Let's get there and then celebrate,' cautioned Anna.

'Who's dealing first?' asked Hubert, still shuffling the cards.

'Why do you ask?' they asked in unison and laughed.

Chapter Fifteen

'Didn't we have a wonderful time?' Anna said after their friends had left on the second day of Christmas. 'You'd better start tidying up.'

For days Eva scrubbed and polished, washed and ironed, forgetting who she was or why she was on her knees, exhausted. The tree started to shed needles though the room was again damp and cold. 'We had too much of a good time,' Eva talked to the over-decorated tree. 'They should never have transplanted you, cutting your roots. I've changed too since I came here. But you wouldn't have noticed, you only arrived recently and will be chucked out soon. I'm still waiting to be disposed of . . . But I have changed. I am no longer desperate.'

'Front room's done!' Eva slumped on to a kitchen chair. 'I deserve a cup of coffee.'

'Take two,' said Anna with a laugh. She was glad Eva did the housework and she could concentrate on dressmaking.

'I'll do the guest room tomorrow.'

'We're spending New Year in town,' announced Anna. 'I hope you don't mind being alone.'

'It's not the first time I've been by myself.' Eva was elated at the prospect.

'I was thinking of the New Year celebration. You might miss that.' Anna would have dreaded a New Year's Eve alone in the woods.

'One day is as good as another. Every day starts a new year.'

On New Year's Eve, when Fred returned early from the city, he brought Arlen as a visitor for Eva. Else had planned this surprise carefully, pulling strings and persuading Arlen that this visit was what Eva needed in her isolation in the woods. When Arlen entered the kitchen, Eva's eyes became blurred for a moment. Then she fought off her joy, her fear, her anger. Why had they conspired behind her back as if she were an idiot whose life had to be planned and arranged by others? Why did they have to lure Arlen into her hideout when it only meant another farewell? What were they to do in the meantime? Play cards, stare at each other, count the minutes?

There he stood smiling, caring, waiting for her joy to be put round his neck like a garland. Instead she put her head on the table and closed her eyes.

'I told you we shouldn't have sprung this on her!' Fred shouted. 'Doesn't hurt to ask her opinion.'

'It was Else's idea,' Anna defended herself.

'Don't worry.' Arlen felt he had to say something. 'Just get ready. We'll be all right.'

'Please go back with them,' begged Eva, in a panic.

'You can't mean it.' Arlen was convinced he could work things out.

'Yes,' she said. 'Yes, I mean it. I can't go through it all again.'

'I'll help you,' he whispered.

'I don't want any more help!' She looked down at her legs as if they were crippled.

Fred started to eat his lunch. 'Sit down, Arlen.' Arlen followed his advice. They ate in silence until Fred pointed at the motionless Eva and said: 'Nerves. Had similar cases in jail.'

'Don't talk as though I wasn't here!' Eva burst out.

'Then sit up or take a walk.'

'I want to make sure Arlen goes back to town with you.'

'I'm staying,' decided Arlen. 'Just get ready. I know how to handle Eva.'

'You don't even know who I am!' she shouted. 'The entire thing is one big joke. Playing house for two days – '

Arlen helped Fred put the bedding in the truck.

'Camping out,' said Fred with a smile.

'Have a good time, and happy New Year.'

'And you. Just give her time. She'll come round.'

'Good luck,' said Anna and squeezed Arlen's hand. Eva still had her head on the kitchen table and didn't move. Suddenly she got up and ran out.

'Please go back. I mean it.'

The truck was moving slowly over the uneven frozen ground, crossing the clearing and disappearing in the woods.

'I'm sorry I'm not happy,' said Eva. 'Other people just jump. Why can't I?'

'We do what we can, that's all,' he replied.

'Finish your coffee,' she said, watching him sit down and pick up another sandwich. 'Finish your coffee! Do you see what I mean? I can't do it for two whole days.'

'Then let's take a walk.'

'No better,' Eva shook her head. 'These woods are so monotonous. Pine trees next to pine trees, the ground covered with brown needles, that's all. No excitement or surprise. There are birds and once in a while you meet a deer.'

They walked along the path. 'In the beginning I often lay awake at night wishing to be back in the bombed city, in my hideous office, finding my way through the dark towards the harbour. I longed to visit Else, to chat with Marion, to phone Darling, to hear Werner's new love-lorn voice and I longed for you. I was rubbing against the pain needlessly, stupidly, daily. During the day I dug potatoes, I worked in the vegetable patch, cleaned the house. Anna had established a routine round our lives which tortured me. But it went on and I kept it up until suddenly something caved in, something won a victory. I became submissive and docile. I knelt in the garden and I scrubbed the floors. I prepared food, I stitched buttonholes and I waited, like Anna, for Fred to come home, to bring the paper and tell us the news. We would have dinner together and afterwards taste that long awaited cup of coffee, lean back in peace, resting, inhaling cigarette smoke, appreciating the moment of leisure before the dishes had to be done, the stove to be cleaned and the fire to be lit in the bathroom for Fred's bath. Towards the end of the day, when the fire burned out and it got colder, Fred gave the signal: "To bed, my girls!" I took my candle and hot-water bottle, wished them good night, walked slowly up to my ice-cold attic room. I undressed in a hurry, crawled under the blanket, clutching my hot-water bottle, and was asleep in a minute. I didn't have time to think any more and if I had time, my thoughts were without dreams. When you arrived today, I realised how shaky my hard-won peace really is. I have to hold on to it, Arlen, I can't start from the beginning again.'

'Perhaps I should have known better,' said Arlen, who really couldn't imagine that Eva wasn't thrilled to see him. 'But I think we won't regret the meeting.'

'For God's sake!' Eva said. 'You're defending yourself.'

Arlen wasn't sure if he should tell Eva that he had given up plenty of invitations just to be with her. He felt uncertain in his position and his surroundings. The house was awful and the woods not very inspiring. Eva had refused to give him a helping hand. Here he was stranded in the middle of nowhere like a traveller at an inn waiting for the storm to pass. At least there was drink in the house. That would save them.

'I came all the way – ' he started.

'Oh, I will be most obliging,' interrupted Eva. 'If you want me to wash windows, I'll be delighted. I also know how to sew buttonholes.'

'Don't rub it in,' he begged. 'If you are unhappy, don't inflict it on me.'

'But you are the one who is unhappy,' she said and laughed. 'I am at peace, leading you through the woods which are quite beautiful in their monotony. I will cook your dinner, offer you wine – we have a gramophone with old-time records, you can admire the Christmas tree which is shedding its needles. I can light a fire in any stove, we can even sleep in the guest room together.'

'You never talked like that before.'

'Perhaps you have changed and not I.'

'You should make plans about your future. The war is almost over.'

'I'll wait and see.'

'Will you live with me?'

'There's no future for us, Arlen. You don't understand me at all.'

'But it was understood – '

'Nothing was ever understood, especially not between us. You flow where the current will carry you, hither and thither, without explanation or intent, returning to me as if I were the truth or God who can grant forgiveness. I'm tired of the same game. And I don't want to hang round your neck in despair. Not any longer, never again.'

'But I helped you,' said Arlen. It almost sounded like a question.

'Do you think I'll ever forget? I remember every moment. But I also know that I never asked for anything and I am not asking now. It surprises me that you've got it all wrong.'

'Did it never occur to you how much I need help?'

'We both needed help but it had nothing to do with you or me,' she said.

'You are just twisting words.'

'I give up.' She raised her arms and let them fall. 'No more serious discussions. It's New Year's Eve and I'm supposed to cook dinner.'

'Stop joking. I can't give up, it's too important.'

'I am going abroad. Would you follow me?'

'But you can stay here once it's over,' he objected.

'It will never be over, not for me. You must understand that much.'

'No, I don't.'

'Then I can't help you, really I can't.'

After dinner Arlen relaxed in Fred's easy chair while Eva sat on the floor leaning her head against his legs. She had shown him the entire house. The twilight had been glowing over the polished ugliness. Eva drew the air-raid curtains.

'We always sit in the kitchen,' explained Eva. 'I think it's less ugly than the other rooms.'

They were anxious to open the wine. During dinner Arlen said: 'I slowly begin to understand –'

'It transforms you,' explained Eva. 'Either it kills you or you adjust.'

Arlen remained silent, holding his wine glass in both hands.

'I had no choice,' continued Eva. 'You would have done the same.'

'In self-defence,' he agreed.

'How easy that sounds. One day I am going away and I'll take my fate along, like a suitcase.'

'You're leaving me,' he said with a sigh.

'I made my position perfectly clear, didn't I?'

'Still, if you loved me –'

'I wonder how we got into this kitchen?' Eva drank down the wine.

'The lamp has its charm.'

'It's burning too brightly.' She turned the handle and dimmed the light. 'Now illusions have a chance.' She laughed.

'I thought you detested – '

'Try to imagine beauty where none exists – ' She looked up at him. 'But you are beautiful.'

They drank against the tide of estrangement. They began to recall their holiday at the Baltic and found only dead words and useless images.

'Others grow closer,' he grumbled.

'I know. Renate would marry you tomorrow.'

'You're a big help.'

They both drifted downstream, swiftly, their hands holding only air.

'Basically,' she brought out with some difficulty, 'nothing exists but you and me. The trouble is I can't find either of us anywhere and I've searched a lot, believe me, I've searched all over.'

'We can keep up the search tomorrow,' he suggested. 'Let's go to bed now.'

'To bed, my sweet,' sang Eva, picking up the lamp from the table. 'Our room should be warm.'

'I've never got this drunk before in my life,' thought Eva while the darkness spun round in her head. They had just been able to take off their shoes, before falling back on their pillows, unable to move, miles apart. Arlen began to snore immediately. Eva's position was more precarious. She felt dizzy, sick and disgusted. What had she done with the precious time that had been granted them? She had spoiled it instead of polishing it brightly like Anna's furniture. Well, it's done, she told herself. Things got lost in the most unlikely places. The spinning motion slowed in the darkness. She listened to Arlen's heavy breathing. 'At least he is alive. Perhaps we'll find something tomorrow. Tomorrow will be 1945. We buried the year. It was a God-awful funeral.'

Suddenly she felt a hand on her shoulder and began to scream, running through streets, screaming, with a dissected hand lying on her shoulder, touching her. She knew that neither running nor screaming would change her situation but she kept on. Others jumped hurdles, she thought, while the hand got a tighter grip on her. 'If I don't do something drastic, I'm in for it.' She opened her eyes and remembered that she'd been quite brave running and screaming in a drunken nightmare, screaming without fear in an act of protest. She felt her head and wondered if she was suffering from a hangover. She touched it like something foreign. Then she detected her left hand lying lifeless on her right shoulder. She lifted hand and arm to her side where it dropped like a dead object. Slowly she felt a prickling sensation in her fingers, some life coming back. She wondered what time it was. She remained motionless until her arm was back to normal, then got up, walked through the darkness, found the door and stepped into the hallway. She drew the air-raid curtains and looked out on to a grey winter landscape with deep, hanging clouds. Tiny snowflakes floated down like birds ready for a landing. The surrounding woods looked like a big dark wall. 'A nice day for a walk,' she concluded. She opened more curtains and looked at the kitchen clock. It was only seven-thirty, much too early for getting up. She felt depressed. It was also cold. She cleaned out the stove and started a new fire. Last night's wine glasses and overflowing ashtrays still stood by the easy chair. She filled a kettle with fresh water and put it on the stove. Then she sat in Fred's chair and tried to fall asleep again. 'What a mess,' she thought. Low air pressure from every angle. The attack on her system was catastrophic. Nonsense. She was exaggerating as usual. What did she expect? Life was broken in this part of the world. She had to be patient. Things would get back to normal after Arlen's departure. They simply had to make it through another day. Water boiling. 'Another day,' she sighed. 'Coffee and something to eat,' she thought as if it would solve her problems. What could she expect? She cut several slices of bread and set the table.

Arlen refused to get up. 'Don't,' he moaned. 'It will be hell.'

'All right, all right,' she tiptoed out of the room. But he appeared after a while, uncombed, unwashed, with wrinkled clothes, looking downtrodden and remorseful.

'Have I behaved very badly?' he asked before sitting down.

'Not that I can remember. We both felt estranged.'

'I wonder what we expected? My vanity is usually at its peak during the night. Mornings are raw and factual. Only this morning doesn't look like one.'

'It's snowing.'

'I haven't eaten so many eggs since the war started,' said Arlen. Apparently his spirits were intact.

'More ham? We have plenty,' she urged, trying to prolong breakfast. 'I'll take a walk in the woods later.'

'I think I am going back to bed. Don't feel like shaving.'

'The trees won't mind. No reason to stay behind.'

'No reason to go,' he insisted.

'Suit yourself.' She looked at his neglected face and was amazed by its beauty. 'Can you imagine breakfast together every day?' she asked him.

'Yes, I can. We would live under different circumstances.'

'They might be worse.'

'You have decided against it anyway –' He pretended disappointment.

'It was a bad idea to start with.'

'Perhaps, I see your point.' He wasn't in the mood to debate an issue of importance. In fact he never debated. He was the perfect drifter.

Eva lit the bathroom stove. She wanted a bath and perhaps Arlen would change his mind and shave off his stubble.

'I've eaten too much,' Arlen murmured with closed lips, making scratching noises with his steel blade, pulling the flesh of his face in all directions.

'Made the same mistake when I first got here,' Eva replied, splashing in the bath water. 'We can walk it off.' She hated this kind of small talk, she hated the faked intimacy of an ordinary life. He could have waited until she'd finished her bath. But he had come in, not asking if she approved, thinking it was his right to shave in the bathroom while she was taking her bath. He had undressed, and was handling his face with the skill of a diamond cutter. She sighed. 'I hope he doesn't keep up the intimacy. I don't want a shaving man in my bathroom. I don't want to listen to the entire record of togetherness while we're miles apart. I'll never be able to live an ordinary life. Aren't we bruised enough?' she thought. 'Why do we have to suffer through another long day?' It was a shame considering the fact that she loved him. She rose to get out of the bath.

'May I have a dip?' he asked. 'I'll wash it out afterwards.'

'He doesn't mind my dirty bath water. What does he mind? Am I allowed to lie?' Of course, that was expected, everybody lied.

Afterwards, when they were sitting in the kitchen again, finishing their coffee, Eva said, 'You don't have to come along.'

'What do you want me to do in this God-forsaken place?' he replied. 'Look, it's only twelve o'clock.'

'There are old newspapers and magazines.'

'No, thanks. I'm not in the mood for anything.'

'It's snowing. Somehow we have to get through this wintery day. Let's take our walk.' Why had she made it worse by saying 'our walk', why couldn't she have just said, 'Let's go!'? Was she in some obscure way enjoying this estrangement which proved what she had known all along, that it would never do, that a life together, ordinary, everyday, was out of the question?

'All right,' agreed Arlen. 'There's nothing else to do anyway.'

They bundled up to their noses and stepped out into the

silent world. It was damp and cold. The clouds seemed to hang motionless in the sky.

'I wonder if I should bring in the Brussels sprouts and the cabbages,' Eva said as they passed the vegetable patch. Arlen remained silent. She had not expected a decision from him. The crunchy noises of their steps in the snow interrupted the silence. The outstretched pine branches were sprinkled with white lace. Once in the woods Eva felt as if she were inside a huge domed cathedral whose source of light was a mystery. She wondered if Arlen saw anything.

'Are you still there?' she asked.

'Hardly,' he replied. 'How can you stand it?'

'There are far worse places. Don't let's harp on circum-stances and surroundings again. We have both changed. What is available to us is nothing but a dead-end street. I won't take it.'

'You are assuming. Give it a try.'

'I am trying right now and nothing comes to life.'

'In this God-forsaken place and never having had a chance – '

'I know. But I am preparing myself for a new life.'

'You told me. You want to leave.'

'I've never lived here like others. It has always been just an overnight stop by the roadside. Then a storm kept me longer than I anticipated. Now the weather is lifting. I can get ready. When the storm is over I'll get out.'

'No ties?' he asked.

'We have a fortune of ties, my pet. Let's cultivate them, not cash in on them with worthless paper currencies. You want the cheap thing.'

'I don't want to feel lonely,' he explained calmly. 'The others make me feel alone.'

'You will have the theatre soon.'

'Oh the theatre!' he exclaimed. His eyelids were half-closed. 'Yes, I'll have the theatre.' He smiled. 'But how will you manage life?'

'Life is going to manage me. It always did.'

'Come back to the city.'

'If I survive.'

Their conversation drifted like the snowflakes, gently falling. Neither of them made an effort to salvage anything – it was as if they had forgotten that some things were worth preserving. They kept up their walk because they were afraid of the emptiness awaiting them in the kitchen, the hours ahead which had to be filled.

'I want to win you back but I don't have the skill. I've never had to conquer women, you know. They run me down in droves. It's really frightening at times, though I'm not complaining. Only occasionally I feel too exposed, too much trampled on. People pointing their fingers at me as if I were a freak.'

'How you exaggerate. Don't play the victim.'

It was still snowing when they sat in the kitchen to have coffee and Christmas cookies. They ate as if it were the only way to ward off enemies. As long as the cookies got crushed between their teeth they felt safe and invincible. Arlen read an old newspaper from a pile destined to light the kitchen stove. Eva decided to make a fresh fire in their bedroom. She also looked into the bathroom to check on its state of cleanliness by Anna's standards. It was a mess. Arlen had not even let the water run out of the bath. The sink was splashed with shaving cream and toothpaste, the mirror spotted. She felt angry, because this was typical of Arlen. Always promising and then disappointing.

'Arlen,' she called from upstairs, leaning over the bannister. 'Come and clean up your mess in the bathroom.'

'Sorry,' he said. 'I'm so forgetful lately. Must be undernourishment.'

'I don't care. Clean it up.'

Later, when the blackout curtains had been drawn, the food was cooking on the fire and the lamp shone brightly, Arlen set the table and began to select a wine from Fred's stock. He opened the bottle with skill, pouring a little in his glass and tasting it. 'Quite good. Not a bad wine.' His mood had lifted in a general way, too general for Eva's taste. They both watched the clock. By the stroke of midnight, they would know that the worst lay behind them.

'You should go more often to Else's if you feel undernourished,' Eva said while they ate their dinner.

'It's not worth it. Hubert always catches me for the entire evening. There's no end to the wine. Finally, I can't stop drinking, I'm trapped and Hubert pulls out his deck of cards, shuffles, deals, while I dance to his tune until two in the morning. It's not worth it. I prefer to be undernourished.'

'Hubert is a little seedy but you can rely on him if you're in trouble. He will never let you down.'

'Well, I don't know. He lives by underworld standards and I love my own.'

'Do we really have standards?' asked Eva.

'At least we keep our self-respect.'

'Not always, not when I had sex with Mr Lindner to buy back Darling's pension.'

'I'm sure he didn't profit from his exploit.'

'No. It made both of us less human.'

'He keeps on paying the pension,' reminded Arlen.

'Underworld talk. It always gets back to that,' said Eva. She lifted her glass and drank the golden wine. 'What an awful way of spending our time together.'

'The wine is good, the place is warm and we've had plenty of food.'

Eva looked at the clock, trying to work out if it was close to ten or eleven.

When they finally went up to their bedroom, arms round each other's waist, Arlen holding up the lamp to light the way, they were singing an old folk song about May and budding trees, swaying slightly from side to side, hitting walls and the bannister, getting out of tune, out of rhythm with their spring song. They didn't mind because they didn't notice. Both felt happy and relieved of all those burdens, burdens they could no longer define. It was like having achieved a great victory. They tried to find their lips and gave up in defeat. They unlaced shoes, and managed to lie stretched out on the mattress, Eva extinguishing the light. The song was over. Arlen stretched his arm to find something of Eva but the bed was too wide and he couldn't reach her.

'Give me your hand,' he begged. She moved her arm towards him. Somewhere they met and each held a hand.

212

'Like cut-out paper dolls,' thought Eva. 'Can't be helped. I won't cry any more. No time left. One day – ' She felt guilty. She accused herself of ending up lifeless, flat, paper-thin and apart on their bed. Yet she had wanted to get that distance between them, had refused to establish a home base. The end of the war would be the beginning of a continuous quest, roaming the world in search of – she didn't know what it was she was looking for. A silly dream perhaps or a world she herself could create. If only it didn't hurt so much to be separated from Arlen; if only it didn't hurt just as much to be with him. 'It's fate,' she concluded, 'someone pulling strings. Always someone pushing my wheelchair in an unforeseen direction and I can't see who it is, they have no face.'

They woke up late and were in a lighter mood. The end was in sight. Arlen was longing for the excitement of the bombed city, Eva wished to return to her state of hibernation.

It was still cold. The sun had come out and made the snow sparkle with millions of tiny lights.

'A brilliant flicker and then gone,' remarked Eva.

'You're always looking for the dark side of things,' complained Arlen, who had not even observed the brilliance of the landscape.

'I don't deliberately look for darkness. I just can't see anything else, unless I'm blind.'

'Will you come back when the war is over?' he asked, stopping her and putting his hands on her shoulders. His face was serious and pained.

'All right,' she agreed because she was tired of discussing the subject. 'You know very well that I will walk on and on, stopping here and there, without credentials or recommendations from anyone, without a passport. I will be one traveller on earth who has nothing but invalid connections. I'll shun the underworld, I'll search for the light. You have always been bright.'

While they were eating lunch Fred and Anna returned. Anna shouted a greeting from outside as if they had not heard the rattling truck.

'We'd better go and help them carry in their stuff,' suggested Eva. Arlen didn't say a word, just got up and followed her into the snow-covered drive.

'Hello, nice to see you, happy New Year.' They said it all. Anna was animated, Fred satisfied and content.

'Just the bedding and suitcases,' said Anna. 'Let Fred rest for a while before he drives Arlen to the station.'

Arlen and Eva put down the things in the master bedroom.

'Take care, my pet,' said Eva, kissing him gently on the lips. 'Take care, so that nothing bad should ever happen to you.' They put their arms around each other as if they were in despair, but both felt relieved.

'Take care. I'll be waiting for you, remember. Always waiting for you.'

Eva thought that they were not honest and that these farewell words sounded like last words spoken on a platform in front of departing trains, recklessly and irresponsibly. Perhaps it wasn't their fault that they couldn't explain their true feelings. They really didn't know where they stood.

'Come,' she urged him, 'we'd better go back downstairs.'

'Nice to be home,' Anna began her report, 'though we have had such a wonderful time, haven't we, Fred? Else's food was simply out of this world and I wasn't allowed even to dry the dishes. Can you imagine, just lazing about for two days? I got nervous from doing nothing,' she laughed.

'Well, you ate a lot,' remarked Fred. 'And you changed your clothes several times. In the evenings we danced and played cards.'

'One night we had an air raid and I was scared to death. Next day Hubert said it had been a mild attack though I remembered it as a fire in hell. Else had decorated the entire place for New Year's Eve and after dinner we put on the radio and danced – just enough room for two couples. Hubert opened a bottle of champagne and we greeted the New Year in style.'

Arlen got restless and left the kitchen. He couldn't stand Anna's holiday report. He walked to the bathroom, pretending to fetch his razor and toothbrush.

'I'd better go and fill up the truck,' remarked Fred. 'Your friend seems anxious to leave.'

'Who knows when he'll get home,' said Eva as if to

apologise. Eva was preparing sandwiches for Arlen to take along. Anna kept up her report, Arlen stayed in the bathroom and Fred filled the tank.

'All set!' he shouted. Arlen came down, thanked Anna for her hospitality, kissed Eva on the hair saying, 'Don't come out,' then disappeared, slamming the door like a statement.

'It's hard to say farewell,' remarked Anna.

'Not this time,' Eva smiled.

'First the war has to end.'

'Has to end,' repeated Eva. 'I suppose it has to end.' She saw Fred and Arlen get into the truck, heard the door slam. Then the engine coughed, started to run and the wheels began to roll. 'I'll clean the guest room tomorrow,' said Eva. 'I'm not in the mood today.'

'You and your moods,' complained Anna. 'Your parents must have spoiled you rotten.'

'I couldn't tell you. Perhaps nobody cared.'

Chapter Sixteen

1945

Spring was late in coming. The end of March brought frosty nights and Eva still walked upstairs to her attic with a hot-water bottle under her arm. During the day it mostly rained. At times the sun came out between the clouds and Eva would take her shovel to dig in the vegetable garden. Anna continued to sit at the sewing machine and turn out more dresses for Eva to finish with buttonholes and hems.

Fred brought truckloads of food and essentials. Every space on the property was filled to the ceiling. On Sundays they cut wood for the kitchen stove.

'We're digging in,' explained Fred.

Eva went into the woods to collect the dead twigs that were needed to start a fire. She carried a rope and bundled the branches together. It was a very busy and useful time. When they permitted themselves an hour of relaxation, they sat back and enjoyed doing nothing.

'Rome is burning,' declared Fred.

'What's coming afterwards?' asked Eva.

'Nobody knows,' he said. 'If we're lucky we'll escape an encounter with the Russians.'

'They can't be worse than the Nazis,' Anna murmured.

'You'll be surprised, my sweetheart, but they are.'

'Don't scare us,' cried Anna.

'I suppose we won't see them. The British are closer.'

'Do you think anyone will find us here?' asked Anna.

'Unlikely,' said Fred. 'Most unlikely. We're away from any road, off the beaten track.'

'Some deserters perhaps or retreating troops. I'm afraid of the SS discovering our storehouses. They'll burn them and shoot us.'

'We haven't had an uninvited guest for years. Why should anybody come now?' Fred was annoyed because he knew Anna was right.

'You're gone all day,' Anna accused him.

'All right, I'll stay at home.' He did for a few days, helping Eva in the garden. He instructed her in sowing and planting. Every bed had to be straight and in perfect shape, no short cuts were permitted. More and more green was visible. Snowdrops bloomed and other spring flowers shot up but did not open yet. Fred promised that one morning they would be in bloom.

'One morning the war will be over,' Eva answered.

'It has to end. Fortunately, it has to end.' Fred talked to himself while turning the soil.

Then the weather changed to a mild breeze and partly sunny skies. The flowers opened overnight. Eva forgot the war, Fred became restless and drove to town again. Anna put her sewing away and sat on a bench in the sun, talking occasionally to Eva about nothing. Eva followed Fred's instructions, measuring the ground before turning the soil and sowing the seeds.

What would she do once the war was over? Where could she go? Would Fred and Anna keep her as a working guest, her prison becoming her home? Perhaps it was better to be in the city, in the thick of all the misery. Yes, she wanted to see their misery and feel no pity. She planned whole ranges of miseries which could, to a tiny extent, revenge the Jews, revenge the cold-blooded murders, revenge her father. Then she didn't want to be near the people but only to run away from them in disgust, never to hear their voices again. Perhaps the Allies would let her out, give her a visa to go to America. She couldn't go back to Hamburg, she had no-where to stay. The office was out of the question. Besides, there wouldn't be any work. They had plundered the world and now had nothing to show for it.

'You really enjoy gardening,' remarked Anna. 'It always gives me backache.'

'Just look at the flowers!'

'Wait until the lilac is in bloom, and the lavender.'

'Do you think I will still be here?'

'That's up to you. No one's chasing you away.'

'You mean I could stay?'

'You're more than welcome.'

'Thanks, Anna. I'd love to stay.' So that was settled. She had nowhere else to go. At the office they might not even have enough money to pay the rent and certainly they had no work, not for her. That part of her life was over. Miss Ehrlich might still go in every day while Mr Schiller and Mrs Richter would have to be dismissed. If anyone could save the company Miss Ehrlich could. She would start a factory that sold sand to wash clothes with, anything, as long as it made them survive. She would engage very skilfully in black-marketeering, Eva was sure. She would carry her mother and Mr Lindner through the hard times with flying colours. Perhaps she would find the courage to do her hair, put on proper dresses and look like a woman. Perhaps Mr Lindner would marry her, out of gratitude, or at least keep up an affair while she was such a valuable asset.

'I'm cutting some flowers for the kitchen,' announced Anna. 'We might as well enjoy them while they last.'

No, she didn't want to see the office people again. Only Marion. But Marion didn't belong to the office. She missed Else's sympathy, her warmth under the matter-of-factness. Else had a deep soul, a deep-sea soul with many colourful tropical fish in it which always came up to the surface at the right moment to sparkle and to hush away dark moods. One forgot aches and pains in Else's presence. Yes, she missed Else with her golden crown.

Then Eva was worried about Werner, the teddy bear, who had to clean the city streets and was in love with a beautiful widow. What did the Nazis have in mind for those half-Jews still under their thumb? Would they just let them go or, in the course of their *Goetterdaemmerung*, kill and murder, enraptured at the sight of blood and death? It was hard to tell, but Eva was rather pessimistic. She wished he would slip away and come here. Fred and Anna could put him up in the guest room. She had to talk about the teddy bear tonight. It was essential to get him away from the supervised street cleaning, out of the hands of the Gestapo.

Darling was probably searching for a partner at cards, and would gladly offer her spare room to Eva if she promised to play two-handed bridge every night. They would talk about the victory and Benny's return. But as much as she liked Darling who had been such a valiant fighter against the regime, she couldn't in the long run endure her dullness, her home-cooked view of the world and life in general. And yet, when she compared her with others, thought of how she had stood alone in her battles, combating her own people, not being Jewish herself, not belonging to the black-marketeers or the underworld, Eva became even fonder of the white-haired, round lady who dealt the cards like someone who hands out bread, fending off starvation.

'I think I'll make us a sandwich and bring it out here to eat,' suggested Anna.

'Our first meal outdoors.'

The sun was shining between diminishing clouds. They still predicted the weather over the radio and had announced fair skies for the following days. They all needed some sunshine, especially her seeds, she thought.

Eva hardly dared to think of Arlen. Of course, she could always find shelter with him if life in the woods should become intolerable. But wasn't life with Arlen worse than her loneliness here? They had come to the end of their road during those New Year days. Nothing was there any longer to hold them up. They had to lie down in order to touch the other's hand and those hands felt paper-thin. Before, when she had thrown herself at him in despair, she had never measured or weighted, had not explained or criticised. She had only evaluated his responses, which had been immeasurable. Now, since she no longer came in despair, nothing was left.

Anna came back balancing a big tray, putting it down on

the bench.

'Come on over and take a break. I'm starving.' Eva took off her gloves and sat down.

'A cup of coffee is precisely what I need,' said Eva. 'Thanks for spoiling me.'

They heard shooting in the distance. 'Cannons or tanks,' remarked Anna. Troops were fighting on all sides, soldiers being killed or wounded, so that Eva might live. She wondered if any concentration camps had been liberated yet, she wondered when the slaughter would stop.

She had to see Arlen again even though they had come to the end of their road. She couldn't imagine leaving without him and she couldn't imagine staying with him.

Anna was carrying the tray back to the kitchen and then she would come out again and sit in the sun. It got hotter. It was already May. Yesterday the mad murderer Hitler had taken his own life but still they were fighting on. Who was in command now? Doenitz or some other general. It was insane. Eva only hoped that whoever was in charge now would beg for peace. She was digging a bed for sweetpeas. She had wanted the flowers and Fred had come up with the seeds. 'Once the lilac bushes are in bloom . . .' Eva thought. Then it crossed her mind again that Hitler was dead but that the killing went on. Anna sat on the bench with closed eyes and Arlen was directing her thoughts. 'I am going away,' Eva said to herself. 'I am definitely going away.' Arlen would pursue his acting career, being Oberon or the Prince of Homburg, the darling of the Hamburg Theatre audience. For how many years? Would she always miss him? For how many years? There would be memories of the devastated streets, the silence of the wasteland. She would remember her walks over miles in search of Arlen when the underworld was closing in. Those times suddenly seemed to be a lifetime, her entire youth, spent in search of Arlen's protection, for his restoration of her strength when it had been depleted beyond endurance. It was over now, her youth, her excessive need of Arlen. She would have to start from scratch, trying to understand what normal life was about, if there existed a standard for normality. It would take her years to find a way, to recuperate from her fears and her anger.

The cannon fire was nearer.

'You would think with Hitler dead they would stop killing,' Anna said without opening her eyes.

'I imagine you have to negotiate first and agree terms. They probably got orders to fight to the last man. Perhaps SS commandos are firing them on.'

'I hope Fred is not getting into any trouble.'

When Fred got home and unloaded his truck he declared that he would not go back into the city before peace. 'The risks are too great,' he explained. 'I don't want to end up a prisoner of war.'

'Look who's coming to his senses,' said Anna. 'Eva is staying with us. She doesn't want to return to the city.'

'That's fine with me,' said Fred.

On the 7 May, Radio Hamburg was silent. At night they heard on the BBC that Germany had signed an unconditional surrender. Still the shooting continued. They heard machine guns and cannon. On the ninth, Radio Hamburg came alive again and declared in a solemn voice that all fighting had ceased, that no more bombs would be dropped, that Germany was at peace. Of course, death didn't stop, it kept on taking its toll. Concentration camp survivors didn't survive and wounded soldiers died at the usual rate. Others wished they could die. And finally the rounding up of the criminals responsible for the disaster began. High drama was under way, with the most disgraceful actors brought to trials so unprecedented that laws got established to fit the crimes. Eva felt uneasy about the proceedings but knew that once involved in the underworld, one couldn't solve the problems without getting one's hands dirty.

'It's over, really over! We are at peace!'

'Let's celebrate with champagne,' declared Fred.

'Do you feel joy?' Eva asked Anna.

'Not like Christmas,' explained Anna. 'But a great relief. Do you realise that nobody can come to you now and say "I'm going to kill you because you are a Jew?"' Eva suddenly realised what a tremendous burden she must have been to Anna and Fred.

'Nobody is fond of Jews,' she said.

'That's a different matter,' shouted Anna. 'Your life is no longer at stake.'

'I wonder what happened to the teddy bear?'

'I wonder what happened to Else and Hubert?' said Anna.

'Don't worry about them. Hubert is a first-rate fox.' Fred poured more champagne into their glasses and laughed.

'I doubt anybody's bothering about the wasteland,' remarked Anna.

'They'll comb it carefully for Germans in hiding,' speculated Fred. 'But Hubert and Else are safe, they live there, it's their home.'

'Renate will look after Arlen. I'm sure she'll seize the opportunity.' Eva watched the bubbles in her glass.

'You and Arlen could get married now.'

'I'm going away and will never marry. I'm not the type. Need my independence.'

'Nothing like marriage,' Fred smiled. 'Is there?'

'You bet!' said Anna and giggled as if she were tipsy from one glass of champagne. 'Perhaps really it is happiness,' thought Eva. Fred wasn't shifty and foxy like Hubert.

They dug in for a peaceful summer. Fred and Eva worked in the garden, Anna did the cooking. The house cleaning was shared by the women while Fred took over the bread making. He was an expert.

'Don't tell me you learned that in prison too,' teased Eva.

'But I did. Worked in the kitchen for a year, in the bakery. One of the worst jobs in the entire place – how we sweated! I wasn't particularly smart at sixteen, couldn't claim any seniority either, so they made me wash the floors first and then promoted me to the bakery.'

'I'm glad they did,' said Eva. 'Your bread tastes delicious.'

The days passed quickly and in harmony. They were conscious of peace and how foolish it would be to quarrel over nothing. Hubert was to make the proper contacts and come out to bring Fred his driver's permit. After that they hoped to resume business on a large scale. But Hubert didn't come.

'Can't expect miracles,' said Fred good-humouredly. 'The British are unapproachable. He might have to get at the Americans, they aren't half as strict.'

'Where did you get your knowledge from?' Anna asked.

'Old experiences,' he laughed. 'I've been in the business for a long time. Used to deal with both countries before the war.'

'Just wanted to check.' She kissed his face. 'So we may still expect Hubert to appear one day.'

'He'll come as soon as he has the necessary papers. No use taking risks. We have enough of everything to last us a year.'

'Longer,' estimated Anna.

They never saw a soldier or a stranger. They were cut off from the world.

'How far is it to the next village?' asked Eva, who got more anxious about her friends.

'Too far to walk,' said Fred.

'Could you drive me?' asked Eva timidly. 'Perhaps the phones are working.'

Next day Fred drove her towards a small settlement in the woods. There were only a few country houses between sandy roads, no town square, no stores.

'Knock on any door,' suggested Fred.

People opened doors, were suspicious and refused, but one woman offered her help immediately. 'Of course, come on in and try to get through. It's not always possible.'

Eva talked first to Else. It was as if they both had returned from a long trip.

'I have so much to tell you!' exclaimed Else. 'No, we're fine. Hubert finally made the right move, we think. American, very nice. I think we can come out and visit you in about a month. Don't count on sooner. These things take time.'

'We're not in a rush. I just had to know how you were. At night, lying in bed, I start worrying. Otherwise life is great in the country. You should see our garden!'

'Can't complain about the city either,' said Else, laughing in a strange way as if she were hiding a big secret or something unusual was going on. 'Call me again.'

Eva phoned again.

'Arlen?'

'My pet, where are you?'

'I don't know. Some settlement in the woods. How have you been?'

'Relieved. My God, what a relief, what freedom! Of course we have restrictions but they're child's play in comparison with the oppressions of old. Aren't you in seventh heaven?'

'I'm gardening all day. There's little change outwardly. Inside I'm – I really don't know, it hasn't sunk in because nothing has changed.'

'There are no trains, no post office. I want to see you.'

'I might come in a month, not sooner. How do you survive?'

'Else is helping, practically keeps me alive.'

Eva was suddenly sure that the two had had an affair. Arlen had started it to secure his food and Else had wanted it to satisfy her vanity.

'Hope Hubert doesn't mind,' she answered.

'Why should he?'

'As long as you are all right – I'll come to town in about a month. If you go anywhere always leave a note.'

'I miss you, my pet. Life is not worth living without you.'

'Then wait for me.'

'I do, I always do.'

After she had hung up she felt depleted. Arlen had lied, so had she, pretending a continuation of their relationship while she knew that they had come to the end of their road. She waited for the telephone operator to announce the amount of money she owed, then she paid and expressed her gratitude.

Fred waited outside the settlement in the woods. She repeated her conversations and mentioned that she had got the feeling that a rift between Else and Hubert had taken place.

'Very unlikely,' said Fred, who enjoyed the prospect of being on the road again. 'But you can't count on foxy Hubert. He's capable of pulling a trick on you out of the blue. Did it to me several times. He has a mean streak in him. Somebody probably mistreated him as a child and the treatment in the orphanage wasn't exactly pleasant either. We were glad when we saw it from far away. All the kids were planning to escape. It was our favourite pastime to think up a plan. Foxy Hubert of course kept his scheme to himself and only told me the night before. But he was right. If we wanted to succeed we had to sacrifice the others. I learned a great deal from him, mainly not to take unnecessary risks. He's cool and collected. Nobody can push him around. There's greatness in that too, you must admit.'

'I wouldn't call it greatness. He is the born egotist and at the moment, I think, he's hurting Else.'

'You're imagining things,' Fred laughed. 'Imagining from one telephone conversation.'

'She didn't talk the way she usually talks.'

'She didn't expect to hear from you.'

Chapter Seventeen

The lilac was in bloom like a painting in a dream. Eva had a bunch in her attic room. At night they sat in the kitchen and smoked, saying very little. Eva tried to work out if she was happy or unhappy. At times she thought that life, at the moment, was more than she could bear. At other times she realised that it was just an ordinary state of mind, a mind without pain. Occasionally she wanted to get to the city, to find the American authorities and apply for a visa. The radio was playing music or giving out the news from all over the world. It didn't touch them greatly. On the other hand they got excited when new plants showed their shoots, when the sweetpeas had grown high enough to be fastened to poles, when Fred surprised them with white rolls for breakfast, when Anna came from her sewing machine with a dress in her hand, specially made for Eva, when the moon shone bright in the night sky like a polished mirror on a blue, velvety background, when the wind rustled through the lilac bushes and the smell of summer hung over them like a strong perfume.

'We are the luckiest people on earth,' Eva then thought. 'I have everything I could ask for.' The next moment she knew she was a monkey in a cage that wanted to be freed and feared its freedom.

On a rainy day at the beginning of August Hubert and Else arrived in their truck. They embraced and kissed as if they'd come for another Christmas celebration.

226

'Got your papers,' announced Hubert triumphantly.

'How did you manage it?'

'It wasn't easy. Tried the British first but without success. Then, after wasting all my time, I got to the Americans, looked around and picked a nice young captain. Had to have someone higher up, I thought. He came to the store and enjoyed our dinner, also liked the cook, I think,' Hubert laughed.

'The cook liked him,' interrupted Else.

'Anyway, I got my permit without any difficulties. But when I asked for yours he hesitated, was afraid I'd taken him for a ride. Else smoothed out things though. He's eating out of her hand.' Hubert laughed again.

'We made no unreasonable demands!' Else laughed loudly.

'That's true. All we needed were truck permits.'

Later the women sat in the living room while the men remained in the kitchen.

'Are you in love with the captain?' asked Eva.

Else was almost in tears. 'You have no idea how I've suffered,' she said. 'When the war ended I was so happy. All I could think of was my wedding. You see, he had promised and I had believed and waited. It was all I ever wanted. And then he laughed at me and told me that he wasn't the marrying type and that if I wanted a paper to make it official, I should have picked somebody else, not a smuggler and outlaw. So I cried for days, thought I wanted to die, still hoped he would keep his promise. Finally I gave up. Oh, we had rows and scenes, we threatened each other, we fought like cat and dog but in the end he always smiled and said, "Nothing doing, my sweetheart. You might as well give up". And I realised one night that it was really final, that either I had to take the risk and keep up appearances or I had to end it fast and look for someone to marry. Now he sleeps in the store, we're business partners but otherwise he's just an old acquaintance. That's all he gets from me nowadays. He doesn't seem to mind. Thinks I'll come crawling back. But I won't. I'm going to marry the captain, you'll see.'

'What about Arlen?' asked Eva.

'What about Arlen? He's fine, I feed him.'

'You are a free woman now,' stated Anna. 'Hubert has a mean streak in him, I always saw that.'

'He does as he pleases and I thought he was right, always right. I think we're brought up that way. Father first, always right, then teacher, always right, afterwards any man, always right. That's why the entire country thought Hitler was right. He said so and nobody doubted it. We're idiots, men are idiots.' Else laughed happily. 'Now my captain is different. With him I am always right and I don't like that either. I told him so. He's learning slowly. No one is always right, what nonsense.' She seemed carefree after confessing her separation from Hubert.

'Do you hear from the office?'

'Occasionally,' Else answered. 'Nothing new. Mrs Richter has met a nice British officer and has her hands full. She also expects her husband home.'

'She looks so honest and trustworthy,' said Eva.

'Who knows what kind of husband she has – '

'Nobody's like Fred.'

'No,' said Anna. 'He's unique. Not one mean streak in him.'

'Hubert knows too many card tricks. He can't play straight,' complained Else. 'But he is a born businessman. Can sniff out a deal like a well-trained bloodhound. Charlie, that's Captain Delmore's name, had introduced us to a few men in charge of supplies but Hubert has done the rest. As a business partner I certainly don't want to lose him.'

'Are you in love with Charlie?' asked Anna.

'I respect him as a person, he is kind and considerate. You see, it's time I got married. I'm over thirty and I want to have kids.'

'Your heart is still with Hubert,' said Anna.

'No, it died for him. How can you love a man who is that dishonest?'

'I don't know, but many a heart does.'

The two continued to talk about love and marriage until Eva got nervous.

'Want to join me in the garden? It's stopped raining. The sun's coming out.' But they wanted to stay indoors and Eva left. Anna and Else hardly felt her absence.

It was amazing how practical and unromantic they were, yet if one looked closely and considered their lives and situations, they really were unpractical and extremely romantic. It all depended from which angle one observed them. Anna had opened the window and the thin white muslin curtains billowed out. Behind sat the two women putting down bricks and cement to form their fate. That's the way it was going to be, for ever, content and happy. No doubt about it.

Fred had taken a test run to the nearest town and had come back in good spirits. No control had stopped his vehicle, nobody had asked for papers. 'Let's all go to the city tomorrow,' he suggested. 'Hubert wants me to meet some business contacts. Eva wants to go to the American mission and Anna can stay with Else.'

'I'll walk through the streets and look at nice, young soldiers,' announced Anna.

'By all means do,' said Fred with a smile. 'They could almost be your sons.'

'I look ten years younger than my age. Everybody says so,' protested Anna.

'You'll find out. Have fun.'

Nothing had changed in the city except that new men in different uniforms paraded. Yet for Eva the entire landscape had a new colour, the seagulls had different shrieks, the waters looked less polluted, the sky had a new height. She drove into the city on the jerky seat like a conqueror into Rome, into a city that had been destroyed through a tremendous catastrophe. When she walked up the stairs at the American mission she had the feeling of utter triumph. The Americans were polite and non-committal. She would be processed like all the others. Bills had to be passed through Congress first. Her fate was uncertain. They would do what was in their power but for the time being they were powerless. They asked her if she had a place to stay and an address where she could be reached. She mentioned Else's store. They would let her know definitely. The man behind the desk understood that she couldn't stay in Germany – he had seen a concentration camp – but she didn't look Jewish. No, but she was. Could he find out where they had killed her father? Of course, the Joint Committee would investigate. Name, last address, when arrested. This man was smooth and gentle. Was he Jewish?

'Are you Jewish?' It didn't matter in America, but he was.

'It always matters,' protested Eva. 'Somebody will let you know, even in America.' The man blushed.

'You had bad experiences,' he stammered.

'I have to get away, do you understand?'

'The difficulty is that you are a German subject. If you were Polish or Hungarian the process would be easy. But you are a special case. I can't put you on the list of Displaced Persons.'

'Do you have any other list?'

'Yes, special cases. Americans are very generous.'

'We all tried to get out before the war but America wouldn't let us in, nobody wanted us.'

'I know,' he said with regret in his voice. 'I think we've learned from our mistake.'

'Nobody regrets the Jewish slaughter,' said Eva. 'The British won't let the few survivors settle in Palestine. They herd them up in camps like cattle. I know, they don't kill them. But do you call that civilisation? What is America doing to put pressure on the Allies? Nothing. The Arabs don't like it, they don't like the settlers in Palestine and Arabs supply oil.'

'World affairs have never been settled in fairness,' whispered the Jewish American soldier. 'The defenceless always remain defenceless.'

'I hope you are going to defend me. I applied for my visa in 1937. Try to get it approved in 1945.'

'I will do what I can.' They were parting almost with tears in their eyes, both thinking of the Jewish fate.

That was all she could do, apply for a visa on a special list for special cases which had to be approved by Congress. It might take ages but it didn't matter as long as she could stay with Fred and Anna, away from the crowd.

She walked to Else's store and was introduced to a nice,

clean-looking officer named Charlie Delmore who had the face of a young man suddenly grown too old, not much muscle in his expression, the sweetness of a choir boy in his eyes and round his mouth. He had eyes only for Else and followed her every mood.

'We're going to discuss business with our new partners tomorrow,' said Else.

Captain Delmore could hardly understand a word. He had taken two years of German at college but couldn't remember a thing. Eva listened to the strange syllables he uttered.

'I had five years of English at school and can't remember much,' said Eva. Captain Delmore thought that she spoke very well and unprompted he gave her a lively picture of his family and background which sounded pedestrian and conventional. They had been good children without any hardship, their parents being such splendid examples of virtue. Here Eva interrupted and asked if he had been a choir boy.

'No,' he laughed. 'We're Methodists. But I taught in Sunday School and liked it. Do you think Else would change to Methodism?'

'If it made you happy,' answered Eva. 'Our Lutheran Church can't be that different.'

'It must be very similar,' he smiled at her.

'What are you talking about?' asked Else, a little jealous.

'About churches,' answered Eva. 'He is a Methodism.'

'Is that bad? Some sect?' asked Else with alarm.

'No, just a branch of the Protestant Church. He asked me if you would join.'

'Aha,' said Else. 'If it makes him happy, why not? One church is as bad as another.'

'You'll have to attend.'

'Perhaps in the beginning. Later we'll stop going.'

'God is a strong opponent,' stated Eva.

'Not for me. Besides, he may keep his God if he can't be entirely happy with me. But he'll learn to rely on me for everything.'

'First you have to be married,' laughed Anna.

'I'm sure I will be.' She tasted the meat sauce that was

simmering on the stove.

'Else has nothing against Methodists,' translated Eva.

'She will be adored by us,' he said as if in prayer.

'I hope she's not rushing into this,' mused Eva.

'I told her the same thing,' said Captain Delmore with a smile. 'Her friend hurt her deeply.'

'Else has a good head on her shoulders,' remarked Eva.

'What are you talking about behind my back?' asked Else, full of pride.

'I just mentioned that you're not stupid.'

'How kind. What else were you talking about?'

'Life in general. What time are we returning? Do you think I could take a short walk to the harbour?' asked Eva.

'Be back in half an hour,' warned Anna, 'we have to return before curfew.'

Eva walked through the wasteland as in days of old. The winter nights she remembered, with the howling wind and the snow on the ground, skipping and sliding like a witch over the snow. It had all been part of the nightmare life, the fears, the bombs, the unmarked graves.

When she returned, Fred and Anna were waiting to return to their house in the woods. The main highways were amazingly crowded with treks of people, people who had fled the Russian zone, trying to find a place in the West where they could resettle. The stream of tired women with children and perambulators looked endless. In between was a soldier on crutches, soldiers with one arm or one leg only, everybody crippled.

The weather remained fine and very hot. Eva worked in the garden, Anna kept up her production of dresses which sold very well on the black market. Fred drove almost every day to the city and was delighted with his new partners and the amount of money he and Hubert could make under this system.

'People are starving,' objected Anna when they had eaten too much and enjoyed a cup of coffee.

'Don't start feeling sorry for them,' objected Fred. 'They didn't have to follow Hitler to their own doom.'

'Enjoy!' urged Eva. They were leaning back in their kitchen chairs, blowing the smoke out into the warm evening air. 'Could you give me a lift tomorrow? I would like to go to town and telephone. I've not heard from Darling or Werner yet.'

'What a summer!' said Fred as they drove slowly through the woods. 'I'm so glad you are getting along well with Anna. Life by herself was very lonely. I'm trying to find a flat in the city and storage space but it won't be easy, everything's in ruins.'

'Yes, I like Anna and I've begun to love your lonely place. The garden could be in better shape but I'm sure we're going to have a good harvest anyhow.'

They had reached the highway, again crowded with an endless flow of refugees.

'They did this to almost all the countries in Europe,' said Fred with anger, 'now they probably feel sorry for themselves.'

'One day it will be over, don't you think? Only for the Jews it will never be over, I'm afraid.'

'Just wait until you are in America!' Fred didn't like Eva's melancholy moods.

Else was in a warm-hearted mood, embracing Eva and saying that she was so happy to have a girl-to-girl talk for once after all the male company she kept.

'May I first make two phone calls?' asked Eva, 'then I'm all yours.' She dialled Dr Kromer's house. His wife answered.

'I'm so glad to hear your voice,' she said. After assuring each other that they were well, Eva asked about Werner.

'They kept him in his work camp up to the last day,' Mrs Kromer reported. 'He looked thin and sick but he only had one thought on his mind, to find a car and to drive to Theresienstadt. The British lent him a car and he was off immediately. He found his mother alive and brought her back. They got a nice, big flat in the suburbs and Werner found a job with the British. Now comes the problem.' Mrs Kromer was silent for a moment. 'He wants to get married right away but his fiancée and her family are Nazis, real

Nazis, and haven't changed. They are making anti-semitic remarks and Werner's mother says she is not going to sit at the same table with such a family. Werner of course is in the middle.'

'How can Werner sit at the same table with *them*? What is the matter with him?'

'We are not going to the wedding,' said Mrs Kromer, 'though we are invited.'

'He is a stuffed teddy bear, not made of flesh and blood. I feel sorry for him, really I do, but this finishes our friendship.'

'We have come to the same conclusion, my husband and I. We did everything we could for the boy.'

'He's madly in love, don't forget. Aren't those mitigating circumstances? Well, nice to have talked to you. My respects to Dr Kromer.' Eva hung up. It seemed that life was continuing on a bumpy road.

'Fred is coming for lunch,' said Else, 'then he wants to drive back.'

'How is Charlie?'

'He loves me as nobody ever did. I think I will be happy with him in America.'

'You will be happy anywhere, Else, you were born under a lucky star. Don't you remember when I told you that during the worst time of the war? You were always sitting there smiling, getting the best out of every minute.'

'My mother used to say: "Natural blondes have it made." ' She laughed.

'Can I use the phone one more time?'

Darling picked up the receiver and said 'Hello'.

'Guess who?'

'My little girl!' cried Darling from the other end. 'How are you?'

'Fine, and you?'

'Lonely, my sweetheart. It's no pleasure growing old – '

'It's going to be lively once Benny is back. I'm sure he is coming as soon as he can.'

'I know, I'm waiting. That keeps me going. But it will just be for a visit. He'll never settle here again.'

'All right, a visit is better than nothing. I am going to the

States.'

'Wonderful! You'll be happy there. A great country. Will I see you soon?'

'Very soon. The people I'm staying with own a truck and can take me to the city for the day.'

'Just come any time.'

'Are you hungry?'

'Often enough. But I don't care. We won the war.'

'Yes, we won the war and soon Benny will be back. How about a game of bridge?'

'All right. I'll see you soon with a food package and coffee.' Darling was crying on the other end of the line and Eva thought it was best to hang up.

Else had set the table. Fred and Hubert returned from their new business ventures. It was hot in the kitchen and Else turned on a fan which Charlie had provided.

'That feels delicious, doesn't it?' asked Else.

'I'm hungry,' said Hubert.

'What a surprise!' Else laughed. She was laughing a lot lately and taking little dancing steps. Her golden hair was freshly washed and pinned on top of her head in a crown. She handed the dishes round and asked what they wanted to drink.

'No heavy alcohol,' said Fred, 'a beer will do.'

They all had beer and felt the breeze coming from the fan. Later, Else and Hubert stood in the narrow street with its ruins on both sides and waved goodbye to Fred and Eva. Eva leant out of her window and waved back as if they would never see each other again.

'It's hard to believe they're going to split,' she said to Fred, once they had turned the corner.

'She is better off with Charlie, trust me. I have known Hubert for a long time and he has a mean streak in him, real mean.'

'Here is a letter for you, girlie,' said Fred one evening after coming home from the city. 'He left it with Else.'

'Who?' asked Anna.

'It's from Arlen,' said Eva, who had read the few lines with excitement. 'He wants me to come on Wednesday and stay till Thursday. I would love to go but I'm in the middle of harvesting the string beans.'

'Never mind, girlie, you go. Anna can take over for two days. She used to do the garden every day. What do you say?'

'Of course I'll do the harvesting if the beans are getting too ripe. Don't worry, just enjoy yourself.'

Eva wasn't quite sure if her meeting with Arlen would be a success. It had been such a failure over New Year. But so much had happened since, she had changed slowly, staying in the country like an invalid who had to recuperate from a long illness.

Fred had taken her to the city and Eva was walking up the dimly lit stairs in Arlen's house, feeling her heart jump and skip. 'Now don't expect anything different from what it has been,' she told herself reasonably. 'Arlen will always remain Arlen, no matter how much you love him.' She had almost reached his floor, when suddenly he stood before her, on the landing, radiant and beautiful, taking her into his arms, just holding her. For a moment everything seemed happy and right. She wished it could last for ever, Arlen and her embracing.

'It's good to see you,' she said, putting an end to the sweet illusion. 'I brought a bag full of food.' She walked into the living room and looked out of the wide open window over the ruined city. 'How has life been treating you?'

'Why didn't you come before?'

'I really don't know, Arlen. I wanted to and then I was afraid that it would be a failure. It's very difficult to predict what will happen. You are a ship without rudder, finding harbours here and there. I can't pull you from the arms of all your girlfriends forever. If it's not Renate, it's Louisa or it's Olga or somebody else. And where do I fit into your scheme of purposeless drifts?'

'I wouldn't drift if you stayed with me,' he promised. They settled on the floor, leaning against big, soft pillows.

'It's so peaceful now,' said Eva, 'no more air raids, no more murders. Do you remember how you had to hold me tight when I came running at night, full of fears – '

'Or when we were lying on the mattress in Ahrenshoop, you holding me? I was close to suicide then.'

'I always wanted to live.'

'They didn't draft you into the army.'

'It's over, Arlen, for you it's over. I have to leave this country, I can't stay here. I've applied for a visa to the States.'

'Will it be soon?'

'No, I don't think so. I am on a special list. It may take years.'

'I don't want you to go.' He embraced her and kissed her lips. 'You just can't disappear,' he said tenderly.

Eva lit a cigarette and suggested some coffee.

'We are going into rehearsals soon,' Arlen said while they were waiting for the water to boil. 'Our old ensemble from the State Theatre is playing *Everyman* in a church. I got the leading part.'

'Are you excited?'

'Nothing could make me happier. You have to come to the rehearsals.'

'I have no time. The garden is full of ripe vegetables and fruit. I start very early every morning at sunrise and work until dusk. Then I take off my gloves, go in and have dinner. Afterwards I fall asleep.'

'Don't die of boredom?'

'You have no idea how damaged I feel, how crippled. This busy, uneventful life gets me through the day. I have no time to think. If I sat down and realised what had happened, I could never stop crying again.' She poured the coffee into their cups. 'What part is Eduard playing?'

'He plays Death. He likes these character roles.'

'Do you know what happened to Olga?'

'Yes, of course. Let me tell you: when the Russians came, to pick up their flock after the liberation, Olga fled into the British Security Office. She didn't want to be repatriated just to get shot. The British protected her and their head of Security fell in love with her. They started an ardent affair. He got Olga a wonderful flat and spent every free moment with her. Olga fell in love too, at least that's what she claims, when one night, as she was going home alone, several men surrounded her. She only felt a slight needle prick. When she woke up she was lying on the couch in her apartment with a bunch of Russians round her. One held a syringe in his hand. The discussion was very short. They reminded her of her situation but, being generous, gave her a chance to make up for previous mistakes. She had to drop the British Security Officer, make the acquaintance of the American in charge of Displaced Persons, marry him, get to Washington, remain there married or divorced, and wait for further instructions. She would be allowed, through the Russian mission, to correspond with her mother as well as her brother. They wanted steady reports on her progress. If she didn't cooperate, well, they had their methods . . . When I met her, she had already broken with her lover, who couldn't understand what had happened. "I'm only telling you, Arlen," she said. "I have to talk to somebody." She's dating the American now whom she neither loves nor cares for. She says he's a bore but that she can divorce him once she's in America and has citizenship. She says she has no choice, that they can kill her and her entire family. Poor Olga, all she wanted from life was love and instead she's got nothing but violence and intrigue.'

'No way out,' agreed Eva. 'Like having cancer.'

'We all have to die,' he replied.

'But we don't have a fixed date. We can look at the stars and think we will always have a chance to look at them again.' She would be looking at the starry sky a million times more and telling herself as many times that life was just beginning, that the future lay far, far on the horizon; that moments like these, together with Arlen, precious and beautiful, would recur again, one day, when she had learned to feel happiness and be well again. She walked to the window and looked down at the garden full of rubble and craters.

'We'll never see Ahrenshoop again, it's in the Russian zone.'

'We live with our memories most of the time,' said Arlen, 'they seem to expand and come into focus much more than the present can.'

'But I want to forget the past. Not you, I'll never forget

you; but what happened here, in this country. I'm getting out as soon as I can.'

'I don't want to talk about it,' said Arlen. 'Come back to me. Don't stand there for ever by the window.'

She lay in his arms, not quite sure of what would happen next. 'It's going to be passion,' she thought like somebody who had to be constantly on guard. But then her eyes suddenly filled. She saw the window extending through her tears. Arlen was there. They clung together, holding on to each other, spinning round with the orbit of the earth, round and round.

'You still have to hold me tight,' said Eva in a soft voice.

'I will, my pet, don't worry. One day you'll be happy. Always remember, we won the war.'

Elisabeth Reichart
February Shadows

Translated by Donna L Hoffmeister

'The emotional impact of this short book is tremendous
. . . a stark reminder of the penetration of Nazism into
every corner of the most ordinary life.'
Miriam Halahmy, *Times Literary Supplement*

It is forty years since the Anschluss, when Hitler annexed
Austria. Hilde was only a girl at the time. Like so many of
her compatriots, she has striven hard to forget a shameful
period in her country's history. It is her daughter Erika
who forces her to remember. Resentfully, reluctantly, she
summons up scraps of memory of that fateful February
when prisoners from the local concentration camp were
hunted down in her village. Did she betray the fugitive her
brother was hiding? Was not the whole village guilty of
trading prisoners for their own survival?

Spare and moving, *February Shadows* won Elisabeth Reichart
two literary prizes.

With an afterword by Christa Wolf

Fiction   £4.95
ISBN: 0 7043 4143 3

Jewish Women in London Group
Generations of Memories
Voices of Jewish Women

'In generously sharing their extraordinary lives with us, the women recorded in this book have added perspectives to our views of Jewish life in this country and in the countries of the writers' parents and grandparents . . . Thank you, Jewish Women in London Group.'
Zelda Curtis, *Oral History*

In this fascinating and unique collection of in-depth interviews, Ashkenazi Jewish women tell their life stories and explore the many ways of experiencing and asserting a Jewish identity. Some are the daughters of refugees and exiles from Eastern Europe, or are themselves refugees from Nazi persecution in the 1930s; others, first or second generation immigrants who made their homes in London's East End or Glasgow's Gorbals. Each has a very different relationship to her Judaism and to her Jewishness, but all have experienced directly or indirectly the painful consequences of migration, displacement and persecution.

Beautifully illustrated with 16 pages of evocative photographs.

Lives/Women's Studies   £6.95
ISBN: 0 7043 4205 7

Leslie Wilson
Mourning is Not Permitted

'A sensitive exploration of the conflict between reported
history and retrospective morality.' *Sunday Times*
Karin is the daughter of a German mother and an English
father. As a Berlin teenager her mother watched for
fire-bombs; her father was part of the victorious occupying
army. Now in her thirties, Karin embarks on a distressing
process of discovery, desperate to believe that her family
were all 'good' Germans.

She struggles to make sense of the anecdotes and
contradictory stories gleaned from three generations of
family recollections; but she also has to face the truth about
her bacteriologist husband's involvement in weapons
research.

An accomplished novel which is also a timely reminder of
the dangers of national amnesia and the importance of
discovering the truth about the past.

Fiction   £5.95
ISBN: 0 7043 4256 1

Manny Shirazi
Siege of Azadi Square

It is the day of the great women's demonstration in Tehran
after the ayatollahs' revolution. Zareen, who runs a
hairdressing salon, Fatemeh, a lawyer, and Malihe, a
seamstress who has herself been imprisoned under the
Shah, march arm in arm. Then the fundamentalist fanatics
charge, the demonstrators are scattered, and excitement
turns to anger and dismay. On the way home, the three
friends come across Goli, a student, who has been raped by
the 'revolutionary' guards . . .

Here is a novel of contemporary Iran, told exclusively from
the point of view of women, determined to evolve their
own methods of resistance to the mullas rather than give in
to the fear and helplessness they feel.

Manny Shirazi is an Iranian writer, and author of the highly
successful *Javady Alley*, the story of the childhood of a
working-class girl in the Iran of the 1950s.

Praise for *Javady Alley*
'A wonderful novel. I recommend it.' Doris Lessing

Fiction   £6.95
ISBN: 0 7043 4264 2